Grave
Undertaking

Also by the author
Dangerous Undertaking

Grave Undertaking

Mark de Castrique

Poisoned Pen Press

Copyright © 2004 by Mark de Castrique

First Edition 2004

10 9 8 7 6 5 4 3 2 1

Library of Congress Catalog Card Number: 2004103311

ISBN: 1-59058-116-4 Hardcover

Poisoned Pen Press
6962 E. First Ave., Ste. 103
Scottsdale, AZ 85251
www.poisonedpenpress.com
info@poisonedpenpress.com

Printed in the United States of America

For Steve Greene
Thanks for keeping the story on the trail

Acknowledgments

Thanks to the many readers and reviewers who encouraged me to keep Barry Clayton and his mountain community alive. I'm indebted to those booksellers who made the effort to introduce their customers to his world. Thanks to Barbara, Rob, Jennifer, Marilyn, et al. of Poisoned Pen Press, the collegial spirit of their authors, and my energetic agent Linda Allen for keeping the process fun. I'm grateful to Steve Greene for his watchful eye and critical ear, to my wife Linda and daughters Melissa and Lindsay for their thoughtful suggestions, to John Patterson for his insights on the funeral business, and to my father Arch for giving Barry his good traits.

Chapter 1

"You beat me to the cemetery," I said.

"Barry, at my age I'll beat most people to the cemetery." The old preacher chuckled and rocked forward, using his ever-present rhododendron walking stick as an anchor in the slippery stones. Reverend Lester Pace had been leaning against the hood of his maroon Plymouth Duster, and the ice-laced gravel of the Eagle Creek Methodist Church parking lot made walking treacherous. "Lovely day for an outing, though I don't think Pearly Johnson will mind the cold. At least the ground hasn't froze to concrete."

Pace's frosty breath bore witness to the chill of mid-December. The early morning sun was only a glow of lighter gray in the snow-laden clouds.

"The TV weatherman says snow flurries before noon," I said.

"He shoulda called me. My bursitis says four to six inches by nightfall." With his free hand, he clutched the shoulder of his battered canvas hunting jacket to underscore the source of his prediction. Then he turned and stepped off the gravel onto the grassy border at the edge of the graveyard. A dark stain marked where the blood of countless rabbits and squirrels had soaked the game pouch of his canvas back. "Come on. Senator Richards is moving in tomorrow and we'd best get his room vacated."

I walked in step beside him. "No need for you to stay out in this cold. Why don't you wait in the church?" I glanced over my left shoulder to the rear door of the white clapboard sanctuary.

"Thanks, but I promised Pearly's family I'd be their witness. Did you know they asked for you to come over here instead of Williams Funeral Home?"

"That's who's handling the senator? Uncle Wayne just told me to be up here to move a grave. I thought it was a favor for you."

"No, a favor for Pearly Johnson's family. They've got a claim on us. You, me, and the Tucker brothers."

He raised his stick and pointed to a spot down the hill. Over the crest, I saw the top of a backhoe. We kept walking until we came to a modest gravestone with Patrick "Pearly" Johnson carved into the smooth granite. A primer-painted pickup towing a flatbed trailer had backed in from a dirt-lane service road. It was parked between Pearly's marker and a wrought-iron fence enclosing a miniature Washington monument that rose at least six feet high, a skyscraper in the landscape of single-story tombstones. Down the shaft were inscribed the words BLESSED UNION FOREVER.

Pace introduced me to two men he identified as the Tucker brothers. They nodded and resumed getting the hoe from the back of the trailer. A limited mountain gene pool had formed their grizzled, unshaven faces into lean expressionless masks. Their soiled denim overalls and floppy-eared leather caps made them as indistinguishable from each other as two Wall Street brokers in pin stripes. I figured they were in their sixties, younger than Pace but not by much.

"What do you mean the Johnsons have a claim on us?"

"Because of what happened to Pearly."

"When?"

"You ain't never heard of the story of Pearly's grave raisin'?" yelled one of the Tuckers from the trailer. He grinned at his brother. "I can't believe Jack Clayton ain't told his boy about that."

His fashion clone elbowed him in the ribs and I heard the whisper, "Jack's got old-timer's."

"Alzheimer's," I corrected, feeling foolish because I knew they wouldn't remember the proper word for the disease any longer than did my father.

"Then you tell him, Preacher," said the first Tucker.

They went back to work, but I could tell they were listening.

As we watched the Tuckers, Pace walked over to the wrought-iron fence and propped his arm along the rusted railing. "Barry, you know how any time your father and I were moving a vault, we liked to have a family member present."

"Yeah," I said. "Uncle Wayne still feels the same way."

Over the last forty years, my father and his brother-in-law, Wayne Thompson, had probably conducted three-fourths of the burials in Laurel County. Uncle Wayne worked for Clayton and Clayton, our funeral home in the western North Carolina mountain town of Gainesboro.

Clayton and Clayton was more than a funeral home to me. It was where I grew up living over the visitation room, the embalming equipment, and the casket displays. It was also where I had been forced to return when my father developed Alzheimer's and Mom and Dad could find no one to run the business.

Buryin' Barry defied Thomas Wolfe by coming home again. To the funeral home.

"That's cause your Uncle Wayne was there with me and your dad," said Pace. "Nearly seven years ago. Hard to believe. Seems like only yesterday we were standing together around Pearly Johnson's grave."

"Yep," the brothers muttered in unison.

"That first time was back up in Whiteside Hollow," said Pace.

"The first time?" I began to suspect I was in for one of the mountain tales the Methodist circuit-riding preacher could spin by the hour. I never tired of hearing them.

There was a rattle of chains as the Tuckers started unhooking the backhoe from the trailer.

"Yes," said Pace. "Pearly was originally buried on family land. That must have been in the Forties. In 1996, they sold their land to developers so that a new retirement community could be constructed. The Johnsons bought more acreage on the other side of the ridge and still came out with extra money to boot. Trouble was what to do with Pearly."

"Well, sounds like Pearly had been permanently retired," I said. "He should have felt right at home."

"Reckon he didn't care much one way or the other, but Pearly's ninety-five-year-old widow didn't want to leave him behind. Your dad and I suspected nothing had been done in a proper fashion when Pearly died, you know, official notifications, death certificate. But, we agreed to help relocate him to the church cemetery, and we had assurance he had been buried in a coffin and a sealed vault. We arranged for the Tuckers and their truck with a hoist. What we couldn't get was a family member."

"I thought they wanted him moved."

"Yes, but they were too superstitious. Even the three grown grandchildren were convinced Pearly didn't approve of the sale, and none of them wanted to be near him until he was securely returned to six feet under."

Pace paused long enough to breathe in a lungful of the brisk mountain air. A network of capillaries had blossomed on his cheeks, but the cold wasn't going to hinder a good story.

"I take it things didn't go as planned," I said.

I heard the Tuckers laugh behind me.

"Not hardly," continued the preacher. "We dug down to the top of the vault. Even your dad and uncle didn't recognize the make. We managed to loop the chains around each end and start the winch. When we had cleared the hole by three or four feet, Barney let out a cry I can still hear. 'Gol-durnit. It's a septic tank. Can you believe it? They crapped in an outhouse and put Pearly in a septic tank.'"

I turned around to see which one of the Tucker brothers would own up to being Barney. They both just grinned at me from either side of their trailer, shaking their heads in agreement.

"Then Barney stopped the hoist motor," said Pace. "Don't know if it was because he was laughing so hard or he thought we wouldn't load a septic tank on the truck. Whatever, it jarred the hoist and set the chains to swinging. I can still see them starting to slip and tipping the septic tank to one side. Sure enough, the whole thing toppled over. The tank landed on one end, cracked open and tumbled Pearly Johnson's pine box onto the rocky ground. Fortunately, the coffin stayed closed, but there we were with an open tank and Pearly's bones only a board-width away from the light of day."

"What did y'all do?" I asked, unable to suppress a laugh.

"Your uncle stayed with the coffin while your dad and I went and told the family what happened. I insisted one of them come with us to decide what to do. You'd think we'd walked in with Pearly's ghost beside us. They all went white as a sheet. I finally got them to agree to cut a deck of cards to see who came out to the grave. In the end, we put the coffin in a real vault and brought Pearly to this new resting place. Ain't that right, boys?"

"God's truth," swore the witnesses.

"And now we're moving him again," I said.

As confirmation of that fact, the backhoe roared to life and the Tuckers began guiding it down the ramps.

Pace raised his voice over the throaty rumble. "Yep, family got an offer on this plot they couldn't refuse. Or so they say. Now Pearly's wife is dead and buried with their daughter in Waynesville. Pearly's going over to join them. Even though they're good Christian people, the grandchildren are afraid of haunts, of unquiet spirits. Said we owed it to Pearly to be the ones to get him settled. In peace and in one piece. And so we will."

"Why'd they sell his grave?"

Pace patted the fence. "Because of this guy. Caleb Turner."

"No-Reb Caleb," said a Tucker.

"Turncoat Turner," added his brother.

"Evidently Senator Richards looked upon Caleb Turner as some kind of personal hero," said Pace. "He paid good money to have his earthly remains buried beside the Civil War maverick. Funny thing, the reason I could get Pearly in this spot seven years ago was because nobody else had ever wanted to be buried beside Turner."

I nodded, now realizing BLESSED UNION FOREVER didn't mean being at one with the Lord.

Pace signaled to the Tuckers to begin digging. One of them crawled up in the metal seat and manned the controls. The jaws of the digger swung out over the plot. I stepped closer to the preacher.

"I've never heard of Caleb Turner," I said. "Was he a traitor?"

"Depends upon which side you take. Even I wasn't alive in 1861, but I know these mountain people were just stubborn enough to rebel against the rebels. About the only slaves around here were owned by the Charleston bluebloods who fled the lowland heat in the summer. Mountaineers didn't care much for them. Thought they were pretentious and pampered. It'd be like the Floridians seceding from the Union today and expecting us to join them because they've got summer places here. You know how that would go over."

"I guess some things don't change."

"Always been some kind of culture clash. But, the outsiders want the summer climate and the locals want the summer cash."

"What did Caleb Turner do?"

"He argued against secession. Then he coordinated a network of spies working between western North Carolina and eastern Tennessee. He knew the hills too well to ever get caught. They say he hijacked a shipment of engraving plates as they were being transferred from Alabama to Virginia. Hard to print confederate money without them."

"Sounds like he wound up a traitor to hear the Tuckers talk."

I looked at the two brothers. Their attention was no longer on the preacher's story but on the task at hand. The teeth of their backhoe bit into the center of Pearly's grave, scooping out a deep wound in the brown, wintered grass. Exposing the vault would not take long.

"Being branded a traitor came later," said Pace. "After the war, Turner joined the Republican party to get in tight with the Yankee carpetbaggers. The mountaineers didn't want to secede, but they sure as hell didn't like Northern reconstruction either. Over the years, the big monument Caleb Turner got for himself became a lightning rod. That's why the church put up that fence back in the 1920s. People used to dump garbage on his grave."

"Well, maybe now Caleb Turner, Pearly Johnson, and Senator Richards can all rest in peace."

I looked out beyond the maligned monument. The land dropped off steeply and the bare hardwoods at the lower edge of the cemetery no longer screened a view of the broad valley below. Thin trails of chimney smoke hung in the breezeless air, marking the resting places of the living on this cold Monday morning.

After a few minutes, I felt Reverend Pace move away. I turned to watch him step closer to the deepening excavation. It sank down at least four feet. The hoe began to make shallower gouges in the soil so that the vault wouldn't be damaged upon contact. Pace nodded his approval to the Tucker brothers. Then he suddenly flailed his stick at the backhoe. I saw a blurred shape topple out of its steel teeth and fall into the pit. It came to rest staring up.

The eyeless sockets fixed on me. The eyeless sockets of a human skull. Centered above those sockets was a single bullet hole.

Chapter 2

"Jesus God Almighty, Barney! Stop it, Barney, stop it!" The Tucker who wasn't Barney punctuated his screams by jumping up on the side of the machine and pounding his brother on the shoulder.

The engine sputtered and died. Barney jumped from the seat and crouched down at the lip of the hole. He looked at the skull and then up at Reverend Pace. "I'm sorry, Preacher. I never felt nothing. I swear to God. I thought it was all dirt."

"Of all people, it would have to be Pearly Johnson," exclaimed Pace.

"We're just to the top of the vault," I said. I sat on the edge, dangled my legs over the side, and dropped to the bottom. I bent down and worked my hands a couple inches into the soil. "Here's the vault. It's not damaged. Somebody get a shovel."

"You heard him," ordered Barney to his brother. He was still shaking and sucking in air.

I stood up and watched the other Tucker brother run to the pickup. The ear flaps on his cap bounced with each stride, and he looked like some deformed bird trying to fly. He pulled a spade out of the truck bed and hurried back.

I took the shovel and gently pried its point under the layer of dirt beside the last gouge of the hoe. I rocked the blade up and down, and a broader section of ground moved as if a root or stick had been dislodged. I withdrew the spade and began scraping away soil with its blunt edge. After a few passes, a dark, moldy piece of fabric broke through the surface. I tossed the shovel aside and dropped to my knees. The Tucker brothers and Pace leaned over the hole and watched in silence as I used my bare hands to unearth more of the cloth.

"Nylon," I said. "Here's a rusted zipper. Must be a wind breaker or light jacket." I felt underneath the exposed remnant, careful not to damage the fragile material. I looked up at the preacher. "Clavicle."

"What's that?" asked Barney. "More bones?"

"Yes, a shoulder bone," I said. "I expect an entire skeleton is here. This isn't Pearly Johnson, Barney. You didn't do anything wrong."

"What'll we do now?" asked his brother.

"We need to call the sheriff. We won't touch anything until he gets here. I know Tommy Lee's number and I've got a phone in the jeep."

Pace shook his head. "No, we're not in Laurel County. We've crossed into Walker. Sheriff Ewbanks has jurisdiction here. And this county's not set up for 911. You'll have to call information."

Pace and I left the bewildered Tucker brothers to guard the site and speculate as to the identity of the skeleton. I started the jeep's engine, hoping a brief blast from the heater would remove the chill which had penetrated my bones. Pace stretched his hands over the vent and shivered.

"What a mess, Barry. It's like Pearly's under some kind of curse."

I forced a smile. "Well, maybe he invited a friend over, or maybe Turncoat Turner is more popular than you thought."

But it wasn't funny. To think that a body had been buried on top of someone else. This was much more serious than a septic tank cracking open.

"Walker County Sheriff's Department." The mountain twang of the man's voice came through the low hiss of the cell phone.

"Yes, this is Barry Clayton of Clayton and Clayton Funeral Directors. I'm calling to report the discovery of a body."

"A body you say?" The voice sounded closer to the phone. "Where?"

"Buried in the graveyard at Eagle Creek Methodist Church."

"You found a body in a graveyard. Look, wise-ass, go chase your refrigerator. It's running." A click and hiss.

"He hung up on me."

"I think you'd better start your story differently," suggested Pace. "Otherwise, we'll be up here all day."

Fifteen minutes later, a tan cruiser with WALKER COUNTY SHERIFF'S DEPARTMENT written on the side pulled into the parking lot. Pace and I got out of the jeep and met the uniformed driver as he emerged from the car.

"You Mr. Clayton?" he asked, talking with a lit cigarette bobbing on the edge of his lip.

"Yes, and this is Reverend Pace."

"I know the preacher. I'm Sheriff Ewbanks. Horace Ewbanks. I'm sorry my deputy hung up on you. Kids give us a lot of trouble." He started walking toward the Tuckers.

"Anybody else coming?" I asked.

"Maybe. Depends on what we got. A deputy's standing by to lead up the state mobile crime lab if it's needed. I'll make that call, Mr. Clayton."

I figured Ewbanks to be in his early sixties. He was shorter than me, no more than five-foot-six, and he looked wiry and tough. White hair stuck out between the upturned collar of his leather jacket and the band of his regulation hat.

"What's Clayton doing burying over in this county?" he asked.

"Pearly Johnson's family asked us to move his grave," I said. "Senator Hugh Richards is being buried here tomorrow."

"Yeah. I knew the senator and his family. You Jack Clayton's boy?"

"Yes."

"Heard something 'bout that. Used to be a police?" He said the word "po-lice" with a couple of extra Os.

"That's right. Till my dad got sick."

"My momma had Alzheimer's."

He stopped and for a second the bantam rooster cockiness left him. "You know the last conversation I ever had with her when she made any sense?"

"No."

"She told me to give up these cancer sticks." He plucked the unfiltered burning cigarette stub from his mouth and flipped it back toward the church. "Promised Momma I'd quit some day." He stuck his hand in his jacket pocket and pulled out a pack of Pall Malls. "But today ain't the day."

Sheriff Ewbanks knew the Tucker brothers. He heard their accounts before going into the grave himself.

"Nothing been touched?" he asked again.

"No," I said. "Like I said on the phone, when I found the jacket and felt the additional bones, I treated it like a crime scene."

"Good." Ewbanks bent over and picked up the skull, cradling it in his right palm like a softball pitcher before his windup. He held the skull close to his eyes and studied it. Cigarette smoke flowed out of his nostrils and drifted around the macabre relic.

"You examine this?"

"No, I didn't."

He looked at it more carefully, turning it over several times before staring into the empty sockets. I thought of Hamlet in the churchyard, making judgments on the skull, on the futility of existence. "Alas, poor Yorick!" Horace Ewbanks didn't strike me as a man who would lose sleep over the meaning of life.

"Amazing, ain't it," he said. "We all look so ugly in the end. Some of us just have a head start." He looked up at me. "You know something about anatomy, and you're an ex-cop. Here, what do you make of this?" He handed me the skull.

"I'd say this hole was made by a small caliber bullet. Twenty-two or twenty-five."

"And?"

"And the owner of this skull was probably dead before hitting the ground."

"Thanks. That's an analysis I understand all too well." Ewbanks looked up at the overcast sky. "Preacher, what time is Richards to be buried tomorrow?"

"Three o'clock."

"All right. I'll call in the crime lab to help dig up the rest of the body. We should be able to finish that before dark, unless this snow sets in. Tomorrow, as soon as it's light, we'll sift through the dirt you dug up here to make sure we don't miss anything. Clayton, if we're clear by noon, will that be enough time to move this vault and be ready for the senator's service?"

"Yes, if the weather holds and I alert the other funeral home."

Ewbanks pulled himself out of the grave. "Well, ain't a hell of a lot I can do about the weather. I'm sorry, but if it runs us late, it'll just have to be that way. This is now the scene of a homicide. There won't be a burying until there's an unburying. I'm going to the radio." He headed for the patrol car, brushing the black dirt from his knees along the way.

Pace and I stood beside Sheriff Ewbanks watching two men from the mobile crime lab carefully remove the dirt from around the bones. Another deputy strung yellow tape in a wide rectangle from the parking lot to at least thirty feet beyond the open grave.

"Why's your man taping off such a wide area?"

"To keep the damn buzzards away," said Ewbanks.

"Buzzards?"

"The press. Same thing. I'll arrest any of them that cross that line, and they know it. Surprised they ain't here by now. Somebody's always monitoring the frequencies. They'll be screaming to get some pictures of our victim down there. Claiming the public's right to gawk." He took a final drag on his umpteenth cigarette, and then crushed it beneath his shoe.

Our victim was now more or less a complete skeleton. Shirt and trousers had rotted away, but traces of a leather belt ended in a silver buckle, the nylon jacket still had green color, and the bones of the feet were encased in moldy remnants of what looked like cowboy boots. One of the lab men delicately slid the hip bones to the side to search the ground underneath.

"Hey, hey, what have we here?" he exclaimed.

The sheriff and I moved closer to the edge. We watched the man reach a latex-gloved hand into the dirt and pull out a small, rusty pistol.

"Looks like he was either packing or the murder weapon was buried with him," said the man as he held the gun up for Ewbanks to inspect.

The sheriff didn't touch it. The lab man turned the pistol so that we could see barrel, clip, and grip.

"Too dirty to make out a serial number," said Ewbanks. "Doubt there's any chance of lifting prints. Colt twenty-five caliber. Chip in the grip. Not the kind of gun I'd expect on a guy wearing cowboy boots. Any sign of a holster?"

"Nothing attached to the belt. Nothing in the nylon jacket."

"Have the lab check the interior clip and any shells," ordered Ewbanks. "Maybe some prints were protected and got etched into the bluing. Alert everyone to look for a twenty-five caliber slug."

I watched the lab man drop the pistol in a clear evidence bag and seal it. Then he went back to fingering through the dirt where he'd found the gun.

"Ah," he said. "I thought maybe he'd have it in his hip pocket." He held up a nylon wallet, the kind held shut with a Velcro strip.

"See if you can open it without damaging it," said Ewbanks. "Maybe we can get an ID."

Carefully, the lab man slid his finger along the edge of the faded blue wallet, breaking the Velcro seal. It unfolded in his hand. I could see the red, white, and blue colors of a North Carolina driver's license in a plastic window.

"Issued in February 1997 to Samuel E. Calhoun," he said. "Asheville address. Caucasian. Date of birth August 21, 1959."

"Calhoun," repeated Ewbanks. "Now where do I know that name?"

"He's carrying more than four hundred dollars in cash." The lab man stuck a latexed finger where additional cards hid.

"Preacher, when was Pearly Johnson buried here?" asked Ewbanks.

"It would have been in the spring of 1997."

"Much go on up here during the week? Meetings? Choir practice?"

"No. The choir rehearses early Sunday before the service. Most meetings are Sunday afternoons. Weddings and funerals about the only other times that aren't Sundays."

"Here's something interesting," said the lab man as he continued to check the contents of the wallet. "Calhoun had a P.I. license. New York."

"Sammy Calhoun," said Ewbanks. "Now I remember. I wondered whatever happened to that guy. He hung around the courthouse, trying to pick up freelance work from lawyers. Struck me as a smart ass. Must have struck somebody else that way too."

His thoughts were interrupted by the sound of tires on gravel. We looked up the hill to see two cars and a mobile news van pulling into the parking lot. The buzzards were circling.

"Don't say anything to the press," said Ewbanks. "I don't want anything reported before I've cleared it. Refer all questions to me, understand?"

We all agreed. None of us wanted to be on the six o'clock news.

"Good. Preacher, why don't you go tell them I'll make a statement in a few minutes. Maybe they'll show you a little respect."

Pace nodded and started up the hill, brandishing his rhododendron staff in his hand like Moses headed out of Egypt. The snow began to fall like manna.

"Here's a babe I'd like to interrogate," said the lab man.

I turned around to look at his latest discovery. Staring at me out of the murdered man's wallet was a photograph of a beautiful brunette that stopped my heart cold—Doctor Susan Miller, the woman I loved.

Chapter 3

I sat in a total white-out. Jumbo flakes swirled around the jeep, but I could still make out the images of Ewbanks and the lab men as they walked up the hill. The white-out wasn't the snow; it was the blank wall of my mind.

The photograph in the murdered man's wallet had jerked me into an unknown past. Sheriff Ewbanks knew Sammy Calhoun must have been put into the grave shortly after Pearly Johnson, while the earth was freshly turned. When I met Susan eighteen months ago, she had told me she hadn't dated since college because the rigors of residency had consumed her time. Med school in New York had been just as tough. So if smart-ass Calhoun wasn't an old boyfriend, who was he? Why would a P.I. have carried Susan Miller's picture? Had he been following her?

Through the jeep's windshield, I saw the sheriff break away from the crime lab techies and head toward the news crew. One of the lab men held the evidence bags under his coat to screen them from the reporters. He and his colleague went to their van. At least Susan's picture wouldn't be given to the press. Not yet.

Ewbanks had released me from the scene. Pace was in the church, telephoning Senator Richards' sister and Williams Funeral Home with news of the delay. The sheriff had told him to reveal as few details as possible, making the pending snowstorm the culprit.

I decided I needed advice, and no one would speak straighter than my friend Sheriff Tommy Lee Wadkins. That meant face to face. I wasn't going to get into the details over my cell phone. I called his back door number to set up a meeting.

"Sheriff's Department. Deputy Hutchins speaking."

"Reece, it's Barry Clayton. Is the sheriff in?"

"Oh, it's you," he replied with as much enthusiasm as if I were selling magazine subscriptions. "The sheriff ain't here."

"Where is he?" Getting information from Reece was like getting helpful hints from the IRS. He was the self-appointed gatekeeper of the department.

"Somewhere close I hope. With this snow coming, we might have traffic emergencies."

"In that case, you're the best man to be in the office," I said, knowing he'd take it as the compliment it wasn't meant to be.

"Yeah, well, Sheriff's out this afternoon. His son Kenny's coming home. I'm going to do my best to keep things under control without bothering him. Something I can help you with?"

"Thanks, Reece, you just did. I wanted to ask when Kenny was coming in for the holidays." I hung up before the nosey deputy could ask why and dialed Tommy Lee's home number.

Tommy Lee's wife, Patsy, answered the phone.

"Kenny get in okay?"

"Just made it. Tommy Lee's helping him unload the car. That boy brings home every stitch of dirty laundry except what's on his back." She laughed and the joy of having her son home for Christmas rang through. "I'll tell him you're on the line."

"No. I'm driving in this mess," I lied. "And my mind shuts down when I talk. Is it okay if I drop by?"

"Sure. We'll save you a spot by the fire."

I looked at my wristwatch. Ten after three. "All right. I'll be there about four."

Tommy Lee and Patsy lived on the side of Laurel County farthest from Pace's Eagle Creek church. The snow-infested two-lane winding roads would keep me under thirty-five miles per hour most of the way. I wasn't going to push it. Four-wheel drive doesn't do a hell of a lot of good if you're tumbling down a mountainside.

I wanted to talk to Tommy Lee alone, but the afternoon activity of his household might make that awkward. Kenny was a sophomore at NC State in Raleigh, and their daughter, Samantha, was an eighth-grader who would be excited about her big brother's return. A roaring fire in the den would be a magnet drawing a close-knit family even tighter.

A good inch of snow covered the gravel driveway to Tommy Lee's house. Both Pace's bursitis weather forecast and my travel-time estimate were right on the money. I pulled the jeep behind a silver Taurus with icicles hanging from the rear bumper. Kenny's car had been hot enough to melt the snow, but now had sat long enough for it to refreeze.

The rambling brick ranch-style house was framed by white pines, now literally white as their boughs bent under the weight of the snow. I stepped from the jeep and took a deep breath. Through the cascading flakes came the sweet aroma of wood smoke from Tommy Lee's chimney. The only sound was the muffled whisper of thousands of tiny particles striking around me. I wished I were ten years old and my greatest concern was sledding with my buddies.

I crunched my way to the side of the house where I could enter through the utility room. Patsy didn't need a melting puddle to come traipsing across her living room carpet. The storm door was unlocked and a rack of coats, hats, and gloves hung from wall hooks just inside. I unzipped my jacket and started to deposit it in a vacant spot when the door to the kitchen opened.

"Well, where's your armload of wood?" asked Tommy Lee. "No one gets by me without paying the toll." His broad shoulders filled the doorway. A red flannel shirt and blue jeans didn't proclaim his off-duty status as much as the pistol missing from his hip. His grin was as warm as the air flowing out around him.

His one eye winked, momentarily blinding him to the fact that I wasn't smiling.

"Why don't we feed the pigeons," I said.

His brow furrowed, puckering the ever-present black patch that covered his sightless left eye. Tommy Lee's tour of duty in Vietnam hadn't come without cost, and the price he had paid was written across his face. "You want to talk," he said.

I nodded and put on my jacket.

Tommy Lee turned around and yelled, "Honey, I'm going to make Barry help with the birds before he falls asleep in front of our fire."

From somewhere inside the house, Patsy called, "Then put on your gloves. You're too old to get frostbite."

"Not me. You tell me I've got the hottest hands in Gainesboro."

He paused, and waited. We both got an earful of silence.

Tommy Lee laughed as he grabbed a gray parka from the rack. "She knows as soon as I come in I'll run my cold hands up her back. Been doing that for nearly thirty years. She hates it, but loves it when I make her mad."

I had to smile. For all his tough talk, Tommy Lee jumped at Patsy's command.

We walked across the back lawn to a wire mesh coop built at the edge of the woods. A chorus of coos originated from a wall that could fairly be described as pigeon holed. Birds nested in mailbox-sized compartments and peered out at the falling snow. The square cage was at least twenty feet on each side and ten feet tall. A dividing mesh bisected the enclosure so that brown birds were segregated from those with white and black markings. Tommy Lee's pigeons numbered more than fifteen, and they all seemed to be speaking their minds.

He uncapped a large rubber trash can, retrieved a scoop filled with cracked corn and held it aloft so that the birds could see it. Then he tossed the grain through the wire and onto the snow. The pigeons dropped from their cubbyholes like bailing paratroopers. The black and white ones began rapidly pecking up the corn, but the browns thrust out their chests and strutted back and forth between swallows.

"The black and whites are the tumblers, right?"

"Yeah, Hanover Tumblers," said Tommy Lee. "On a clear calm day, I need to have you and Susan come see them. They fly in an upward spiral, and then take a wild acrobatic fall hundreds of feet that would make an F-16 pilot hurl lunch."

"Why?"

"Why does any guy take a tumble? For a dame. Sex."

"How do you get them back in the cage?"

"What's more important to a guy than sex?"

"Food?"

"Right. Barry, what's so complicated about life? Why don't women understand us?"

"Who are these guys?" I asked, pointing to the brown pigeons huffing and puffing on their side of the mesh.

"They're the ones who screw it up for the rest of us. German Magpie Pouters. The males bloat themselves up, ruffle their own feathers, and try to intimidate. At least the tumblers actually do something."

"Guess they're like people."

"Like a lot of the pompous assholes I lock up, except these guys behave better in their cage."

Tommy Lee walked to the side of the coop and opened a screen door. He stepped in with the tumblers and began breaking the thin ice on the water trough.

"So, you want to talk about birds or people?" he asked.

The wire mesh between us provided a psychological barrier that kept his question safe, like the screen in a confessional. The distance helped me relax. We were having a conversation while he did some chores.

"I want to talk about a body."

"One that's at the funeral home?" He stopped fooling with the water trough. I had gotten his attention.

"No. One that was dug up out of the ground at Eagle Creek Methodist Church. Only it wasn't the expected resident. The grave had been sublet as a duplex."

"In the coffin?"

"On top of the vault. Appears to be a bullet wound to the skull. The body is nothing but a skeleton and remnants of clothes and cowboy boots. Sheriff Ewbanks came up to investigate."

"Hard-ass Hor-ass." Tommy Lee undid the wall of wire separating the two breeds and stepped in with the pouters. As he cleared their water, several males strutted around his feet as if giving an ultimatum.

"What kind of sheriff is he?"

"Good enough, I reckon." Tommy Lee let a wide grin break through. "Not as good as me, of course. Horace Ewbanks is old school. Been there since the Sixties and pretty much runs things his way. Lets the mountain boys make shine as long as they don't sell so much he has to do something about it. Doesn't have much use for Yankees, though he knows their tourist dollars get more important each year. He and I stay out of each other's way. Worst thing you can do with Horace is tell him how to do his job. You'll have to give a statement, but after that, you can put it out of your mind."

"I wish it were so easy."

"Why? Is there something else?"

"Mobile crime lab found a pistol. Might be the murder weapon. They also found a wallet. Samuel E. Calhoun, assuming the wallet belonged to the skeleton."

"Never heard of him," said Tommy Lee.

"Ewbanks had. New York P.I. evidently trying to get work down here. Had a North Carolina driver's license recently issued."

"Recently?"

"I mean recently related to when Ewbanks thinks Calhoun's body was buried. The original grave had been dug in the spring of '97. It would make sense that whoever shot Calhoun put the body in a fresh grave where no one would notice turned earth. The driver's license was dated February '97."

"That's good. Gives Horace a point to backtrack."

"There was also a picture in the wallet the sheriff will backtrack."

Tommy Lee stared at me through the wire. A few flakes rested on his black patch, but his good eye was clear and curious. He sensed we had come to the reason we were standing out in the snow. "Whose picture?"

"Susan Miller."

For a few seconds, all I heard was the cooing of the pigeons. Tommy Lee stood as frozen as the snow around us.

"I haven't said anything to her," I added.

"Well, you're going to have to. I take it you didn't tell Ewbanks."

"No. He didn't know who she was. Reverend Pace was there for the grave transfer, but he'd gone up to talk to the reporters before the photograph was discovered."

"Reporters?"

"A NEWSCHANNEL-8 crew arrived. I doubt if Ewbanks told them much of anything. The lab men took the photo along with the other evidence. Then I came here. The sheriff wants to sift all the dirt before we move the vault. That might be after the storm."

Tommy Lee looked up at the sky. "Could be a couple days. Now that we've broken the ice, let's get by that fire. I want to hear everything that happened."

Chapter 4

Susan opened the door before I had a chance to ring the bell.

"I'm so glad you came over." She stood smiling on the threshold wearing a long-sleeved denim shirt hanging over black jeans. Her brown hair was pulled back in a ponytail, and her face glowed with a vitality impossible to capture in any makeup bottle. She held up her hands and puckered her lips, a kiss-but-don't-touch gesture. Tufts of white feathers sprouted from her fingers.

"Are you molting?" I asked, giving her a quick peck on the mouth.

"I'm feathering my nest." She looked past me to the swirling snowflakes visible in the light spilling from her open door. "Isn't it wonderful? I couldn't help myself. I had to stop."

She was giddy. I felt sick to my stomach. My news would melt her joy faster than an August sun. "Stop from what?"

"You used to be a cop," she teased. "Figure it out." She pointed to her Subaru Forester in her parking space and then down at the ground.

I could see a depression scooped in the snow from the rear of the Subaru to her front door.

"I'll give you a hint," she said. "It's not a body."

She didn't know I had a body on my mind. But, that was what it looked like—a body dragged up the sidewalk and into her condo. Then I noticed scattered green needles peeking through the white powder.

"You got a Christmas tree."

She clapped her feathered hands together like a six-year-old. "Lying on a sheet in front of the fireplace. That's how I dragged it in. Old lady Grimshaw across the way was peering from her window. Probably thought it was a victim of my surgical skills. She's as much as told me women should have babies, not careers."

I looked back across the parking lot to the opposite condo. A sliver of light winked out as the nosey neighbor yanked closed the crack in her drapes. "And now the undertaker shows up," I said. "Well, let's hope she stays awake all night wondering if she's next."

Susan stepped back and beckoned me into her living room. "Come on. I want to introduce you to a Miller tradition."

I stomped my feet on her welcome mat and followed her into the condo where the heavy scent of evergreens hung in the air. I heard an a cappella version of "White Christmas" and thought this could be The Mormon Tabernacle Choir meets Robin Hood in Sherwood Forest. In front of the gas fireplace, a blue-green Fraser fir lay on a damp white sheet with its aromatic limbs bound in a mesh straitjacket.

"Usually the nest goes in the tree, not the other way around," I said.

She plucked feathery strands from her fingers. "And usually these are stuck on the bird."

Her glass coffee table had been shoved against the sofa so that the fir could be pulled into the room. Three unopened boxes of Christmas tree mini-lights were stacked on the hearth along with a shiny red tree stand and a tinsel star. A new CD case was propped up on the mantel, and the title A Mormon Tabernacle Holiday verified I'd been half right.

"While I was at the hospital, I realized Christmas is less than three weeks away, and I haven't done one thing to get ready. Not an ornament, a wreath, or even a sprig of mistletoe. After my rounds, I stopped at Wal-Mart and bought some instant traditions. Except for the tree decorations which I'm making myself.

Rather, I was until you came to help me." She gestured to the dining table just off the kitchen. "Angels in a bag."

Newspapers covered the top of her table. The jumbo-size container of Elmer's Glue sat beside a clear plastic bag which overflowed with fluffy white feathers. A smaller bag contained wooden beads. Clothespins spilled out of an overturned box. Behind the box, a row of angels had come into being from glue, wood, and feathers.

I walked over and examined the six-foot tree. Sap oozed from the severed trunk, and I guessed no more than a day ago it had been on a mountainside within fifteen miles of here. Next to apples, Christmas trees were the largest crop in Laurel County.

"You didn't buy this tree from a rustler, did you?"

"I got it from the Boy Scouts' lot on Church Street, but now that you mention it, they did look a little shifty." She held out her hands. "Here, give me your jacket. It's dripping. I'll put it in the sink before it ruins the feathers." As she walked to the kitchen, she asked, "You serious about rustlers?"

"Tommy Lee told me Earl Statton lost two acres of trees last night," I said over the sound of the opening refrigerator. "Must have been a well-organized theft with trucks and laborers. He figures they hit between midnight and five. Those trees are probably already on lots from Charlotte to Charleston."

Susan returned bearing a glass of chardonnay and a mug of Newcastle Brown Ale. Her festive spirit wasn't making my mission any easier.

"That's despicable," she said. "How long did it take to grow those trees?"

I took the ale and sat at the table, careful not to disturb the pile of feathers. "From twelve to fifteen years."

"Those creeps. They not only stole the trees, they stole all the time some poor family put into raising them." She slid into the dining room chair beside me and took a healthy sip of wine. "And at Christmas too. It's almost sacrilegious."

"And in a few weeks, those trees will be worthless. It's nearly impossible to recover them and get them back in time to salvage any profits."

"Did Tommy Lee call you for help?" she asked. Then she mimicked a Texas drawl. "You in a posse fixin' to ride the range in search of them rustlers?"

"No." Suddenly, I felt closed in. Susan was right beside me. She was getting ready to make Christmas decorations on her dining room table, and I was ready to get a buried body out on the table.

"Good," she said. "Then we can get started on these angels. Stevie taught me how to make them. The clothespin's the body, the wooden bead is the head, and two white feathers are the wings. Then you clip them on the tree. The Miller tradition is a tree with nothing but lights and white-feathered angels."

"Sounds easy enough."

"It is." Her voice lost its bright edge. "The first craft I remember learning. We used to decorate a fir by Stevie's grave with them each Christmas. I guess Dad stopped after I went to New York and I never picked it back up."

I had learned about Susan's brother on our second date when I asked her if she had any brothers or sisters. "Only Stevie," she had said. "He died a long time ago." The way she had said it kept me from pressing for more information and she had offered none.

Susan twirled a feather between her fingers, and then stroked the plume across the back of my hand. "You would have liked him," she said.

"If he was anything like his sister, I'm sure I would have."

Susan shook her head. "He wasn't like me, but I sure wanted to be like him. Stevie was the adventurer, the first to jump off the wet rocks into the darkest creek waters, the first to climb white pines so high the limbs became thin as fingers."

"He was older, right?"

"Seven years. I was only five when he was killed." She took another sip of wine, and tears formed in the corners of her eyes.

"Late one afternoon, Stevie took me out to a lightly traveled, narrow two-lane blacktop that ran at the end of our dirt road to teach me how to ride his bicycle. He thought if I could get the feel of my balance without having to pedal over gravel or dodge roots, I could master it. He couldn't do anything about the seat set too high or the boy-style crossbar, so I had to mount the bike like a pony, throwing my leg over the saddle and then pedaling while standing up."

"Must have been a challenge for a five-year-old."

"I guess, but if Stevie could do it, then I wanted to learn. He had me stand by the edge of the road as he demonstrated how to get the bike rolling downhill while swinging a leg up over the crossbar. He'd just pushed away when I heard the sputter of an engine behind me. A pickup crested the hill, weaving and swerving as it sped down toward us. I screamed at Stevie, and then jumped across the ditch to hug the fence post on the other side."

Susan took a deep breath. She looked down at the feather. "I can still see him looking back over his shoulder, squinting against the fireball of the setting sun and trying to balance as the bike slipped onto the dirt shoulder. The truck veered away from me, crossing over into the other lane. Then the driver must have realized he was on the wrong side of the road and cut back sharply, sending the pickup straight at Stevie. He tried to jump off the bike, but it was too late. He was in mid-air when the right fender caught him on the thigh and slammed him against the strands of a barbed wire fence. The driver spun the truck out of the ditch, dragging the mangled bicycle under the rear axle. He never stopped."

She wiped her eyes with the back of her hand. I said nothing, knowing she had more to tell me.

"The state police found the pickup truck a mile away, side-swiped against a tree. The driver was unhurt and so drunk he couldn't remember how he got there. Stevie died at the rural clinic because there wasn't a surgeon able to get to him in time." She laughed bitterly. "The backwoods of North Carolina wasn't a lucrative place to practice. So, here I am, the rural surgeon who wasn't there for him."

I wasn't surprised those clothespin angels had become a tradition. Amid the joy of the Christmas holidays, Susan would always grieve for Stevie. I stared at the feathers, beads, and clothespins and knew I couldn't wait another minute. I stood up, crossed to the bookshelf and turned down the stereo.

"What's wrong?" asked Susan. "I didn't mean to upset you."

"Tommy Lee didn't call me about tree rustlers," I said. "He told me about them when I saw him this afternoon. I needed his advice."

Susan set the feather on the table and gave me her full attention. "About what?"

"About what was found this morning up in the Eagle Creek Methodist Church cemetery."

Susan didn't ask the obvious question. She patiently waited for me to tell her. I skipped all the preliminaries and jumped right to what concerned me. "Did you know a Sammy Calhoun?"

She looked away and reached out for her glass. I sensed she was stalling for time. Whether it was to try and remember Calhoun or decide what to say, I didn't know. The tremor in her hand sent a ripple through the wine as she brought it to her lips. She swallowed, and then whispered, "Sammy Calhoun, I haven't heard that name in a long time."

I waited.

"He used to work in Asheville. I met him through my Aunt Cassie. He was a detective. Last I heard he moved to Texas. Why? Is he back?"

"I'd say he never left. This morning a skeleton was found buried on top of a vault. The original grave was dug nearly seven years ago."

The blood drained from Susan's face. "And you think it's Sammy?"

"The sheriff of Walker County found a wallet with the bones. Contained a driver's license for Samuel Calhoun. He was buried with moldy cowboy boots and a green windbreaker."

Susan's gaze wandered around the room, never lighting on anything in particular. "I'm sorry to hear he's dead." Then she made the connection. "If another sheriff is handling it, why did you see Tommy Lee?"

"Because there was something else in the wallet. Your picture."

She flinched, as if my words slapped her. "My picture?"

"Yes. I didn't want to say anything to Sheriff Ewbanks till I talked to you, and I didn't want to talk to you till after I checked with Tommy Lee."

"I met him through Cassie," she repeated. "I can't help who has my picture. Was it just me?"

"Yes, a close-up smiling at the camera. I only saw it for a second, but it was long enough."

Susan stood up and started pacing in front of the kitchen. "Could you tell where it was shot?"

"No. Looked like some buildings behind you. What difference does that make?"

"Just that it could have been taken by anybody. Sammy could have gotten it from my aunt. He's not in it, right?"

"No, but it's still in his wallet. Tommy Lee says you should come forward. I can tell Ewbanks I saw it but wasn't sure it was you."

"Why get me involved in something like this?"

I was surprised at her defensiveness. To me the easiest way to get uninvolved would be to make a simple statement to Ewbanks and let him follow other leads. "Look, Susan, I went to Tommy Lee because you are involved. Like it or not, yours is the only photograph in a murdered man's wallet."

"Murdered?"

"Yes," I said, letting my exasperation get the better of me. "He didn't bury himself."

Susan started to cry.

"I'm sorry," I said. "I'm upset that you're upset. Maybe you're right. We can wait a day or two and see what happens. Maybe they'll get a lead off the gun."

"Gun? What gun?"

"They uncovered a pistol that could be the murder weapon. Rusty but they might get a trace on it. Little Colt semi-automatic. Twenty-five caliber."

Susan reached out and steadied herself against the wall. "Excuse me," she managed to say as she headed for the bathroom.

I turned up The Mormon Tabernacle Choir until I could no longer hear her vomiting.

Chapter 5

Susan waved to me from the front door. I honked a goodbye like everything was normal, like a shadow hadn't fallen across our relationship, a shadow cast by a skeleton.

She had emerged from the bathroom, shaken and apologetic, claiming to have been stunned by the fact that someone she once knew had been murdered. She begged me not to say anything to Ewbanks. "I don't want to be dragged into an awful crime I know nothing about," she had said. "If I could help, I would." I had looked into those tear-filled brown eyes and melted.

Now, driving through the snow-filled black night, I felt uneasy. Had I made a mistake involving Tommy Lee? Would he feel obliged to talk to Ewbanks? Or was I letting Susan's emotional reaction cloud my judgment? The real problem was that my own curiosity had been aroused, but I had no business prying into a past Susan wanted closed.

One thing I did know—the bodies of Pearly Johnson and Senator Hugh Richards wouldn't be going anywhere tomorrow. Sheriff Ewbanks would be dealing with snow on the grave and snow on his county roads.

The radio weathercast now predicted six to eight inches. Even Pace's bursitis had underestimated the accumulation. I had the choice of driving five miles out to my cabin or spending the night at the funeral home. The only obligation I had at the cabin was my roommate, George Eliot. George was a Peruvian long-haired guinea pig, and her three water bottles and self-filling feeder ensured she would survive the blizzard for a few days.

Although the jeep could navigate the roads without any trouble, it wasn't the roads I was worried about. Other drivers were the greatest hazard to my safety. Give a southern good-ol' boy a snow-packed road and he'll do something stupid with it every time, usually involving a souped-up Camaro and a six-pack. I decided I'd enter the funeral home vertically instead of horizontally.

I drove down Main Street without passing another vehicle, which in my hometown wasn't unusual after eight at night. The light from Gainesboro's streetlamps became pyramids of animated snowflakes, and the dying business district took on a charm that temporarily masked the ravages caused by the strip malls along the nearby interstate. At least Wal-Mart wasn't offering funeral services—yet.

Clayton and Clayton Funeral Directors operated from the same white antebellum home my grandfather purchased in 1930. Set back on a rolling hill on the outskirts of town, it projected a tranquility and stability that served our clients well, and it was also a home in every sense of the word. Mom and Dad still lived on the second floor.

Jack Clayton had been a pillar of the community, a revered citizen and friend to those in need. So, when one day he pulled out of a funeral procession and passed the hearse, not only was the family he was driving shocked, but the whole town was shaken by the revelation: my father suffered from the early onset of Alzheimer's.

That had been over six years ago. For the next three years, he and Mom tried to run the business while searching for a buyer. None of the chains were interested, and my uncle Wayne had neither the finances nor the desire to take on full responsibility. By then Dad's condition had deteriorated to where there were more bad days than good days and all the cheat sheets and memory tricks he had devised no longer served to get him through basic interactions.

So, I left my job on the Charlotte police force, abandoned my criminal justice studies at the university, and returned home to help. The choice cost more than my career; my marriage didn't survive the strain and Rachel had moved to Washington D.C. and all the things Gainesboro was not. Although the divorce was amicable on the surface, bitterness filled my life and threatened to consume me with self-pity.

Then about two years ago I met Susan Miller. She had appeared at a graveside ceremony, standing with the family of a seven-year-old girl her skills had not been able to save. Their grief was her grief, and her tears had touched my heart. Now I feared an intruder in the grave of Pearly Johnson would become an intruder between Susan and me. Where one grave had brought us together, another might tear us apart.

I turned onto the unblemished snow-covered side street by the funeral home. The second floor lights were on and I caught a glimpse of my father peering through his bedroom curtains at the wintry spectacle captured by the outside floodlights. He could have been standing there for a minute or for an hour.

The garage behind the funeral home had been constructed to shelter four vehicles: a hearse, a family limousine, a personal car, and an ambulance. From 1930 to 1962, Clayton and Clayton Funeral Directors also provided emergency rescue service for Laurel County. Dad told of many a night being roused from his bed to transport a birthing mother whose baby wouldn't wait or a bleeding driver who had tried to straighten out a mountain road. When the county established its own paramedic unit, my father and my uncle Wayne gladly sold them the ambulance as backup. I had always wondered why the community wanted a business whose revenue came from burying the dead to be responsible for keeping someone alive. It must have been a tribute to the integrity of Clayton and Clayton that no one saw the conflict of interest.

I parked my jeep in the bay once occupied by the ambulance and tromped along the hidden sidewalk to the back door. My Docker moccasins were no match for the snow and I felt the cold powder penetrate my feet from heel to toe. Fortunately, I kept extra clothes and boots in a spare closet just for such an unexpected overnight visit. Weather respects neither the living nor the dead.

I slipped my shoes off on the back porch and entered the kitchen in damp stocking feet. Mom stood at the kitchen sink, wearing a calico apron and washing up the supper dishes. "Trying to sneak up on me?" she asked without turning around.

"I knew you saw me through the kitchen window."

She looked over her shoulder and smiled. "Yes, and for a moment your hair was as white as mine. Dry it with a towel before you catch your death."

Mom and Uncle Wayne both had hair the color of cotton, but where she stood a smidgen under five feet, my uncle topped six. Mom was a rotund bundle of energy; her brother, an easy-loping "tall drink of water," as the locals described him. Walking together, they looked like a bowling ball and a bowling pin.

"Do you want something to eat? There's some cold chicken in the refrigerator."

The mention of food triggered a pang in my stomach. My last meal had been a bowl of granola and apple juice at breakfast. "Thanks, and I'll finish cleaning up. I'm here for the night, if that's all right."

Mom grabbed a plate from the shelf. "I'll rest easier knowing you're not out on the road. Sit down and I'll fix you a plate."

I slid into my customary place. The chrome and Formica kitchen table had been in the funeral home as long as I had. Mom set a blue and ivory dinner plate in the spot once reserved for my favorite "Peter Rabbit rounding the cucumber frame" bowl. She retrieved a platter with three pieces of cold fried chicken and a Tupperware container of coleslaw.

"I can make you something hot if you'd like."

"No, this is fine."

She gave me silverware, and then said, "I'll put on a kettle for tea."

She brought a gas burner on the white enamel stove to a blue flame and centered her kettle over it. "Your dad was fascinated by the snow. That's why we ate so late."

"He was still at his window when I drove in."

Mom untied her apron and hung it on a peg under the red electric wall clock. It was nearly eight.

"Oh," she said as she sat across from me. "Before I forget, your uncle Wayne wants to talk to you."

"I hope he's not thinking of driving in tomorrow."

"No, talk by phone. He asked me to have you call him as soon as I heard from you. He doesn't like leaving messages on that answering contraption."

"Mom, he needs to get used to it. The world's turned into a bunch of machines talking to each other. People expect it."

"Not your uncle."

I didn't argue. Mom would vigorously defend her brother and I saw no upside to offending my favorite source of fried chicken. "Yeah, Uncle Wayne probably has the only rotary phone left in the county."

"And it still works fine," Mom said. "So, call him when we finish our tea."

"Tonight?"

"He said it was important. He'll be up late. His GRIT Magazine came today."

I laughed out loud. GRIT Magazine made Reader's Digest look like a sleazy tabloid. The publication dated back to the 1880s and used to be sold by kids door-to-door in rural communities across the country. Uncle Wayne said it was his first job and his first reading primer. For years, he insisted on keeping a copy in the family visitation room because "the happy stories will lift their spirits." I finally got him to stop when the Yankee retirees kept mistaking it for a southern cookbook.

"Then Uncle Wayne might be up till nine," I said. "Maybe even nine-thirty. I'll call him after I see Dad for a few minutes."

"Your father had a good day," Mom said. "I think the snow kept him focused."

"One day at a time," I said. It was how we lived with Dad—on a rollercoaster of emotional ups and downs, learning to communicate with fewer and fewer words. His medical treatment now included Aricept, which seemed to have slowed the degenerative progress of the disease, but neither that drug nor anything the doctors foresaw on the horizon promised the return of husband and father to our family.

"How was your day?" asked Mom. "You get finished at Eagle Creek before the storm?"

"There was a complication, a serious complication."

"Oh?" The wrinkles in Mom's round face deepened.

Before I could continue, the shrill whistle of the kettle penetrated the kitchen. "Why don't you make our tea, and I'll tell you about it."

A plate of Mom's Christmas butter cookies had been served with the tea, but my description of the events at the cemetery had so far kept either one of us from eating them. I was grateful for Sheriff Ewbanks' admonition not to tell anyone too many details. Although I'd confided in Tommy Lee and Susan, it gave me an excuse to stop the story with the discovery of the wallet and to emphasize the official procedures the sheriff said he would have to follow.

"Of course, it should be kept a secret until they notify next of kin," said Mom. "I wouldn't want to know."

"I expect they'll be able to do that quickly." I relaxed and grabbed a cookie. Mom's reaction was more of concern for possible loved ones than curiosity about the body.

"And poor Senator Richards' family," she added. "A delayed burial and now all this snow."

"Reverend Pace said the public memorial service can go on as scheduled. It wasn't tied to the interment."

"That's a blessing. Reverend Pace is the perfect man to comfort them."

"Pace said there isn't much family. Evidently Richards' relationship to his sister was cool at best, and the senator had been divorced for years. That's another reason he wanted to be buried next to Turncoat Turner."

"Don't speak ill of the dead, Barry."

"Sorry. I just meant there weren't family ties to keep him from resting beside his hero."

Mom took a cookie. "Must have paid a pretty penny to get Pearly Johnson moved. If someone ever wants my plot, you get a good price."

"Mom, I'd never sell your grave."

"Don't be silly. Your dad and I will be in a better place than a patch of dirt. And he'll be in his right mind again. If you're in your right mind, you'll take the money. Just keep us together, and maybe not too close to a road. They're always widening them."

"Tell you what, Mom. When the snow melts, we'll go look at some backup plots."

She laughed and got up from the table. "Why don't you take a glass of milk and the cookies up to your father. Then you'd better call your uncle."

I found Dad still standing at the bedroom window, his head rhythmically bobbing up and down as he watched the flakes tumble through the floodlight. His face was so close to the pane that his breath fogged the glass. His right hand rested against the sill. One suspender dangled to his knee while the other looped over his shoulder. Belts had been traded for suspenders since they were easier for him to manage when using the bathroom. A pair of gray flannel pajamas lay across the foot of his bed. I suspected he had started to get undressed and caught a glimpse of the snow. Perhaps during the time he had eaten dinner, he had forgotten about it.

With cookies in one hand and milk in the other, I couldn't knock on the open door. I cleared my throat softly, and then whispered, "Dad."

His reaction came a few seconds later. He turned and the light of recognition sparkled in his eyes. It was a wonderful sight. "Barry," he said.

"Yes," I replied.

"It's snow," he said, and turned to make sure the snowflakes still fell. "Snow," he repeated.

When my father spoke, he kept his sentences short. Too often his words collapsed in on themselves as the thought he wanted to express evaporated.

"Yes, Dad. Snow."

He kept staring out the window.

"Dad, I brought cookies and milk."

Again, I waited for him to respond. After a few seconds, I started to speak again.

"TV," he said to the night sky. Then he turned around and looked at the cookies. "TV."

He had made the association. We always had our cookies while watching television.

I helped him change into his pajamas and walked him to the den at the end of the hall. He settled in his easy chair and I spread an afghan over his lap. I found the remote control on top of the set and started flipping through the channels. I'd glance at the screen and then at my father's face to see if the picture caught his interest. As usual, he grunted approval when I reached the Cartoon Network.

I sat on the sofa and watched a couple minutes of Yogi Bear and Boo Boo trying to outsmart the ranger. At first Dad would look over at me every few seconds to make sure I was still there. Then his attention became focused on the talking animals. When the on-screen action was at its most frenetic, I got up and stepped in front of the set. "Bathroom," I said.

He shook his head and waved me aside.

"I'm going to the bathroom," I explained.

"Go," he said.

Mom and I were blessed that Dad still could handle his own toilet functions and he never questioned when we said we had to go. It became the easiest excuse for leaving him.

I met Mom as she came up the stairs.

"I'm going to call Uncle Wayne," I said. "Dad's changed and in the den."

"I'm sorry. Did you want to use the office? I've already locked up and turned out the lights."

"No, the extension in my room is fine. I'll be back in a few minutes. Uncle Wayne talks on the phone like he's paying by the word."

My bedroom was officially the guest room, but it still bore the décor of my youth. Mom had kept my model cars and planes, various sports pictures and trophies, and a sprinkling of favorite knickknacks on the shelves and bureau. It wasn't so much a preservation for my benefit as a haven for Dad. Old memories are the strongest and wandering down the hall and into my bedroom would reassure him he was in familiar surroundings.

I closed the door and sat on the side of the single bed. Nine-fifteen. My uncle should still be awake. I dialed the number.

His black rotary phone sat on an end table in his living room, hardwired into the original jack in the baseboard. I always expected at least eight rings before he answered because Uncle Wayne was never in the living room. After his wife, my Aunt Nelda, died in 1983, Wayne spent all his time at the kitchen table in the winter and on the screened back porch in the summer. He claimed no one ever called him but us, so if he didn't get to the phone in time, he just dialed the funeral home.

After the tenth ring, I heard his raspy voice announce "Thompson."

"Uncle Wayne, it's Barry. Did I wake you?"

He cleared his throat. "Oh, no, just haven't used my voice in a while. I don't talk to myself—yet."

"So, are you reading about a woman who grew a turnip that looks like the Pope, or a man who built his own fighter plane?"

"A husband and wife who drove their Airstream trailer around the world. Lived in it on board freighters."

My uncle took his GRIT seriously so I moved on. "Mom said you wanted me to call."

He cleared his throat again. "I didn't mention it to Connie, but when I was in the office this morning, we got a call from some man named Ted Sandiford."

"Sandiford? Never heard of him."

"That's cause he was calling long distance, though you could have fooled me. Sounded clear as you."

Since Wayne didn't like answering machines, I wasn't about to get into the wonders of digital technology. "Long distance from where?"

"Atlanta, Georgia," he said with the same awe as if the city had been Paris, France. "He said he was interested in our market."

"Our market?"

"I didn't know what he meant, either. I asked him if he was talking about Winn-Dixie or Ingles. One's good for meat, the other for produce."

"That's not what he meant."

"Right. Wished you'd been here. He said we were a growth market and he wondered if we'd be interested in selling the business."

I stood up from the bed and looked back to make sure the door was closed. "He wants to buy Clayton and Clayton?"

"Yep, but not him personally. He's with some company. Hoffburg or Hoffton."

"Hoffman?"

"That's it. You heard of them?"

"It's a huge chain with funeral homes all over the southeast. What else did he say?"

"Not much cause I told him to save his breath."

My stomach inverted and I struggled to keep my voice below a shout. "You did what?"

"I said you'd be making any decisions so he should talk to you. I didn't want to leave a written note in case Connie found it. Figured you'd want to handle it quiet like."

I sat back on the bed and took a deep breath. I should have realized Wayne would know exactly what to do. When you calm and console grieving families, you become adept at avoiding anything that causes anxiety. Mom didn't need to worry about any business issues until we were more certain of the possibilities.

"Did he leave a number?"

"Yes, you got a pencil?"

I fished one out of the nightstand drawer and wrote Sandiford's number on the back of a magazine. "Thanks, Wayne. I'll call him tomorrow."

"What are you going to tell your mom?"

"That you wanted to check our work schedules. That okay?"

"Yep." He paused, and then cleared his throat a third time. "Barry, you know I don't mind working, but you do what you think is best."

"I'll find out what this Sandiford is proposing, and then we'll see what's best for Mom and Dad."

"And what's best for you, Barry. It's okay to think about that."

He hung up, leaving me uncertain about what to do. Since my father's illness, my uncle had made his own sacrifices, taking on more responsibility than a man his age should. We only had one part-time assistant and at times the funeral business can be overwhelming. Wayne had never complained. Now I wasn't sure how to read his reaction. Did he want to keep working or was he just saying that so I wouldn't feel forced to take a less than reasonable offer? I traced over the Atlanta number again, darkening it while the numbers were fresh in my mind. I would call first thing in the morning.

For the next forty minutes, I watched television with Dad while Mom, beside me on the sofa, knitted yet another sweater for her church mission board. Somewhere in the Balkans, an entire village must be wearing Connie Clayton originals.

An episode of "Rocky and Bullwinkle" had just begun when I heard the dialogue of moose and squirrel grow interlaced with my father's snoring. "Looks like Dad's good day is ready for a good night."

"We'd better get him to bed," said Mom. She looped the excess yarn into a skein and tucked her needles in her knitting bag. "I think I'm going to turn in as well. Stay up if you like. The television won't bother me."

I gently shook Dad's shoulder and he woke up with the bewildered look a normal sleeper quickly loses. He remained disoriented until we got him into his bed. For a moment, he stared at the window, but the pulled shade masked the snow. If he remembered the magical scene outside, he showed no curiosity. Mom sat on her adjacent bed. Dad rolled over where he could see her. Then he closed his eyes.

"What time do you need to be up?" asked Mom.

"Seven-thirty or eight. Since there's nothing going on, it'll be a good morning for me to start year-end inventory." I kissed her goodnight and returned to the den. I lost myself in the cartoons until I had to face the real world on the late news.

At eleven, I grabbed the remote control and switched stations. Graphics swooped across the screen, building NEWSCHANNEL-8 ELEVEN O'CLOCK REPORT in brash gold letters against the panoramic helicopter footage showing the twinkling lights of Asheville nestled among the mountains under a starry night sky. I guess they didn't have a snow special effect to add to the stock footage. The title scene froze as the theme music reached crescendo, and the scene dissolved to a solemn-faced anchorman with the graphic MATT MARKLE boldly displayed across his chest.

"Good evening," Matt said in a mellow, well-modulated voice. "A white Christmas has been delivered early. We'll have complete weather details and traffic conditions in a moment, but first tonight's lead story."

The camera zoomed out from Matt Markle, leaving room in the upper right corner for the word MURDER to appear in red over his shoulder.

"As we reported at six, human skeletal remains were found this morning buried atop a vault in the Eagle Creek Methodist Church cemetery."

Videotape rolled of the snowy graveyard. I saw myself walking up the hill from the backhoe. I looked dazed, but the camera zoomed past me and focused on Sheriff Ewbanks and the crime lab team.

Matt Markle continued his voice-over. "Sheriff Horace Ewbanks was called to the scene when preparations for the interment of the late State Senator Hugh Richards led to the grisly discovery. Interviewed in a NEWSCHANNEL-8 exclusive, Sheriff Ewbanks said—" a close-up of Ewbanks appeared with the cemetery out of focus behind him; he looked defiantly into the camera, his burning cigarette on his lip—"we'll know what we've got here, when we know what we've got here, and when I have something to say, I'll have something to say."

Some exclusive. The report cut back to Matt Markle at the anchor desk. The hallowed words NEWSCHANNEL-8 EXCLUSIVE had replaced MURDER on the screen.

"Less than an hour ago, NEWSCHANNEL-8 learned the body is suspected to be that of Samuel Calhoun, a private investigator believed to have left the Asheville area in the spring of 1997, a time consistent with the condition of the remains."

The photo I had seen on Calhoun's driver's license appeared full-screen. Somebody was on top of things in the newsroom. I wondered if Susan had tipped off her aunt, the show's producer.

"Sheriff Ewbanks refused to confirm Calhoun is the victim, but sources close to the case state both Calhoun and the murder weapon have been identified. We take you live to Cliff Barringer, our investigative reporter on the scene at the Walker County Courthouse in Tyler City for an interview with District Attorney Darden Claiborne."

A tall man in a dark blue suit stood on the snowy steps in front of a courthouse. Several print journalists gathered around him, jotting notes as if he were uttering the Sermon on the Mount. The camera panned left to reveal a middle-aged reporter with a neatly trimmed beard standing on the sidewalk a few yards away and clutching a hand mike close to his lips. The NEWSCHAN-NEL-8 logo appeared on his jacket and the mike.

"Thank you, Matt," he said. "District Attorney Claiborne has agreed to give NEWSCHANNEL-8 exclusive comments regarding his progress in determining who murdered the man discovered in Eagle Creek cemetery." He called to the D.A. "District Attorney Claiborne, can you share with our NEWSCHANNEL-8 viewers the status of your investigation?"

The D.A. held up his hand to the print journalists as if to say, "Sorry, boys, TV is calling." He took the arm of an attractive woman standing beside him and descended the steps to Barringer.

The reporter thrust the mike in the D.A.'s face like Zorro attacking the Spanish commandant. The camera zoomed in and a name appeared in the lower third of the screen: Darden Claiborne. District Attorney. Walker County.

Claiborne, mid-forties with the perfect touch of gray in his temples, exuded confidence. He peered straight into the camera and spoke dramatically. "The citizens of Walker County can rest assured that my department will get to the bottom of this murder. Although I must be careful not to compromise the case we are building, I expect both the identity of the victim and a suspect in the killing to be named soon."

"Is the victim Samuel Calhoun?" asked Barringer.

"The name is being withheld until attempts to reach next of kin have been exhausted."

"Has Sheriff Ewbanks taken anyone into custody?"

"The sheriff and his team are pursuing promising avenues of inquiry that I expect will culminate in an arrest." Darden Claiborne then actually took a step closer to the camera. "My fellow citizens, again let me stress that the safety of our community is my main priority. I have no reason to believe any of you are in danger, but I ask if you have any relevant information, please contact my office. We'll be working round the clock to see that justice prevails. And now my wife, Carol, and I wish you a good night. Rest well."

The camera zoomed back to reveal his wife wearing a plastic smile. Her lips quivered at the corners from the cold. Claiborne then turned away and led his wife into the falling snow like two-bit actors in a late-night movie. The camera panned to the reporter, who said "Thank you, sir" to the shadows, and then stared into the lens. "There you have it. District Attorney Claiborne's first official comments. We will stay with this rapidly developing story wherever it leads. For NEWSCHANNEL-8, I'm Cliff Barringer live at the Walker County Courthouse. Back to you, Matt."

I clicked off the set. Claiborne had been quite the grand-stander. Why would he be outside in a snowstorm at eleven o'clock at night unless he wanted the face-time? And having the spousal accessory on hand for the photo-op. Vintage political campaigning. I remembered he was rumored to be consider-ing a run at Attorney General. In North Carolina, that was a frequent launching pad to the governor's mansion. Claiborne hadn't denied the victim was Sammy Calhoun, and he seemed pretty confident a suspect would be named. I hoped that would happen without involving Susan.

As I sat down on my bed, I glanced over at the magazine on the nightstand and saw the phone number for Ted Sandiford. Tomorrow promised to be a busy day. I turned out the light and lay down, but sleep didn't come for hours.

Chapter 6

"Barry, wake up. Your father's gone."

A bucket of ice water couldn't have jarred me awake any faster. Mom retreated outside the door as I grabbed yesterday's clothes from the closet.

"I heard him get up and go into the bathroom," she said. "Then I fell back asleep." She was close to crying.

"You're sure he's not in the house?"

"I've looked everywhere."

"What time did you hear him?"

"About forty-five minutes ago. His boots are gone and there're footprints leading off the front porch."

I jammed my shirt tail in my pants and pulled on my socks.

"He saw the snow and got excited. Can you tell if he wore a coat?"

"He took his raincoat and boots, but I can't find his pajamas. He must still be wearing them."

I hurried past Mom to retrieve my boots from the cabinet on the back porch. A quick glance at the thermometer outside the screen door showed twenty-five degrees. How long could Dad survive in sub-freezing temperatures wearing pajamas and a raincoat? Where was he headed? He had enough trouble finding his way without being adrift in a sea of white.

Mom handed me a coat and gloves. "What can I do?"

"Call the neighbors. And call the sheriff's office. Someone might spot him. He can't have gone far."

I pushed open the back porch door, scraping away at least eight inches of snow. I ran around the funeral home and found the tracks heading straight down the walk until they veered off toward one of the large spruce trees at the edge of our lawn. The snow had weighed down the branches and turned it into a thirty-foot igloo. As a kid, I had loved to crawl inside. My child-like father might not be any different.

His trail circled around the tree at least two times and then led to the street. The footsteps disappeared into a packed tire rut that made walking easier. Another passing vehicle had obliterated his trail and I wasn't sure whether he had turned right or left.

Our funeral home was on the edge of town where the street name changed from Main to Green River Highway and the speed limit increased from twenty-five to thirty-five. I looked in both directions, but the road was deserted. Overhead, the morning sky promised a Carolina blue day, the kind of crystal brilliance that would hurt the eyes. Already the clear arctic air stung my face and I knew the snow clouds had been driven out by a high-pressure wintry blast that would send temperatures lower even as the sun rose higher.

I jogged in the direction of town because that would be the way most familiar to Dad. No other footsteps split off, and I had gone a couple blocks when a Pepsi delivery truck, grinding gears as it struggled to accelerate, headed toward me. The driver kept the wheels in the ruts as closely as a train to the tracks. He gave a beep of the horn to warn me out of the road. I stepped into the deep snow between the grooves and waved my arms over my head.

The transmission sounded like it would fall into the street. A double-clutched downshift slowed the rumbling vehicle without sending it into a skid. The cab rocked to a halt about six feet in front of me, close enough to see Pepsi—Born in the Carolinas written above the grill and anger written across the driver's face. His shaggy brown hair and beard encircled his scowl like a ragged oval picture frame. I forced a smile and walked to his side window.

He cranked down the glass and snarled, "I don't sell off the truck."

The absurdity of his statement blew right by me. That I would be standing out in the snow, flagging him down for a cold soda would only seem possible to a man who believed in his product or was duped by its advertising.

"My father wandered off this morning," I said. "Did you pass an older man walking into town? Raincoat, maybe pajamas showing underneath."

The Pepsi driver shook his head. "He sick?"

"He gets confused."

"Sorry. And sorry I barked at you. Just worried about getting down the mountain on time."

"People want their Pepsis."

"You got that right. My granny drinks one every morning instead of coffee. Claims it keeps her regular."

I thought that was Dr. Pepper's claim to fame, but I knew better than to argue with a man risking his life to drive carbonated sugar water down snow-covered mountain roads. "I'm not sure what direction he took. Would you keep an eye out?"

"Yep. Listen, I just turned onto Main back at Rockland. If your daddy went beyond there, I wouldn't have seen him."

"Thanks." That meant town was still my best bet and I started to walk away.

"Hey," he called, "if I find him, where do you want me to take him?"

"Where's your next stop?"

"Hell, I'll carry him back for you. I'm sure you'd do the same for my daddy."

In the rural south, daddy is the permanent term even if the child is seventy-five. "Clayton Funeral Home," I told him.

His eyes widened in boyish wonder and my estimate of his age dropped from forty to thirty. "You lost another relative?"

"He's Mr. Clayton. He lives there."

"Well, don't you worry none. If he's headed my way, I'll fetch him or my name ain't Joshua Crowder." He pulled open his frayed leather jacket to reveal Joshua embroidered on his blue shirt in Pepsi-like script.

"Thanks, Joshua. Drive carefully."

As I passed his rear axle, the three-ton truck lurched forward, spewing black-blue exhaust onto the pure snow like a smoker's cough smudging a white handkerchief.

In the next block, any hope I had of trailing Dad from the road was obliterated by the blade of a snowplow. I retreated to the safety of the sidewalk and watched as a three-foot wall rose between me and the street. I called to the plowman but he only raised his chin in acknowledgment and kept his attention on the curb.

At a few minutes after eight, most businesses in Gainesboro would have been closed even on a normal day. The town would be slower to stir this morning. Old man Larson's drugstore used to open at seven-thirty to sell coffee and prepackaged Little Debbie cakes, but his arthritis and an abundance of breakfast franchises on the interstate had caused him to start opening at nine.

Beside Larson's Discount Drugs, there was movement behind the plate glass of Fats McCauley's furniture store. Although the McCauley name had been scraped from the window, its ghostly image stained a milky memorial to the family that had been a Main Street fixture for over fifty years. A young couple from Atlanta had bought the store without having to share the town's grisly memories of Fats' murder. They planned to turn it into an Appalachian artisans gallery. Through the window, I saw a lanky young man wearing a wide tool belt stretch a measuring tape across a countertop—ambition personified on a wintry morning.

I started to rap on the pane when I heard someone shout my name. Up the street, standing atop the plow's snow bank like Sir Edmund Hillary on Mount Everest, P.J. Peterson waved frantically. "Barry, he's here, he's here!" His white barber apron flapped around his sides, turning him into a snowman with wings.

Dad sat in the first chair, eyeing himself in the wall-length mirror. When he saw my reflection, he smiled and said, "Haircut."

"I called your mom," said P.J. "She said you were looking for him. I kept stepping outside hoping to catch sight of you. I didn't dare leave him."

"Glad you were open."

"Haircut," repeated Dad. He looked at P.J. expectantly.

"I wasn't." P.J. reached for a clean barber's cloth to snap around Dad's neck.

If my father hadn't been sitting in his pajamas, the scene could have been from a Norman Rockwell painting. P's Barbershop hadn't changed since P.J.'s father opened it nearly seventy years ago. With Fats McCauley's death, P.J. and Larson became the last remnants of the simpler, innocent small-town era of the 1950s.

"I was upstairs debating with myself whether to open," continued P.J. "I heard pounding on the door. Guess he came here because your mom just brought him in for a haircut yesterday."

"Maybe," I said, but I suspected it wasn't yesterday's visit. Dad had been a lifelong customer. It was more likely a boyhood memory guided him there and into the first chair, the one that hadn't been used since P.J.'s dad died nearly twenty-five years ago.

"I'll give him a quick trim on the house," said P.J. "Man hikes through all this snow it's the least I can do."

"Want me to move him to another chair?"

"No, that's okay. Kinda nice cutting the hair of someone my dad barbered all those years. His customer in his chair."

"Just a little off the top, Pete," said my father.

In the mirror I saw Pete Peterson Junior blink back tears at hearing his dad's name. "Yes, sir, Mr. Clayton." He hesitated, looking at his time-traveling customer through the mirror in a way that pulled him back into his own images of the past. Then he ran a comb straight through my father's hair and began snipping air.

"There's some Pepsis in the back, Barry. Help yourself. Ain't had a chance to put on coffee."

"No, thanks. Better save them in case the snow causes a Pepsi shortage for the regulars."

P.J. nodded without understanding my private joke.

"How'd he get out?" asked the barber.

"Just walked out. He woke up and saw the snow."

"Reckon y'all have to do something. How about them invisible fences?"

I stared at P.J.'s reflection, expecting a wink. The man wasn't kidding. "Wear a dog's shock collar?" I asked.

"Ssshh," he said. "I don't mean to upset him." P.J. stepped around to the front of the chair where we could talk eye-to-eye. "Maybe something that would ring a bell or sound an alarm. They got all sorts of high-tech stuff these days, you know, for keeping criminals prisoner in their own homes."

I realized P.J. meant well. Although he considered my dad to be his father's customer, Pete Peterson Junior and my dad were both in their sixties. Like so many others in Gainesboro, P.J. found it painful to see a lifelong friend disintegrating before his eyes. Was keeping Dad a prisoner in his home being suggested for my father's security or for P.J.'s? An undertaker bears the extra burden of reminding a community of its mortality. An undertaker with Alzheimer's shows that death may approach in insidious increments that can keep a body above ground long after the person has ceased to exist—a fate far more fearful.

"Well, we'll have to do something," I admitted. "Can I use the phone? I'd better call my mother."

"Sure. Tell her I'll run you home. Main Street ought to be plowed by now."

As I dialed from the wall phone at the rear of the shop, I watched P.J. and my dad framed against the bright whiteness outside—two boyhood friends: one sat falling into shadow, the other still stood in the light.

Mom met us at the back porch with dry slippers for Dad and a mug of black coffee for me.

"Did you let the neighbors know?" I asked.

"Yes, and I notified the Sheriff's Department everything was all right. A man telephoned a few minutes ago. Wondered if we found your father."

"Who was he?"

"I'm not sure. Hard to hear because he was talking beside a highway. Do we know a Joshua?"

I eased Dad into a kitchen chair and pulled off his wet boots. He hadn't bothered to wear socks and his feet were like ice cubes. "Drives a Pepsi truck," I said.

Mom dabbed melted snow from my father's hair and neck. "He told me P.J. must give a good haircut and that he'd have to try a store-bought one sometime."

I was touched by the stranger's concern. "Joshua's a nice guy. I met him on the road out front. I think we should start stocking Pepsis to offer families."

"I think I'd better take your father up for a hot shower," said Mom. "Then I'll get you some breakfast."

"Don't bother. I can fix myself an English muffin." I looked at the clock. Five minutes after nine. "I'm going to work on year-end inventory and I've got some calls to return."

Mom led Dad upstairs. I locked the deadbolts on the front and back doors and set the keys where Mom and I could easily find them. An invisible fence was out of the question, but something needed to be done. The morning episode had been an adventure I didn't want repeated. Perhaps Ted Sandiford offered a solution.

I closed the office door behind me, laid the magazine with Sandiford's number by the phone and pulled a new legal pad from the drawer. Overhead, I could hear the shower running.

"Good morning. Hoffman Enterprises." The woman's voice was crisp and pleasant.

"Ted Sandiford, please."

"May I tell him who's calling?"

"Barry Clayton, from Gainesboro, North Carolina."

"Yes, Mr. Clayton. Mr. Sandiford told me to put you right through."

Everyone likes to feel important, and the idea that I was being given preferential treatment gave my ego a boost.

"Barry, Ted Sandiford here. Thank you for returning my call, especially since the Weather Channel says the sky fell on you."

"Looks like we'll have a white Christmas." I jotted "Christmas" on my legal pad as if it were some significant point. Writing down my own words only happened when I was nervous. "My uncle said you called."

"Yes, a delightful gentleman." Sandiford sounded like he was in his late fifties and his mellow southern accent had overtones of an Eastern education. "I'll get straight to the point, Barry. You know anything about bird dogs?"

"Bird dogs?" I asked. I scribbled the word under "Christmas" and wondered if Uncle Wayne had gotten the message confused and this man was trying to sell me something.

"Yes sir, because that's what I am. Hoffman Enterprises pays me to spot what they're hunting. I'm a pointer. When I see something I like, I point it out to them."

"So they can shoot me?" I laughed, although being in the funeral business had already gotten me shot once.

"I don't want this to come out wrong, but I know a little bit about your situation. Four years ago, we looked into bringing Clayton and Clayton into our company. I was the bird dog and I liked what I saw."

"I never heard about it. Did you speak with my father?"

"No, it never went that far. At the time, we had just come through a major expansion and capital funds were tight. We had to get the operation phase of our new acquisitions under control. And, frankly, the situation in Gainesboro worried us."

"Too small?"

"Too unstable. We knew about your father's illness, and although we could have approached you with a price favorable to us, the management team was leery of picking up a property with uncertain operational variances."

The phrase was so corporate sounding I didn't bother to write it down. "What's that mean?"

"Barry, Hoffman Enterprises is a business. We utilize all of the strategic and managerial tools available to operate at a fair profit."

"Right, so why didn't you make a fire-sale offer when you learned my father had Alzheimer's?"

"Because that wasn't the issue. You were the issue."

"Me?"

"Yes. I may have a string of degrees and years of business experience, but I also understand the uniqueness of our industry. I'm a second son."

"Second son?" The man was losing me in a conversation of meaningless phrases.

"You're an only child, Barry. You've probably never heard of what I call second son syndrome. My family ran a funeral home in Irondale, Alabama. I was the second son, and there wasn't enough business to support two families, even though at the time I wanted the home more than anything. My brother was older by ten years, he made a buy-sell arrangement with my father, and I got tuition money for Harvard Business School instead."

"Want more than anything" went on my pad.

"So I know a funeral home is about relationships with the community," continued Sandiford. "There was no continuity we could see at Clayton and Clayton. You had taken a different path."

"And that made a difference?"

"Absolutely. Our business model is to buy family funeral homes, keep the family as employees, and run the business with the efficiencies of a large corporation able to buy equipment, supplies, and services at discount volume."

Wal-Mart has come to the funeral business, I thought, except the people saying "Welcome to Wal-Mart" are all kinfolk.

"Without that family link," said Sandiford, "we decided we couldn't afford to take a chance on re-staffing while we had so many other operations in transition."

"What's changed?" I asked. I drew a line across the page, figuring we were getting to the heart of the matter. There was a knock on the door behind me. "Hold on a second," I told Sandiford. I tore off the sheet and stuck it in the magazine just as Mom came in with a plate of toasted English muffins.

"Oh, I'm sorry. I didn't realize you were on the phone. You never made your muffins." She set the food on the magazine beside me and retreated. I waited until her footsteps faded down the hall.

"Go ahead, Mr. Sandiford."

"Ted, please. A couple things changed. Four years have passed and our operations are running smoothly under the Hoffman umbrella. We're profitable and we need to re-invest in our own company. Otherwise, certain tax advantages will be lost. And then there's you. You've returned and from my conversation with your uncle, I gathered you've done an outstanding job interfacing with your community."

"Interfacing?"

Sandiford laughed. "Now that's a word that's just full of it, isn't it? I mean people think highly of you, Barry. You provide a good service. Clayton and Clayton is in good hands and I'd like to know if you're interested in joining hands with us. We have a lot to offer each other."

"Maybe, but I need more information."

"Of course. So do I. There is one consideration about the timing."

"What?"

"Our fiscal year ends December 31st. If we can fast-track this thing, it helps our bottom line, and some of that help can be passed on to you."

"You mean the sooner the deal, the better the deal?"

"Exactly."

I looked at the calendar hanging above my computer screen. Today was the 9th. Ted Sandiford was talking three weeks with Christmas thrown in the middle. "That's awfully fast, Ted. I don't see how we can get everything worked out."

"We don't need everything worked out. If we have some key documents completed and notarized by year end, our team of accountants and lawyers can massage the details."

I didn't have a team other than my archery buddy Josh Birnam who did our taxes and Carl Romeo who had drafted my parents' wills. I was David with an abacus going into negotiations against a massaging, interfacing Goliath who had invented his own syndrome. Ted Sandiford heard the silence.

"Barry, I want you to think what's best for you and your father. You'll come out with cash and a job. We offer corporate health care, a 401-k profit-sharing plan, administrative support, and you don't even have to change your commute."

"What about my parents?"

"You can use the money to get them into a proper home or a facility that handles special needs. I know this has hit you out of the blue. Like I said, I'm a bird dog. The corporate tax lawyers let me off my leash and I'm looking for the best game I can find. I hope we can at least go to the next level."

"What's that?"

"Meet face to face. Bring you down to the Atlanta office. You can get some numbers together for me and I can give you more specifics and start to hammer out a potential deal. What do you say? Is Thursday or Friday better for you?"

The dates on my calendar were as empty as a roadside wine bottle. "You know this business," I said. "Hard to say. Right now I could probably swing Friday."

"Great. I'll keep both days open in case you need to adjust your schedule. Now here are some things you should pull together."

Sandiford spent the next fifteen minutes listing the information I was to bring. In essence, he wanted our company books with the expense and revenue figures for the last three years. He also wanted purchase details of all our funeral supplies, furniture, embalming equipment including serial numbers, and company vehicles. His team would do a depreciation analysis which would affect the categories of the financial package Hoffman might offer. I hung up the phone with a head and legal pad swirling in numbers.

My first concern was explaining to Mom why I would be going to Atlanta. I didn't want to lie but I didn't want her to worry about a deal that might go nowhere. I decided to call Uncle Wayne. To my shock, he picked up the phone after two rings.

"Are you okay?" I asked.

"Fine. Why shouldn't I be?"

"You're right by the phone."

He laughed. "Getting ready to telephone you. See if you need any help. People always die when it's least convenient."

"Nobody's died, but we did have a problem." I told him about Dad's pursuit of a haircut.

"Well, no two ways about it," stated my uncle, "we got to figure a way to keep your dad from wandering off. Come spring-time some tourist will run over him."

"There might be an answer before then," I said. "I just talked to Ted Sandiford in Atlanta. I think Hoffman is going to make an offer for the funeral home."

My uncle said nothing for a few seconds. All I heard was shallow breathing.

"Uncle Wayne?"

"Could be the best thing, Barry. It's up to you and your mother."

"I want your say in it too, Uncle Wayne. And they want us to stay on."

"An old coot like me?"

"Come on. You know more than any of us. And you have to admit most of our business is old coots."

That got a chuckle out of him. "You told your mother yet?"

"No, and that's a problem. They want me in Atlanta Friday to talk about a deal. What do you think? Should we have a family meeting?"

"Yes, when we've got something specific to discuss. But give your mom credit, Barry. She lives every day with the uncertainty of your father's condition. She can live with the uncertainty of a business deal. Tell her you got a call and you're going to at least listen to what they have to say. You're the one with the future stake in all this. We're here to support you."

I thanked him and hung up. His advice made sense. Lunch would be the time to bring it up. Family decisions were always best discussed around the kitchen table.

I spent the rest of the morning compiling the figures for Ted Sandiford. Most of the information would be required for our business tax return anyway. Over tomato soup and turkey sandwiches, I told Mom about my Friday trip. She seemed more concerned about road conditions than the actual meeting. I suspected she didn't want to discuss the implications of a sale as far as what she and Dad would do. Like Uncle Wayne, she kept deferring to whatever I thought best for me. I wanted to say what's best for me is to know what's best for you, but I held my tongue. Uncle Wayne was right. We needed more information.

At three o'clock, I was cross-referencing purchase records for embalming fluid and reconstructive cosmetics when a loud rap shook the office door.

"Wake you up?" asked Tommy Lee. He came in and eased into the red leather chair beside my desk.

"Why? Is this normally nap time in your department?"

"Not today. We had to work. Too many crazies out in the snow." As he spoke the last words, his rough face reddened as he remembered Dad's escapade.

"Present company included?"

"You know I didn't mean that. One of the reasons I dropped by was to see how he's doing."

"He's fine, but it looks like Mom and I have to become jailers. Any tips?"

Tommy Lee shifted in the chair, catching his holstered gun on the armrest. "You might consider installing inside electric locks. They work with a magnetic plate and a keypad. Punch in the code and the door opens. Then you're not worrying about using a regular key to lock and unlock the doors."

"Beats P.J.'s suggestion of an invisible fence," I said.

"You could put a fenced area in the backyard. Give your dad a little roaming room without being able to wander off."

The idea had merit, but not if we were moving. Although I wanted to talk to Tommy Lee about selling the business, I decided to wait till after my Atlanta trip.

Tommy Lee unbuttoned the chest pocket of his uniform jacket and withdrew a postcard-sized piece of cardboard and handed it to me. A color photo of a young blonde girl was on one side and descriptive information and phone numbers were on the other. The girl's name was Tammy Patterson. Her picture looked like it had been taken for a high school yearbook.

"This girl's gone missing," said Tommy Lee. "Two weeks now. Everybody but the parents is convinced she ran away to Atlanta with her twenty-five-year-old boyfriend. Her father had these printed up and distributed to law enforcement offices in five counties."

I knew where Tommy Lee was headed. "If Dad wanders off, you and your deputies could have them all ready."

"Right. All of my deputies know your dad by sight, but the cards are also good for showing other people. I could keep them in the patrol cars. Take this one. The company's name is on the back." He shifted again, edging forward in the seat.

"You want to move into the front room? That chair's pretty uncomfortable."

"No, I'd rather talk here," he said, and glanced at the door.

I realized he had closed it behind him.

"There's something else," he said, dropping his voice. "I have a friend in Sheriff Ewbanks' department. I asked him a few questions, unofficially. He's taking a chance for me so none of this can get back to Ewbanks."

"I understand."

"Seems like Hard-ass Hor-ass was livid last night that someone leaked Sammy Calhoun's name to the TV station. I figured you told Susan and I know her aunt works at NEWSCHANNEL-8."

"I told her not to tell," I said. I wished I felt more confident she had listened to me.

"Sure," said Tommy Lee. "The information could have come from any number of sources. Ewbanks is also pissed at the D.A. for making this case a showpiece. That just ratchets up the pressure and the media coverage. Suspects get dragged into the spotlight before a case has been built. I'm sure the same thing happened in Charlotte."

Tommy Lee was right. Although I had only been a patrolman, I had heard the detectives complain about how too much pressure on high-profile cases created leaks that undercut their investigations.

"They've got something already?"

"They found the slug in the dirt. Must have stayed in the skull and fallen out when the backhoe uncovered it. Ballistics report came this afternoon. The Colt twenty-five fired the fatal shot."

"They pull a number from the gun?"

"Yeah, and believe it or not prints were on the clip, but nothing's been matched yet. They got lucky with the serial number too. The gun's owner registered it. My contact says Ewbanks plans to drop by his house unannounced this evening. After the newscast and after most of the reporters have gone home. He doesn't want any press tailing him."

"You know who owns the gun?"

Tommy Lee nodded. "Walter Miller. Susan's father."

Chapter 7

When it rains, it pours. Or in this case, when it snows, it dumps. Tommy Lee had no sooner stunned me with his revelation about Susan's father than Mom knocked on the office door.

"I hate to interrupt," she said. "The McBee family or at least a goodly portion of them are in the front room."

"Who?"

"Claude McBee. He died this morning at the Springhaven nursing home and four grandchildren have come in a four-wheel-drive pickup to make funeral arrangements."

"I think we're done here," said Tommy Lee. He stood up and Mom backed into the hall.

"Tell them I'll be there in a moment," I said. "I'll see Tommy Lee out." I walked him to the back porch where we could talk a minute before I met with the family.

"If you need me later, I should be at my desk," said Tommy Lee. "Afraid I don't have any advice other than to play it straight with Ewbanks."

"I'm not going to bring up the picture unless he directly asks me about it."

"And he might not ever ask. Ewbanks now has a connection stronger than whether you recognized a photograph."

"I appreciate the advance warning."

"I trust you to use it appropriately." He zipped up his jacket and stepped onto the unshoveled walk. "And here's another tip.

If Stony McBee is here, don't let him leave without frisking him. That man's got magnetic fingers."

I watched him trudge to his patrol car in the driveway. He and someone in Ewbanks' department had gone out on a limb for me. I'd be very careful not to saw it off.

"I called Wayne," Mom said behind me. "He's coming in."

"I wish he wouldn't do that. Freddy should be available." Freddy Mott worked as our on-call assistant, and I'd rather have him on the roads than my elderly uncle.

"He's taken care of calling Freddy. Wayne says he knows the McBees won't do anything before Saturday and he wants you to keep your Atlanta appointment."

"All right," I agreed, but I resented Uncle Wayne preempting my decisions. In some ways, I would never outgrow being little Barry, the favorite nephew. "I'll make the arrangements with the McBees and then I'm going to snow-blow everything. It's my responsibility to see Clayton and Clayton is open for business."

I met for about half an hour with Claude McBee's four grandchildren. They were representing Claude's son and daughter, who were still at the nursing home. They wanted "to get in line," as a granddaughter phrased it, in case somebody else died. I gave them basic information to take to their parents while watching the lanky young man named Stony. Although it may have been my imagination, he seemed to be casing the room. We set an appointment for a more detailed consultation, and I made it a priority to shake Stony's hand and eye his pockets for suspicious bulges.

After they left, I cleared the snow from the walks and driveway. The mindless chore let my thoughts ramble. I kept thinking about the pistol in the grave. I was surprised that Walt Miller even owned a gun. Maybe he bought it as a paperweight. Walt made his living with a calculator and tax forms, and if Central Casting were asked to supply a CPA for a movie scene, Walt Miller would be the guy. The idea that he could outgun a private eye and then bury him on top of someone else was so preposterous as to be laughable. Except I couldn't laugh away the picture of Susan in the murdered man's wallet.

Between the top and bottom of the handicap ramp, I made the connection how I could get information from Walt without compromising Tommy Lee's informant. Ted Sandiford's phone call gave me my cover.

The winter sun raced toward the Appalachian ridges as my jeep moved slowly but steadily along Highway 25. It wasn't quite four-thirty, and I became concerned I hadn't allowed enough time to travel from Gainesboro to Walt Miller's cottage north of Asheville.

Susan's father was a sixty-five-year-old widower who had found himself surrounded by too many memories. Three years ago, he had sold the house where he and his wife had lived and moved to a two-bedroom stone cottage purchased from a client's estate. Although he maintained an office in Asheville, thanks to email and the Internet, most of his accounting practice was being handled from his house. I expected to find him there, but I wanted to catch him alone. As dusk deepened, the prospect grew that Sheriff Ewbanks might arrive at Walt Miller's sooner than I would.

I turned onto his drive and relaxed. The snow was unblemished.

"Barry? What are you doing out in this weather?" He met me at his front door with a quizzical expression that immediately changed to panic. "Susan? Is Susan okay?"

"Yes, Walt. She's fine. Sorry to drop in unannounced. I was driving around doing some thinking and I realized you were nearby. I stopped in on the chance you'd have a few minutes to talk business."

His relief that nothing had happened to his daughter over-rode any question as to why I'd be twenty miles from home in the snow.

"Sure. Come on in. Is this a den discussion?"

"You might want to make some notes."

He led me back to the second bedroom, which served as his office. Through the rear window I could see snow covering the border of grass between the house and bare hardwoods. The long twilight shadows of tree trunks and twisted limbs spread across the white canvas, soon to be lost in the evening darkness.

Walt crossed the room to his oak desk where stacks of client files became a barricade between us. Susan had told me that for as long as she could remember, Christmas had been celebrated with tinsel, trees, and IRS forms, just as Easter had meant colored eggs, chocolate, and April 15th tax returns. Walt stood braced against the back of his desk chair, looking at me curiously. The collar of his red flannel shirt bunched around his neck, and errant strands of thinning gray hair radiated from his head.

"So what's on your mind?"

"I'm thinking of selling the funeral home." I eased into the chair opposite him.

Walt pondered my statement and nodded. Then he rolled his swivel chair to the end of the desk where he could look around the mountain range of papers. "You going back to Charlotte?"

"I don't know. Probably not right away."

"Have you told Susan?"

"No. I haven't told anyone. The preliminary meeting with the buyer is Friday in Atlanta. I want to keep it confidential. The whole thing may fall apart."

"Happens more often than not," he said. "What can I do?"

"Josh Birnam's been our accountant for years so I'll bring him into it, but I'd like to get a second opinion, a paid opinion on the best way to structure things. You may have more life experience."

The chair squeaked as Walt leaned back and laughed. "That's probably the most diplomatic way I've ever been called an old geezer. Sure. Glad to help. But this consultation's on the house. Josh is a good CPA. I may have some suggestions to protect your parents' estate. I assume they'll be moving."

"Mom will at some point. Dad's going to need supervised care soon. He took an arctic expedition on his own this morning."

"Is he all right?"

"Yes. Luckily I was there to look for him." I tried not to let the tension come through my voice as I cast my bait. "Guess that was one good thing about the body at Eagle Creek cemetery."

"What body?" Walt brought the chair forward and leaned across the desk corner.

"You didn't see the news last night?"

"I don't stay up past ten and today's newspaper is somewhere under the snow."

"We were doing a routine grave transfer yesterday and found a skeleton buried on top of the vault. By the time I got through with the sheriff and crime lab, the weather was so bad I stayed at the funeral home."

"They know who it was?"

"NEWSCHANNEL-8 said the body has been identified as Samuel Calhoun."

Walt Miller didn't speak. His face turned as gray as the twilight snow. I just sat there.

"You found Sammy Calhoun?" he whispered.

"I found a skeleton. All I know is what I heard on TV."

Clearly, the news startled him. I tried to analyze deeper reactions; he seemed reluctant to say more.

"So, you knew him?" I pressed.

Walt looked at the papers on his desk. "Not really. Someone Susan met in New York."

"New York?"

"When she was in med school."

The ground suddenly shifted under me. Susan had told me she met Sammy Calhoun through her Aunt Cassie. That she couldn't help who might carry a picture of her. I thought about the photograph. The street and buildings in the background could be New York. No skyscrapers but the eclectic storefronts of lower Manhattan. Susan had asked me if she were alone in the picture. Was that to make sure there wasn't evidence tying her to

Sammy Calhoun? I sorted through the jumble of contradictions with the mind of an ex-policeman and the heart of a lover.

"He was bad news," said Walt. "I thought he moved away."

"He followed her to Asheville?" I asked.

Before he could answer, a solid knock sounded from the front door.

"Who could that be?" asked Walt.

I followed him, knowing Horace Ewbanks had arrived.

The sheriff stood straight as a new fence post. The only thing different in his attire from when I'd last seen him was a toothpick dangling on his lip instead of a Pall Mall. He planned on coming inside.

Behind him, a deputy slouched against a stone column of Walt's porch, his easy grin in contrast to the sheriff's scowl.

"Mr. Walter Miller?" asked Ewbanks.

"Yes."

"I'm Sheriff Horace Ewbanks from over in Walker County. This is my deputy John Bridges. We need to talk with you a few minutes." He looked at me. "Evening, Mr. Clayton. Small world ain't it?"

"Mr. Clayton's here for an appointment," said Walt. "Is something wrong? Has there been an accident?"

"No. Just a few questions. Where can we talk in private?"

Walt looked back at me as if I somehow had a say in the matter.

"It's all right. I'll wait."

"Okay," said Walt. "I have an office, Sheriff."

"That'll do. Bridges, keep Mr. Clayton company. Have a little chat. I don't think we'll cut into his appointment too long."

"Y'all can use the den," said Walt.

The fact that Ewbanks gave me a keeper rather than follow a two-on-one interview procedure made me nervous. He wasn't pleased to discover the man who found Calhoun's skeleton in the home of the owner of the murder weapon.

Deputy Bridges trailed me into a pine-paneled room with a stone fireplace at one end. An oval, brown and tan braided rug covered the hardwood floor between a cracked leather sofa and the high hearth.

"Have a seat," I said. "I'll tend the fire." I dropped the kindling on the glowing coals and heard the crackle as new flames greedily devoured the dry oak strips. For a few seconds, the acrid smoke leaked from the fireplace until the air warmed enough to carry it aloft through the chimney. I added split logs, and then I sat down on the hard hearth. The long shadows of the andirons danced like animated bones on the floor between us.

"That was quite a surprise yesterday," said Bridges. He angled his body in the corner of the sofa and propped one leg across a cushion, careful to keep his damp boot clear. He looked about forty. Close-cropped black hair. A moustache starting to turn gray at the edges. Everything about him was easygoing except his eyes. "Who would have thought to hide a body in a graveyard?"

"You didn't take my call yesterday, did you?"

"No. That was Clint Carson. I hear he hung up on you. Failed to see the humor in the situation."

"So did I."

"It's no laughing matter, that's for sure."

Bridges closed his eyes and took a deep breath. "Sheriff was lucky you were the undertaker."

"How's that?"

The deputy ignored the question, content to enjoy the warmth of the fire. After a few minutes, I thought he might be squeezing in a quick nap. Then he opened his eyes and looked at me as if he'd been watching me through his closed lids all along. "Tommy Lee Wadkins says you're a good man. I heard all about that Willard business last year."

Dallas Willard had killed his brother and sister at the funeral of his grandmother. He'd turned the shotgun on me but didn't go three for three. I had a nice scar on my shoulder as a souvenir of the adventure and a closer friendship with Tommy Lee because of the collaborative success we had in bringing a killer to justice.

"You've worked with Tommy Lee?"

"Used to be his deputy. My wife died about ten years ago and Tommy Lee arranged a job with Ewbanks so my thirteen-year-old daughter and I could move to Walker County and be closer to my parents. Raising a teenager and working the crazy hours of law enforcement was a recipe for disaster. I knew I needed help."

"Glad it worked out."

"For a time. A girl without a mother was a handful. Since she turned eighteen, we've hardly spoken."

I didn't know what to say, and so I just nodded and stared at the fire.

"But Tommy Lee was there for me when I needed him. He knows he can count on me." He let the statement hang out in the air.

I got the message. John Bridges was Tommy Lee's conduit of information.

"I mentioned the skeleton to Walt Miller," I said. "He hadn't heard anything about it."

"Surprised him?"

"Yes, but didn't alarm him."

Bridges nodded. We were having a conversation on two levels and each of us knew it.

"What did you tell him?"

"I gave him last night's news report. The possibility of the body being Sammy Calhoun."

Bridges grunted his disapproval. "That leak put a burr up my sheriff's butt."

"I haven't talked to any reporters."

"Miller react to Sammy Calhoun?"

"Yeah. He knew him. Not well he said but enough to be shocked he was dead. Walt thought he'd moved away. I'd have to say his surprise was genuine. Why's Ewbanks talking to him?" That was my bullshit question. Bridges probably suspected Tommy Lee had told me about the gun, otherwise what was I doing there? But I asked it so he could repeat it to Ewbanks and keep everything tidy and innocent.

Bridges smiled. "Yeah, Tommy Lee said you were a good man. Charlotte police?"

"That's a lifetime ago."

Our conversation shifted to Tommy Lee. I found out Bridges had been the one to get Tommy Lee interested in pigeons.

"I started with homing pigeons," he said. "Tommy Lee took an interest. He'd ride out with me some weekends when I was training them. I lived on one side of the county, he on the other. I gave him a couple birds and we'd swap messages."

"Must have driven Reece Hutchins crazy."

Bridges erupted with a belly laugh. "Man, you got that right. He lives to monitor the police radio. Tommy Lee and I gave up on homing pigeons because hawks were killing them, but I wouldn't be surprised if Reece had taken up falconry. I suspect you've had your run-ins with him."

"He's all right. Just a little insecure."

"Tommy Lee always assigned him some duty that was just his. And Reece would perform to perfection. You just had to suffer through his windy descriptions of his efforts."

"Ain't that the pot calling the kettle black." Ewbanks stood in the doorway to the kitchen, a slight smile on his thin lips. "We'd better head out, Bridges, before you get too comfy. Hate to have you pushing the patrol car if we get stuck."

I stood up and the sheriff came over to the fire for a last dose of warmth. Walt followed behind. He looked ten years older and had to steady himself by grabbing the back of a chair.

"Well, here's a pretty woman." Ewbanks reached out to the mantel and picked up a silver-framed photograph. Susan sat on a rock ledge at one of the scenic overlooks along the Blue Ridge Parkway. The golden light of the setting sun created a portrait far superior to anything from a studio. The sheriff looked back at Walt.

"My daughter, Susan," he said flatly.

Ewbanks glanced at me.

"Downright glamorous," I said, hoping the sweat on my forehead would be chalked up to the fire.

Ewbanks set the picture down. "She's a looker all right." He held his hands out to the flames. "Getting hot in here. You might have to open up some air." He turned around. "And we'll let you fellows get back to your high finance discussion. No need to show us out. Thank you, Mr. Miller. I'll be in touch."

They left the house. Walt and I stood motionless until we heard the car engine start.

"Let's bag the high finance discussion," I said.

"I'd like a drink," said Walt. "Will you join me? All I've got is bourbon."

"A light one with ginger ale. I want to stay out of the ditch going home."

While Walt mixed the drinks, I jabbed the poker aimlessly into the burning logs. Sparks swirled up with every blow. The sheriff was right. Things were getting hot and I couldn't see a way to keep the sparks from flying. There was no doubt in my mind Ewbanks had recognized Susan. He now had the murder weapon owned by the father of the woman whose picture was found on the dead man. Ewbanks played it cagey, not saying anything to Walt until he gathered more information on Susan and her tie to Calhoun. Maybe the sheriff thought I was being cagey as well, keeping quiet so he could have a free hand. Maybe Ewbanks thought I didn't know Susan well enough to recognize her. He'd know better as soon as he asked a few questions and I surfaced as the boyfriend.

I'd neatly boxed myself in. I'd promised Susan not to tell her father about the photograph and promised Tommy Lee not to act in a way that could harm his confidant. I wondered what Walt would ask me to promise.

"Here you go," he said, handing me a highball glass with liquid too brown for my taste. His was even darker. "Sit down."

I sat in the sofa depression left by Bridges, and Walt took the wing-back chair beside me. He swirled his ice for a few seconds, and then sighed.

"You know what's going on?"

"The deputy was asking about the skeleton. I assume it has something to do with Sammy Calhoun."

"It has something to do with Sammy Calhoun all right. They found a gun with the remains." He paused as the circumstances dawned on him. "But you were there, you know that."

"I only found the skeleton. Lab man dug up the pistol." I don't know what difference that made other than make me feel somehow less responsible for Walt's predicament.

He eyed me over his drink. "Are you really thinking about selling the funeral home? That's quite a coincidence, your being here when the sheriff showed up."

"I got the call from Hoffman Enterprises this morning. I'm driving to Atlanta on Friday like I said. I wanted your opinion."

He shifted in the chair and took another drink. "Then I guess I'm lucky you're here. You know how these people operate. I'd appreciate your not mentioning anything to Susan."

I shook my head. I had run out of promises. "No."

My refusal put color in his face that the drink couldn't. "What do you mean no? Susan plays no part in this. I don't want her upset."

"You don't have a choice, Walt. First of all, you haven't told me any specifics about the sheriff's visit. I do know how these people think, but unless you tell me what Ewbanks asked you, how can I know what they're thinking? And second, anything you told them is going to require confirmation. The first person they'll ask is Susan, and I'll look like a jackass if she finds out I was here and didn't tell her. You know your daughter better than I do. She's going to be royally pissed. You're putting me in a hell of a bind."

"Okay, okay," he said, and threw up a hand in surrender. "It's just that it looks worse than it is."

"The gun's yours, right? That's the only reason I can think of that would bring Ewbanks here."

"Yeah. I bought it ten years ago, legal, proper, and registered."

"So, what happened?"

"I lost it. That's what happened. I kept it in the glove box of the Mercedes. I think one of the guys at the maintenance shop took it, but I didn't have a shred of proof."

"Okay," I said, finding the story plausible and convenient. "Ewbanks then asked why you didn't report the theft to your auto insurer."

"Right. I said since I couldn't be sure, I didn't want to get anyone in trouble where a gun was concerned. I also didn't know how long it had been missing."

I tested the bourbon and ginger. Walt had hit it with a heavy hand. I set the drink on the floor where I couldn't unconsciously drain it. "A gun in a glove box is a concealed weapon," I said. "Registering it doesn't give you the right to carry it that way. I suspect Ewbanks didn't like that."

"I'm an accountant, not a lawyer. My old car is prone to break down and I felt safer with the pistol."

Walt's twenty-year-old 240-D Mercedes could be cantankerous. He once said when he drove into work on cold mornings, kids along the road would pick up their book bags thinking he was the school bus coming around the bend. Yet, Walt loved his old diesel. I wouldn't be surprised if he asked me to bury him in it.

"Did Susan know about the gun?"

"Yeah. I showed her how to shoot it."

"You're asking me not to say anything to Susan, yet Ewbanks will go straight to her with questions about a gun and Sammy Calhoun. They're going to blindside her."

Walt ran his fingers through his thin hair. "Then I should be the one to tell her."

It was what I wanted to hear. I asked a question whose answer I didn't want to hear. "You never finished telling me about Sammy Calhoun. Susan met him in New York, but he wound up in a grave at Eagle Creek."

"Sammy Calhoun." He said each syllable like it came wrapped in a persimmon. "My sister Cassie introduced them."

"In New York?"

"Right. When Cassie worked for CBS and Susan started med school."

I felt a little better. Susan's lie had been one of omission. She let me assume Calhoun had been a casual acquaintance she met through Cassie in Asheville. "Soon after Susan got there?" I asked.

"Yes. Calhoun was a P.I. doing some work for the news division. He started asking her out. He was ten years older and knew the ropes of the city. At first, I thought he'd be good protection. Margaret had just died and losing my wife meant all of my worry got transferred to Susan. Then I'd pick up things from Cassie that Calhoun wasn't the kind of man she felt was good for Susan."

"Did one of you talk to her?"

He laughed and took the last swallow of bourbon. "You said yourself we both know Susan. How do you think she'd react to that conversation?"

"The more you tried to interfere, the more she'd defend the guy."

"Exactly. She's got my mother's hardheadedness. Like Cassie."

Like you, I thought. When it comes to protecting your daughter.

"I figured Calhoun would disappear when she returned to Asheville for her hospital residency. I just hoped she wouldn't do something stupid like marry him."

"When did he arrive?"

"About six months later. She wasn't glad to see him. I think he came looking for money, not knowing residents work a hundred hours a week for less than minimum wage."

"But eventually that changes," I said.

"Eventually. I thought Calhoun wouldn't wait. I heard he moved to Texas and I thought we were done with him."

I stood up and walked to the far end of the sofa, away from the heat and away from Walt.

"But you aren't done with him. So how did that gun come to be in the grave?"

He stared at his empty glass and shook his head. "I don't know, Barry. Maybe Calhoun stole it from me."

"But he didn't shoot himself. And he sure as hell didn't bury himself."

"Ewbanks wants my fingerprints," murmured Walt. "They must have something to match."

"That's my guess. If there's a print, it has to be in a protected spot, probably up on the clip." I knew damn well that's what they had.

"So even if it's mine, there's an explanation. I never denied handling the gun."

"That's correct. The fact that a print survived all those years in the ground is remarkable enough. No one can say for sure when it was originally made."

"Good." Walt got up. "I'd better call Susan and warn her. Do you want me to say you were here?"

"Yes. You can mention the funeral home sale. Tell her I'd planned to talk to her in person after I knew more."

"Okay." Walt bent down and picked up my full glass. "Maybe you'll feel like sharing a drink when this is over."

"Right, Walt." I looked at Susan's face smiling at me from the mantel. Somehow I knew this was only the beginning.

Chapter 8

I decided to brave the secondary roads and return to my cabin for the night. George Eliot, the guinea pig I had acquired when my wife divorced me, tolerated my absences as long as she enjoyed plentiful food and water. The shrill whistles that greeted my arrival told me provisions had run low and her Highness was not amused.

"Just a second, George."

The cries intensified. I stripped out of my parka and let it drop to the wide plank floor. The room felt cozy, heated by propane and moistened by a humidifier. The modern interior stood in contrast to the exterior of nineteenth-century logs culled from three other cabins. A psychiatrist from Charleston had found the rustic shells while hiking the Appalachian Trail. He had arranged for their purchase and reassembly on five acres outside of Gainesboro, and then became too ill to enjoy his retirement retreat. I found his blend of old and new to be the perfect spot for me to reassemble my life.

As I walked to the kitchen, I noticed the red message light blinking on the answering machine. I suspected Walt had talked to Susan and she had immediately called for my version of events.

The sound of the opening refrigerator door sent George into more frantic squeals. My low-tech alarm system never failed when it came to protecting our food supply. I dropped a handful of lettuce in her cage and scratched my long-haired Peruvian pal gently behind the ears. All was forgiven, or simply forgotten in the face of the feast.

I returned to the refrigerator for my own treat, twisted the cap off a Bud, and sat down on the sofa by the telephone. I punched the replay button. "Barry. This is Cassie. Susan's aunt. Call me please. Don't worry about the time. Try the cell first." She left a string of numbers, cell—work—home, so fast I had to listen three times to jot them down.

I had met Susan's aunt last Thanksgiving when we ran by Walt's after stuffing ourselves at Mom's table. Susan warned me she was a piece of work. Her father's sister and her only aunt, Cassie had gone through the journalism school at the University of North Carolina at Chapel Hill and landed a rewrite job for the Associated Press. In the mid Sixties, she joined the local newsroom at WCBS in New York as an assistant producer for a throwaway early morning newscast.

Her energy and quick wit enabled her to advance at a time when women weren't part of the good ol' boys' club. She came to the attention of the network brass, who brought her into the hallowed CBS News sanctuary of giants like Walter Cronkite and North Carolina native Charles Kuralt. She was a tough-skinned, no-nonsense, hard-talking producer who could hold her own with the best of them. Must have been mountain stubbornness that served her so well.

She rode the tumultuous waves of countless management changes and survived the passing of the crown from Cronkite to Rather. Then eight years ago, she quit. Burned out and aged out, she had come back to the mountains to find herself. She had been fifty-three, and as she succinctly told Susan, "tired of seeing the fucking world through a god-damned TV monitor." Aunt Cassie could wilt a fleet of sailors' ears.

Four months later, she went to work at NEWSCHANNEL-8, trading in the big rat race to be queen of the local news scene. The station owner wanted her to shake up the town and "knock the pompous newspaper on its ass." She proceeded to do just that by launching an investigative series that exposed a cozy relationship between the highway contractors and transportation department officials. Bid-rigging. The impact of her report resounded all the way to the state capitol at Raleigh. Cassie became a force to be reckoned with—a force I would have to reckon with.

I knew her call had to do with Sammy Calhoun. There was no other reason she would seek me out so urgently. Walt's revelation that Cassie had introduced Calhoun to Susan made me anxious to talk to her as well. It was only a few minutes past nine. I picked up the receiver and heard Susan's voice in my ear.

"Barry?"

"Yes."

"The phone didn't even ring."

"I just picked up the phone to call you." I rubbed my nose to keep it from growing. "Did your father reach you?"

"He doesn't know about the photograph." She hid the question in the statement.

"Neither Sheriff Ewbanks nor I mentioned it," I confirmed. "I didn't see a need to alarm him. What did you say?"

"That he shouldn't have lied."

I stood up and walked with the cordless receiver to the front window. The moon gave the snowy landscape a bluish glow. An animal track crossed the footprints I had created minutes earlier, the only sign that the outside world wasn't frozen in time. Inside, I waited for Susan to unfreeze the conversation.

"Dad didn't lose that gun in his Mercedes. No one stole it. I gave it to Sammy."

My chest tightened. I didn't like where the conversation was headed. "Are you sure you should be telling me this?"

"Who else can I tell? My father just cut me off, claiming he distinctly remembers losing the pistol. I know him. That means he distinctly remembers not losing the gun and he's trying to protect me."

"Why?"

"Why didn't you tell Ewbanks my picture was in the wallet?"

"I just couldn't imagine you tied to something so horrible."

The faint warble of a sigh came through the phone. "That's what I keep telling myself."

"When did you give Calhoun the gun? Sometime in New York?"

"Hmmm," she murmured, realizing her father had brought that part of the story out in the open. "No, not then. He asked me for it here, a few days before he left for Texas."

Except he never made it, I thought. "Maybe you should come forward now," I said. "Tell Sheriff Ewbanks what happened. At least it accounts for the gun being in Calhoun's possession."

"I don't want my father to get in trouble if I contradict his story."

It was a little late to worry about that. Walt's testimony would crumble with Susan's first truthful answer unless she perjured herself. "The sheriff saw your photograph on your father's mantel. He didn't say anything, but the look he gave me left no doubt he recognized it."

"He didn't say a word?"

"Ewbanks is backtracking," I said. "He'll piece together whatever he can, and then hit you and your father with it."

She mulled over her options. I imagined her sitting amid the feather angels, realizing no choice was a good choice. "All right," she said. "I'll talk to Ewbanks tomorrow."

"Tonight," I insisted. "It'll disarm him. Your father called you about the sheriff's visit. You told him about loaning Calhoun the gun, and you contacted the proper authorities immediately. What can Ewbanks say?"

"He'll want to know about my relationship to Sammy."

"Then tell Ewbanks as little as possible." I forced a laugh. "You didn't shoot him."

"But I wanted to."

Again, the empty silence was filled with my unasked questions.

After a few seconds, she said, "I'll think about it, Barry. You're probably right."

"I'm right about one thing."

"What's that?"

"I love you." Fortunately I got the words out before I could think how corny they might sound.

"I love you too," she said softly. "I really do. Let's talk tomorrow." She hung up, and I wanted to drive through the snow to be with her, protect her with more than words from a past unearthed in a mountain cemetery.

Cassie Miller answered on the first ring of her cell phone. "Barry," she snapped, "what's going on?"

Caller ID. Hearing my name blurted out instead of hello always startled me.

"Barry?" she repeated, this time a question.

"Yes. Have you talked to Walt?"

"You'd think Walt would talk to me. But no, I have to call him because I learn my brother's gun is a god-damned murder weapon from an anonymous tip to the newsroom. A tip to that asshole Cliff Barringer of all people. Walt told me you were there. You seem to be popping up everywhere."

"What do you want to know?"

"I want to hear your version of what happened so I can verify Cliff's information before I air it."

I gave Cassie my rundown of Ewbanks' visit, omitting the details of the photograph on the mantel and the sheriff's reaction to it. If Susan was going to approach Ewbanks, I didn't want Cassie breaking the story on the eleven o'clock news.

"What are you putting on the air tonight?" I asked.

"Believe it or not, more than I want to. If I hold back, it looks like I'm shielding my brother. The competition, both the newspapers and other TV stations, would have a field day."

"Do I have to be mentioned?"

"You have something to hide?"

I could see her reporter ears perking up. "No. I was at Walt's getting some financial advice. Nothing to do with this. But people will make the wrong assumptions because I'm dating Walt's daughter. There's no reason to bring Susan into it."

"Uh huh," she said skeptically. "And you found the remains and you show up in the home of the owner of the murder weapon. Quite a coincidence. I don't like coincidences."

The statement could have come straight from the lips of Sheriff Tommy Lee Wadkins.

"Who was Sammy Calhoun?" I asked. "If I'm going to be nailed by a coincidence, then I'd like some information."

"Sammy Calhoun was trouble." Cassie's husky voice descended to a growl. "Look, I don't have time to go into it now. I've got a newscast to put together. I'll be back at work tomorrow after two. Talk to me then."

"And tonight?"

"You and Susan aren't in the story. Since the tip to Barringer didn't mention you, I'll keep it that way. But don't screw me over on this, Barry." The phone went dead.

Cassie wasn't mad at me. She was mad because she didn't know what was going on. For a news reporter, there's no worse predicament.

I took a slow swallow of my beer and settled back in the sofa cushion. Who had called the newsroom? As cagey as Ewbanks was playing Susan's picture, I couldn't believe he would have leaked information to a television station. Was Bridges sharing the case's progress beyond Tommy Lee? And who was this Cliff Barringer that Cassie Miller called an asshole? His source might be Bridges or anyone else in the sheriff's office.

By tomorrow, Susan should have talked to Ewbanks and her story would explain both the gun and her photograph. The big question was, would Ewbanks see her story as an explanation or an implication?

Chapter 9

The next morning I allowed extra time for the drive to town, but discovered I had the road to myself. Most county people were still digging out or taking care of the livestock whose winter grazing pastures lay smothered under a frozen barrier.

When I arrived at the funeral home early, Mom made an egg and sausage breakfast casserole, and we sat at the kitchen table with Dad. Our conversation consisted of sporadic threads that abruptly snapped and then veered off on whatever tangent next broke from his tangled memory.

Uncle Wayne and Freddy Mott arrived in time to finish the coffee and casserole and to hear Dad mix his recollection of JFK's death with the current plot of "General Hospital." Freddy had been with us part-time for over ten years. He also worked as a carpentry handyman, specializing in odd jobs for wealthy retirees, but with their understanding that his funeral duties took priority. Since most of his clients were at the stage of life when funerals were as common as an afternoon of golf or an evening of bridge, Freddy could juggle building and burying with their cooperation.

I studied the faces around the table. We worked well together, providing comfort and consolation to our community. Even Dad showed no signs of anxiety when the five of us were together. What impact would Hoffman Enterprises make on this scene?

My thoughts were interrupted by the ring of the phone. I motioned for Mom to keep her seat, and I grabbed the receiver from the wall. Susan recognized my voice.

"Can you talk a second? I'm between rounds."

"Hold on." I turned to Mom. "I'll catch it in the office."

She took the phone, ready to hang up when I came on the extension.

I closed the office door behind me. "Okay, Mom." The kitchen line clicked off.

Susan said, "I telephoned Sheriff Ewbanks last night. The dispatcher took my name and said he'd track him down. Ewbanks called me back about midnight."

"Was he surprised to hear from you?"

"Hard to say," she said. "He was too angry."

"At you?"

"At NEWSCHANNEL-8. The station broke the story about my father and the gun."

"Did he think you called them?" I grabbed a pencil and started jotting words on my notepad—"Cassie" and "Ewbanks."

"No. He wanted to know if any reporters had tried to reach me earlier. I said I'd only heard from my father."

"Did he say anything about your picture being in Calhoun's wallet?"

"He didn't. And I couldn't bring it up since I'm not supposed to know about it."

"But you told him about Calhoun."

"How I met him in New York and then how he followed me to Asheville. I volunteered the information about the gun."

"What did he make of that?"

"Not much. He thanked me for contacting him."

"So that's that for now," I said.

"That was that for last night," she said. "This morning at six I got another call requesting me to go to Walker County for fingerprints. I told the officer I had two surgeries scheduled and that I couldn't get there till early afternoon."

The word "fingerprints" went on the pad with an underline. "I guess they just want to rule you out," I assured her.

"You want to have dinner this evening?" she asked. "I'd like to talk."

"Fine. Where?"

"My place. Just bring your appetite."

We agreed on five-thirty. After I hung up, I realized I hadn't told Susan about my conversation with Cassie. Just as well. I had more questions for Susan's aunt, and I wouldn't be asking them over the telephone.

Freddy and I spent the morning preparing Claude McBee's body. Uncle Wayne met with the family, which had now grown to eight plus local Baptist preacher Calvin Stinnett. A funeral by committee. While Freddy and I pumped Claude full of embalming fluid, Wayne walked the entourage through the casket displays, encouraging the financially strapped family to choose from the lower-priced models without insinuating that they couldn't afford the deluxe solid mahogany costing more than a room full of furniture. A compassionate funeral director protects mourners from emotionally overspending and makes them feel good about their economical choices. Uncle Wayne knew how to do that better than anyone.

By lunch, both the burial plans and Claude were in good shape. Visitation would be Friday night with the funeral at Crab Apple Valley Baptist Church set for one on Saturday afternoon.

After devouring a bowl of Mom's beef stew with Wayne and Freddy, I told them I needed to drive to Asheville for office supplies. The thermometer had risen into the mid-forties and road conditions posed no problems. I could run by Office Depot and still be at the TV station by two. Cassie Miller would begin her day with an unexpected interview.

The studios and offices for Channel 8 perched halfway up one of the ridges surrounding Asheville in nearby Buncombe

County. Higher above, on the ridge crest, the transmission tower rose majestically into the clouds, flashing red warnings along its vertical shaft of interlaced steel. Officially, the station was WHME-TV, "Where Heaven Meets Earth," but the days of cable television and the hard-fought competition for local news viewers made such a picturesque slogan obsolete. Now it was simply NEWSCHANNEL-8, one word, the be-all, end-all mantra glorifying the six o'clock newscast. Cassie had told Susan that's where the station made one third of its money. "Where your treasure is, your heart will follow," the scriptures say. News was the heart of Channel 8, and Cassie Miller was the heart of the news.

I parked in a visitor's spot along the iron picket fence which protected the employees' cars and the millions of dollars of equipment rolling around in the LIVE-EYE vans. Channel 8 didn't have a helicopter, but that was about the only piece of glitzy hardware missing from its news-gathering arsenal. I grabbed my cell phone from the charger on the jeep's dash and clipped it to my belt. When in Rome, at least look like a Roman. No one in this communication citadel would take me seriously unless it appeared I needed to be constantly in touch with someone.

Security was tight at the visitor's entrance. I entered one set of doors, and a receptionist behind a thick window asked if she could help me. Another set of glass doors barred access to the lobby until I could assure this electronic gatekeeper that I had legitimate business within.

"I'm Barry Clayton. I'm here to see Cassie Miller."

"Is she expecting you?"

"Yes," I lied. "She called me last night."

A buzzer sounded and the doors automatically opened. I was surprised they hadn't thought to add celestial music. The lobby was richly furnished with a large mahogany coffee table, burgundy leather sofa, and two matching wing chairs. On the walls, numerous award plaques and statuettes basked in the reverential glow of spotlights positioned in the high ceiling. The photographs of network celebrities mingled with those of the local wannabees who were either on their way up or on their way down.

I turned to the receptionist, whose desk was now clear of the bulletproof glass of the airlock.

"I've notified the newsroom," she said. "Please have a seat."

Before I could sit down, a young man entered the lobby from the far end. He wore a headset around his neck and carried the unplugged jack in his hand. "Did you just get here?"

"Yes."

"Come with me, sir."

Impressed with the NEWSCHANNEL-8 efficiency, I followed my guide down a hall and through huge, wooden, double doors marked STUDIO B. We walked behind three cameras aimed at a living room set. The walls and fake fireplace were draped in Christmas ornaments, and an artificial tree in the corner shone with miniature white lights. A woman who looked vaguely familiar sat in a chair opposite two men. One of the men wore a clerical collar. An empty chair beside them had a microphone draped over its back.

A voice boomed through an invisible speaker, "Get him in place and miked. We've already got color bars. Rolling tape in forty-five seconds."

The woman stood up, and our confused faces must have mirrored each other. "Who are you?"

"I'm Barry Clayton."

"Did Dr. Elbertson send you? Isn't he coming?"

"I'm here to see Cassie Miller."

"But this is 'Pastors Face Your Questions.'" Her eyes searched the studio beyond the glare of the lights. "Sid," she yelled sharply. "I told you to meet Dr. Elbertson in the lobby. From Long Creek Baptist Bible College."

"Barry, what the hell are you doing?" Cassie strolled onto the set as if it were her own living room. She was no more than an inch or two above five feet, barely higher than the cameras. Her dark pants suit hung loosely on her thin body, and she wore no jewelry other than gold hoops sparkling in her ears. Her short hair was shoe-polish brown and framed against a strong-boned face which revealed her sixty-one years only when it wrinkled in a wicked grin. She spoke to the reverends. "I'm sorry. He was supposed to come straight to the newsroom, but he's a Pastors Face Your Questions groupie and has a thing for Charlene."

The host, who I gathered was Charlene, flushed crimson. "Cassie. Really!"

"It's the price you pay when you're into public affairs, Charlene, dear. You are the best at public affairs. I'll take care of the moon-struck boy for you." She ceremoniously escorted me from the studio, and then broke into laughter as soon as we were in the scene shop and out of earshot. "That'll chap Charlene all day. She's such a god-damned prima donna."

Cassie didn't say anything else until she closed the door to her office. She motioned me to a chair and plopped down behind her cluttered desk. "Okay, why are you here? What's going on?"

"You know more than I do. Who's Sammy Calhoun?"

Cassie leaned forward, resting her elbows on the desk and lightly touching the tips of her fingers together. Her eyes widened with the curiosity bred into every good reporter. "Why don't you ask Susan?"

"For the same reason you called me last night," I said sharply. "I want to know what's going on, and the answers might be ones that I'd prefer to learn without Susan having to tell me. She and her father are too distracted and distraught to handle both a police investigation and the press leaks that are flooding your newsroom."

"You really like her, don't you," she said. "Not exactly the match made in heaven, a surgeon and an undertaker." She paused and smiled. "On second thought, it could be convenient. Okay, I'll tell you about Sammy Calhoun, but you didn't learn it from me. I think Susan is in love with you and prefers to keep private what is an embarrassing relationship from the past."

"I'm just trying to understand how to help her. A skeleton doesn't give me much to work with."

A shudder rippled through Cassie's body and I remembered the skeleton had once been a flesh and blood person to her.

"First of all, any mistakes Susan made were aided by my own stupidity," Cassie said. "I had lived in Manhattan over thirty years when Susan came to the city. I took her on as a project."

"Project?"

"Turn the mountain girl into a New Yorker." She shook her head at the absurdity of her quest. "I was very proud of my niece. She'd not only left the hills like I had, but she was entering a prestigious medical school at twenty-two. My feminist battle flag proudly waved over my protégée, and I waltzed her around to impress as many of my friends as I could. One of them was Sammy Calhoun."

"A private detective?"

The question must have carried a judgmental tone because Cassie scowled at me. "You're an ex-cop," she stated. "You know you make or break a case by getting information. Sammy was smooth and ingratiating. That was how he worked his sources. I didn't stop to think that's how he would work my niece."

"She fell for him?"

"Like he was Sam Spade or Philip Marlowe. Susan had never had time for a boyfriend, not that her looks wouldn't fetch a passel of guys with their tongues hanging out. She was focused on getting into med school. Sammy cut through all that at a time in her life when she began to look around. I had helped open her eyes and then put the wrong object in front of them."

"Was he abusive?"

"No. Sammy was a user. Not drugs, people. Within three months, they were living together. Susan was carrying a full course load and waiting on him hand and foot. He'd turned my feminist charge into a school girl doting on a man ten years older."

I had difficulty imagining Susan as fawning over anyone. Her independent mind was the defining trait of her personality.

"He must have been something."

"Sammy was that all right. I guess he finally ran into someone he couldn't charm."

The intercom on the credenza behind her desk buzzed. "Cassie," said a man's voice.

"I've got someone with me," she said, and punched a button blocking further interruptions.

"Did they break up before she left New York?"

"I gathered the relationship started to cool the last year of med school. When Susan came back to Asheville for her residency, Sammy had already returned to his old haunts. I used him on a few assignments. He was a good investigator. Knew surveillance and had all the latest high-tech gadgets."

"How'd he wind up here?"

"Looking for work. Sat in the very chair you're in now and spun me this sob story about how he wanted out of the New York rat-race. I'd been down here about six months and I gave him a sympathetic ear. He told me he'd walked in on a convenience store robbery a block from his apartment and when the gun smoke cleared, he'd killed the armed holdup man and the store owner's eleven-year-old daughter who ran through the crossfire."

"Jesus, that's every policeman's nightmare."

"Yeah, and I bought it. So, I gave him an assignment to tail a road paving contractor we'd heard was a little too successful. Two days later Sammy showed up in this office with glossy photos of some good ol' boys walking out of a hotel in Charlotte. Sure enough, the guy had met three of his competitors and a bid supervisor for the Department of Transportation. They were screwing the taxpayers out of millions on overpriced work. I paid Sammy an advance for his services and he went through Dumpsters, phone logs, checkbooks, and whatever else it took to expose the scheme. The bid-riggers never knew what hit them." Cassie smiled, savoring the memory. "Sammy was good."

"And he reconnected with Susan," I said, getting back to what interested me.

"I think he tried. I warned her he was in town, and she told me she could take care of herself. I believed her."

"Did you think Calhoun went to Texas?"

"That's what I heard. Figured it was as likely a possibility as anything. I wasn't giving him any more work."

"Why not? You said he was good."

"The son of a bitch lied to me. That story about the holdup and the dead girl. It was a crock of shit. A friend at CBS called to congratulate me on the bid-rigging story. I gave Sammy credit and said I was glad he'd bounced back from the tragedy. It never happened. My friend said Sammy skipped New York after he tried to blackmail a mobster with information he'd collected for a client—playing both ends of the game for the biggest payoff."

"You think he could've been hit down here?"

"I doubt it. Sammy would've wound up in cement, not some mountain graveyard." Cassie thought a moment. "Sammy would've appreciated that. He was always talking about how people overlook the obvious. Said that's what made him a good investigator." A bittersweet smile crossed her lips. "Hidden in a graveyard. Like that Poe story, 'The Purloined Letter.' Who'd look for a body in a cemetery?"

"Was he working on anything here that would get him killed?"

"I don't know. The last I heard from Sammy was a voicemail he left pitching a story. Really big he claimed. Something about sex in the criminal justice system."

I knew enough about news ratings to know that was a potent combination. "Sounds like a winner."

"Sammy said it would make the bid-rigging scandal look like a Sunday morning, feel-good puff piece. But by then, I'd had it with Mr. Sammy Calhoun. I erased the message and put one of our reporters on it instead. He sniffed around the courthouse and jail but nothing came of it. And I never heard from Sammy again."

I leaned forward in my chair, intrigued by the possibility that Sammy Calhoun had gone up against something he couldn't control. "Susan said she loaned him the Colt twenty-five a few days before he disappeared. Any reason that's not true?"

"Sammy had a license to carry in New York. He owned several pistols."

"Maybe they weren't small enough." I thought about the remains in the grave. "Calhoun always wear cowboy boots?"

Cassie looked surprised. "Cowboy boots? He liked Gucci street shoes." She mulled the implications. "A twenty-five would slip in a boot, wouldn't it?"

Before I could answer, a sharp rap came from the door and a man stuck his head in. "Sorry. I couldn't get through the intercom."

He didn't look sorry at all. A mischievous smile came through his neatly trimmed brown beard. I recognized him as someone I'd seen on TV.

"That's because I didn't want anybody to get through the intercom," snapped Cassie. "I'm busy."

The intruder looked at me and shrugged. "Okay, but I thought you'd want to know Mr. Darius needs to see you at three. In his office."

"Fine. Now I know. Close the damned door."

As the latch clicked, I heard Cassie whisper, "Asshole."

Cliff Barringer. I placed the face with the name thanks to Cassie's ranting the night before. Barringer had broken the story of Calhoun and tied Walt to the gun.

"Who's Darius?" I asked.

"The station owner. Nelson Darius is the one person I have to listen to when it comes to running this department." She looked at her watch. "I wonder which advertiser we've pissed off now."

She glanced down again. I sensed I'd have her attention for only a few more minutes.

"I'm afraid I'm not much help," she said. "All I can do is speculate."

"There's no speculation that Sammy Calhoun was buried in that grave in the spring of 1997. If it wasn't something he was working on and it wasn't from New York—"

"I can't say that for sure," she interrupted. "I was thinking hypothetically. A dead body trumps a theory." She snatched a pen from a chipped mug and wrote something on the back of her hand. "Hard to lose a hand," she said. "I'll call my friend at the network and see how seriously Sammy pissed off the mob."

"What about the bid-rigging scandal? Any motive there?"

Cassie pursed her lips and thought for a few seconds. "The case hadn't gone to trial yet, and the Charlotte prosecutor was mad that Sammy had left."

"Charlotte?"

"It's where the conspirators met. The indictments were issued there."

"So Sammy was a star witness?"

"He was to testify how he got the evidence."

"Did the case fall apart?"

She shook her head. "No. The prosecution had Sammy's deposition and I took the stand to tell how I'd hired Sammy and seen all of his evidence firsthand."

"But someone might have thought his testimony would be more damaging with the jury."

"They still pulled jail time."

"Yeah, but I doubt that was any consolation to Sammy. Who were these guys?"

"The local crook was a contractor named Duncan Atkins. He's still in jail. I don't know about the others." She scowled. "I'll have to ask Cliff Barringer. He was our court reporter at the time. He'd have notes on the other men as well, if the jerk bothers to keep them."

I got up, realizing I'd gotten as much information as I could. "Thanks. Let me know what you find out," I said. "This visit's between us."

"Play it however you want." She stood up but didn't walk around the desk. "Tell Susan to relax. I'm sure Sammy managed to get himself popped without any help from her or Walt. Probably a two-timing husband who got caught on camera."

I opened the door, and then turned back. "You don't really believe that, do you?"

"Hell no."

The first thing I noticed when Susan opened her door was the table was no longer covered in feathers and glue, but set with good china and silver for two. The gas logs burned low in the fireplace and the tree at the edge of the hearth sparkled with white lights and a host of angels. The Mormon Tabernacle Choir shared the air with the aroma of brownies. "Wow," was all I managed to say.

"Just a little something I threw together after work. I hope the tossed salad doesn't taste like ink." She held up her stained fingers. "This stuff is murder to get off."

I took her hand and kissed a fingertip. "I'll suggest to Ewbanks they try a new flavor."

"The London broil just has to sit a few more minutes. Would you change your standard beer order for a glass of merlot?"

"I'm in for the whole package."

She returned from the kitchen with two rounded wineglasses and we sat on the sofa. The light in the room glowed with the mixture of candle, fireplace, and tree. I'm not the most romantic guy, but the scene made me feel we should have been on a Harlequin cover. And I liked it.

"To us," I said, clinking my crystal glass against hers.

"To us."

We sat suspended, wineglasses in hand, ignoring the rings from Susan's phone. Then the speaker from her answering machine overpowered everything.

"Susan," said Cassie. "God-damn-it, I'm sorry. I just got free to call and I hoped to reach you before the broadcast. They're idiots and I'm off the story. Get Barry and get a lawyer."

Chapter 10

After the dramatic open culminated in the title NEWSCHANNEL-8 SIX O'CLOCK REPORT, Matt Markle appeared on Susan's TV, barely able to contain his excitement. The well-coiffed anchorman looked like he wanted to crawl over his news desk and into the room with us.

"NEWSCHANNEL-8's ongoing coverage of the case involving the body discovered in the Eagle Creek Methodist Church cemetery has learned a major breakthrough came this afternoon. With details, here is NEWSCHANNEL-8 investigative reporter Cliff Barringer."

The camera zoomed out to reveal Barringer sitting smugly on the right of the set. He nodded to his colleague, and then gravely stared into the camera as if ready to announce an impending nuclear attack. The shot changed to a close-up with *Cliff Barringer, Investigative Correspondent* written underneath him. The guy must have gotten a promotion during his on-air introduction.

Susan grabbed the remote and turned up the sound. Wine and dinner were forgotten.

"Thank you, Matt. Sources close to the investigation have told me Sheriff Horace Ewbanks of Walker County has identified a print on the alleged murder weapon which could break this case open. Last night, my exclusive report named Walter Miller, a local CPA, as the owner of the gun. In Mr. Miller's statement to authorities, he asserted that the pistol had been stolen from him at an unspecified time in the past. The identification of a fingerprint now puts that claim in doubt."

The camera zoomed back to allow room for a visual to appear over Barringer's left shoulder. A composite of two photographs shared the screen—a grainy black and white of Walt that looked like it had been enlarged from some Kiwanis Club speaking event and a cleaner one of Susan at last month's groundbreaking ceremony for the new O'Malley Surgical Clinic. NEWSCHAN-NEL-8's graphics department had placed a highlight effect on her smiling face. I heard Susan take a sharp breath.

Barringer paused to make sure the director had brought in the pictures, and then continued, "The print on the pistol is unmistakably that of Dr. Susan Miller, a surgeon with the O'Malley Clinic in Laurel County and the daughter of the gun's owner. Sheriff Ewbanks would neither confirm nor deny that Dr. Miller is a subject of his investigation, only stating that he expects her full cooperation wherever the evidence might lead."

Mercifully, the photos of Walt and Susan disappeared as the camera zoomed back to Barringer.

"However, I have learned," continued the correspondent, emphasizing his favorite pronoun, "that Dr. Susan Miller is the estranged live-in girlfriend of the victim, private detective Samuel Calhoun."

"Estranged live-in girlfriend!" Susan erupted beside me. "I dumped the bastard," she shouted at the bearded wonder destroying her life. "Why don't you just pronounce me guilty and be done with it?"

Whether Cliff Barringer did declare her guilty was impossible to tell because Susan's outburst covered his closing comments. The camera switched back to Matt Markle.

"Thank you, Cliff," effused the anchorman. "And there is a further twist to this rapidly unfolding story. Our own newsroom is not without personal connections to the case. News director Cassandra Miller is the sister of the gun's owner and the aunt of Dr. Susan Miller. In the interest of the unbiased reporting you have come to expect from NEWSCHANNEL-8, we are taking special measures to insure our coverage remains above reproach."

The camera zoomed out to reveal the anchorman now joined at the desk by a distinguished, older, white man with gray hair and chiseled features. He wore a pressed blue suit, burgundy tie, and crisply starched white shirt. His pale blue eyes stared straight into the camera. He had the bearing to be sitting in the Oval Office of the White House.

"And now, with some additional comments, here is the Chairman of Mountain View Broadcasting and owner of WHME-TV, Nelson Darius."

"Good God," muttered Susan. "The station owner. What's he going to do, fire Cassie on the air for being my aunt?"

"Thank you, Matt," said Darius in a tenor voice not quite devoid of its mountain twang. "And thank you, viewers of NEWSCHANNEL-8, for making us your number one choice. Ten years ago, I made a commitment that WHME-TV would be the premier information source for western Carolina. To help me in that quest, I recruited and hired Cassandra Miller, a native of our region and an experienced, award-winning producer for CBS News. Under Cassie's guidance, the NEWSCHANNEL-8 team has operated with integrity and dedication to fulfill my dream. They will continue to do so."

Darius turned his head. A second camera framed him in a close-up, and his tone shifted from serious to grave. "However, the body unearthed in the Eagle Creek cemetery has taken Cassie Miller from news manager to relative of those involved in the case. She and I have agreed this is not the appropriate perspective from which to produce this particular story. Although I have total confidence in Cassie, our newsroom policy dictates that she not be involved in the coverage of this investigation. Instead, I shall personally direct our reporting efforts with the capable assistance of WHME-TV's Public Affairs Manager, Charlene Kensington, and the full-time assignment of Cliff Barringer. I want to assure our viewers we will follow this story wherever it leads, without bias and without compromise." He paused and leaned a little closer to the lens. "You have my word."

The camera pulled back to include the anchorman again. Matt Markle nodded respectfully to his boss. "Thank you, sir. We welcome you to the news team."

"What a suck-up," said Susan.

The station took a commercial break and Susan turned off the set. Immediately, the telephone rang.

"Would you get it?" she pleaded. "It might be Cassie, but if it's not, I'm out."

The caller asked for Susan and identified herself as Melissa Bigham of The Gainesboro Vista.

"Hello, Melissa Bigham of The Gainesboro Vista," I replied warmly. Susan shook her head that she didn't want to speak with the reporter. "This is Barry Clayton."

Melissa worked for the small daily in town. Last year the young woman and I had collaborated on a news story that trapped a killer. It proved to be an exclusive that gave the novice journalist a national byline when the wire services picked it up. I trusted her as much as anybody can trust a reporter.

"Hi, Barry. You want to give me Susan's official no comment."

"No comment." Susan stiffened and I winked at her. "Now that we've gotten her official response out of the way, what do you think's going on?"

Melissa laughed. "You're questioning me? Well, off the record, I'd say Cliff Barringer is trying to skewer Cassie Miller."

"What?"

"Newsroom politics, pal. It's payback time. Maybe you were gone, but when Cassie joined NEWSCHANNEL-8, the first thing she did was remove Barringer from the anchor spot. She couldn't fire him because he had a contract. He was reassigned to court reporting. The man's ninety percent ego and ten percent bullshit, but he knows where a lot of bodies are buried and will get his exclusive now and then."

I thought of the irony. Cassie demoted Barringer and he wound up covering the trial of Sammy Calhoun's big story. "Who's his source on this one?"

"Wish I knew. I've talked to several guys in Ewbanks' department and been stonewalled. Same for the other reporters. Maybe Barringer's bugged the sheriff's phone."

"Maybe."

Melissa made another attempt for information. "What do you think the comment Susan is not commenting on would be if she was commenting?"

"Nice try. My turn to say no comment."

"Not even about the estranged live-in girlfriend?"

Melissa knew how to punch the right buttons.

"She dumped him," I said. Susan shot me an alarmed glance. "Years before he disappeared," I added.

"Years?" questioned Melissa.

"Yes, two qualifies as years."

Susan stood up and started toward me. I should have taken that as a sign to shut up.

"Melissa, let me say no one is more surprised than Susan by this turn of events. If she fired her father's pistol for target practice, a fingerprint is perfectly consistent with that use."

"So, she did fire the gun for practice?"

"That's far more likely than she shot an old boyfriend, hauled his body up to Eagle Creek cemetery, and buried him single-handedly."

She laughed again. "You're right. I can't see her doing it single-handedly. Where were you seven years ago?"

"Patrolling the streets of Charlotte. Look, I promise when Susan is ready to comment, you'll be the one I recommend she contact."

"Fair enough." She gave me a string of numbers and had me repeat them just to check I had written them down.

As soon as I placed the phone on the cradle, it rang again.

"I can't take this," said Susan. "Don't answer."

The voice on the machine was a reporter from the Asheville paper.

"Let's take dinner to the cabin," I said. "They can't bother you if they can't find you."

The twenty-minute drive from Susan's condo proved to be a good transition from the paralyzing shock of the newscast to the practical actions we could take to go on the offensive. When we parked at the cabin, Susan was determined to make three phone calls—one to Sheriff Ewbanks protesting the public disclosure of her name, the second to her Aunt Cassie to find out what had happened at the station, and the third to Melissa Bigham giving an exclusive on her relationship with Sammy Calhoun and her reaction to the events.

I would make one call. I wanted to know what Tommy Lee thought Ewbanks would do next and how we could best defuse it.

While I set out plates for our progressive dinner, Susan dialed the Walker County Sheriff's Department. Ewbanks was in and immediately took her call.

Susan managed to inject her voice with the proper degree of indignation, and I gathered from her end of the conversation the sheriff tried to appease her anger. Then the expression on Susan's face shifted.

"Who's Mabel Potter?"

Ewbanks must have told her because she sighed and lost the accusatory tone.

"Yes, I was angry," she said. "Sammy had borrowed the gun and skipped town without returning it. It belonged to my father and I wanted it back." A long silence served to intensify the color in her cheeks. "That's not true," she argued. "I thought maybe he'd left it in the apartment. I had a key and found the apartment cleaned out. That was after he left. She's got it wrong!"

Ewbanks made the mistake of giving her an order.

"I'll say what I want to the press. The problem will be finding a reporter not flooded by the leaks from your department." She slammed down the phone.

"Well, I'd say that went well," I quipped, trying to bring Susan down off the ceiling. "Who's Mabel Potter?"

"Sammy's landlady. She told Ewbanks I came over to his apartment looking for him with a gun."

"That's not good."

"She's botched the timeframe. I went there after he'd moved out. This Mabel Potter told me she'd received a letter from Sammy with a month's rent in cash and a notice that he'd moved to Texas. I was furious. I probably said I'd like to kill him and I was looking for my gun. Now that he's been found murdered she's got the sequence out of order."

"What happened to his stuff?"

"That's the weird part. Potter said movers had showed up and loaded everything on a truck. Nothing was left behind."

"And no record of where it was delivered?"

"Gone without a trace."

"Anybody could have sent movers," I said.

"What are we up against?"

"You said something about a key."

Tears broke through her fury. "Oh, Barry, it's not what it looks like. Sammy mailed me a key soon after he got the apartment. He said he wanted me to have it. He made it sound like an innocent request—someone he trusted to have access to his apartment in case he was gone for awhile. I meant to send it back. I swear I never used it till I went looking for Dad's gun and that's when the landlady found me there. God, was I stupid."

"Did he say why he wanted the gun?"

"He had a meeting and needed some extra insurance. I knew he had a license in New York, and my pistol would be easier to conceal."

"How'd you get it to him?"

She paused and thought for a moment. "I met him in the hospital parking lot. He said he was working on another big story for Cassie. I guess I felt sorry for him. She had told me about the shooting in New York."

"The convenience store holdup?"

"Cassie told you?"

"Yes. She also said it was a lie. He used it to get her to hire him."

Susan started pacing the length of my fireplace. "That snake. Aunt Cassie never told me. She hates to be duped."

"Give her a call and then Melissa. I can guarantee this landlady's story will leak and you'd better get your version out first. Even though the Vista is a small paper, the other news outlets will have to take notice and quote it."

Susan got an update from Cassie. The situation stood as Nelson Darius described it. Cassie was removed from all aspects of the Sammy Calhoun investigation. She had considered resigning, but thought she had a better chance of helping Walt and Susan if she went along. It wasn't the policy of being detached from the story that bugged her as much as the terrible judgment Nelson Darius and Charlene Kensington had used in putting Cliff Barringer's reports on the air without independent confirmation. Barringer wouldn't reveal his source, and Darius savored the exclusives too much to hold them.

We decided I should call Tommy Lee at home before Susan contacted Melissa Bigham. He answered the phone.

"You see the news?" I asked.

"No. I was at the office and just got in. Patsy gave me the summary. What a damn mess."

"They're convicting Susan on the news set. We're going to fight back."

"She get a lawyer yet?"

"No. Her Aunt Cassie said she should."

"Hold off a day. Sometimes getting a lawyer just makes you look guilty. Nobody's charged her yet. I bet the most Ewbanks will do right now is to label her a material witness. I'm going to call my contact in Ewbanks' office and see if I can get more information."

Bridges, I thought, but I wasn't supposed to know that. "You think there's any chance your source is talking to this Cliff Barringer?"

"No way. Every officer I know hates the squirmy son of a bitch. Especially Ewbanks. There's some other agenda here. Barringer must have some dirt on somebody."

"What else can we do?" I asked. "I don't know where to start."

"Find the real killer," Tommy Lee said. "That grandstanding D.A. Darden Claiborne and Horace Ewbanks are searching for facts to convict Susan. She's got the most circumstantial against her. I guarantee you they'll miss anything that leads to another conclusion. You need to discover who else wanted Calhoun dead."

"That's the sixty-four-thousand-dollar question all right, and I understand why you can't help me find the answer."

"Barry, who said that? Between us we've got three eyes, four ears, and a brain and a half. Hell, I'd take them on with less. I just can't do it publicly."

"Cassie told me that Sammy Calhoun was supposed to be a witness in the trial of the bid-riggers. You know the case?"

"Oh, yeah. It was big news. So, Calhoun died before he could testify?"

"Yes. Cassie's working that angle. Maybe you could mention it to your source."

"I will. The more suspects the better."

"Unless you're trying to solve the case."

He laughed. "But it's not my case. I'll be in touch."

While Susan talked to Melissa Bigham, I fed George Eliot and made a pretense of walking around the outside of the cabin searching for God knew what. I knew Susan didn't want me hearing her describe her relationship with Calhoun to a reporter. When I came back in, she was still on the phone. Her soft voice broke into laughter a few times, and I began to relax. The overdone London broil, salad, and wine were on the table when she finished.

"Melissa's going to do everything she can to get her story in before deadline," said Susan. "She's a sharp woman."

"Feel better?"

"Yes, I do."

I lifted my wineglass. "Then where were we? Ah, yes, to us."

We finished dinner and took our wine to the fire, and then the fire to our bed. Life held promise.

That promise was kept in the morning edition of The Gainesboro Vista. Melissa Bigham's story carried the headline A RUSH TO JUDGMENT. She refuted Cliff Barringer's assertions piece by piece, using the information Susan provided and mixing her rebuttal with descriptions of Susan's work at the hospital and her fine standing in the community. Melissa tied in the fact that Calhoun had died before appearing as a prosecution witness in a high-profile trial, and she broke the news about him fleeing a mobster in New York.

Susan left for her hospital duties in good humor. I decided to delay going to the funeral home till later in the morning. Wayne was in, and our only scheduled visitation was for Claude McBee the next night.

Not only had Melissa Bigham made her deadline, but the story had been picked up in time by the Associated Press to hit the wires. Tommy Lee called to say he'd read it in the Asheville Citizen and the Charlotte Observer. At nine o'clock, Darden Claiborne's office issued a statement that Susan Miller was not currently a suspect and any reports to the contrary were erroneous.

An hour later I was nibbling on a day-old doughnut when Cassie Miller telephoned.

"Which do you want first?" she asked. "The good news or the bad news."

"The bad."

"Damn, I should have said bad news, bad news, good news." She sounded chipper for someone who had just been yanked from a major story."

"Don't play with me, Cassie."

"I heard from my old associate producer at CBS. The guy Sammy tried to screw over in New York got iced seven and a half years ago."

"Seven and a half?"

"That's right. Means he'd already been dead six months."

"How's your friend know this?"

"Have you seen the movie *Married to the Mob?*"

"No."

"Well, let's just say if the Sopranos ever have a Christmas episode my pal Jerry will be the honest guy who can ask the blessing without being struck by lightning. His wife's the daughter of a don."

"No one else was after Sammy?"

"No. The beef with Sammy was small potatoes, if I can mix my food groups. It's called organized crime for a reason. They keep their hotheads under control. We aren't talking about a street gang that wastes some dude for looking at them funny."

I took a deep breath. The New York angle had been a long shot.

"I know you're disappointed," said Cassie, "but there was always the problem with the gun. A New York shooter would have brought his own hardware and not used my brother's old twenty-five for the job."

"What about the crooked contractors?"

"That's the other bad news. Barringer won't give me his file. I'd like to work that myself, but he said it's part of the story. He'll whine to Darius if he thinks I'm horning in. And there might be another problem."

"What?" I wondered when we were ever going to get to the good news.

"That local contractor who went to jail, Duncan Atkins. Guess who was his accountant?"

"Not Susan's father?"

"Bingo. Walt had been cleared of any wrongdoing, but now you have his gun as the weapon that killed the witness against his client. People may draw some unpleasant conclusions."

"Barringer's running with that?"

She chuckled. "That's the good news. Nelson Darius took Cliff Barringer to task for overstating unsubstantiated conclusions last night about Susan. Cliff's not about to risk a libel suit with some preposterous claim that my brother was a hit man for Duncan Atkins. He'd be the laughingstock of Asheville."

And I'd told Tommy Lee to have Bridges check out the possibility the contractors had Sammy killed. I'd only managed to make things worse.

"That may be the silver lining in this whole screwed-up affair," said Cassie. "Give Barringer the rope and he'll hang himself. Gotta go."

She hung up. Probably had a to-do list written halfway up her arm.

I spent my time in the funeral home office assembling the paperwork for my trip to Atlanta. The detailed ledgers, financial statements, and inventory lists took my mind off Sammy Calhoun, and before I knew it, the winter sun disappeared behind the ridges. I declined Mom's offer of dinner and decided to eat at home. Susan was spending the evening with her father, reassuring him that she wasn't on her way to the gas chamber.

I turned in early. Tomorrow's meeting was set for ten, and I needed to leave by six to time my arrival after the Atlanta rush hour.

At seven the next morning, I joined I-85 at Greenville, South Carolina. The mountains and most of the snow were in my rearview mirror and traffic whipped along at ten miles over the speed limit. Obey the posted sign and you wound up on the grill of an eighteen-wheeler.

My hope of avoiding commuter congestion vanished as I neared the major interchange of I-85 and I-285. Ted Sandiford had given me directions to Hoffman Enterprises that didn't take into account that the expressway would be a high-speed, bumper-to-bumper parking lot. His corporate headquarters lay in an office park along the I-285 beltway, and I nearly crashed into a piling trying to maneuver across three lanes in time for the I-285 ramp.

If the interstate loops were the arteries around the heart of Atlanta, then a cardiologist would pronounce the patient dead of clogged vessels. Given the manners of the drivers, an intestinal blockage was a more appropriate analogy—the city and its commuters could benefit from a giant enema.

I found the building housing Hoffman Enterprises without further mishap. It was one of a series of long, pink granite monstrosities that were separated from each other by black asphalt and green lawn trim. If you added handles to the rectangular edifice, it would look like a casket.

I walked in, black attaché case in hand, and announced myself to the receptionist in their lobby. Her smartly tailored business attire told me casual Fridays had not infiltrated the Hoffman corporate culture, and I was glad I had chosen a funereal charcoal suit for the occasion. The woman had my name on a list of expected visitors and asked me to make myself comfortable while she buzzed Mr. Sandiford.

I amused myself by examining the wall of photographs and the plaques of commendation for the Hoffman Family of Fine Funeral Homes. I guess the title phrase had been designed to create the sense of a single-family funeral home like Clayton and Clayton, even though the business was run out of this corporate machine. I tried to envision my name added to the brass plates of Funeral Director of the Year. Maybe they had an Embalmer of the Month Club with the coveted award of a reserved parking space.

"Barry. You made it."

I turned to see a man with a bad brown toupee coming toward me from a side door. His tan face was split by a broad smile of capped teeth. He was without a suit coat, and his white shirt was rolled up at the sleeves. Casual Friday after all. He pumped my hand like he was extracting a pail of water.

"Welcome to Hoffman. You folks digging out up there?"

"Things are getting back to normal."

"Good, good." He grabbed me by the elbow and steered me like Uncle Wayne guiding the bereaved to the graveside.

We passed through the door and into a wide hallway. Ted Sandiford wasn't what I expected. In my mind, I had created him in the mold of NEWSCHANNEL-8's owner Nelson Darius. But the Hoffman executive was closer to a guy you'd meet at a neighborhood bar than a country club banquet. Sandiford softened the contrived image portrayed by the soulless display of the Family of Fine Funeral Homes.

We entered a well appointed conference room, and the friendly bird dog pointed me to a leather chair at a large elliptical oak table.

"Did you bring the paperwork?" he asked and eased into the chair beside me.

I opened my attaché case and handed him four file folders bound together by two rubber bands.

"Excellent," he said. "Let me take these to our acquisitions analyst. Then if he has any questions, we can get them after lunch. When do you have to head back?"

"I need to be on the road by two-thirty. We've got a visitation tonight."

"Did you include it?"

His question stumped me. "Include what?"

"The upcoming funeral. It will help with the projections."

I reached for the files. "No. I didn't think about it."

"Never mind," he said. "I'll stick a note on this." Sandiford got up. "Want a cup of coffee?"

"No thanks."

He started for the door. "I'll be back in a few minutes. We've got a little promotional video you might find interesting." As he left the room, he flipped a toggle switch on the wall.

The lights dimmed and a whirring noise harkened the descent of a screen from a slot in the ceiling. A video projector mounted above my head flickered to life, and the mellow voice of a Hal

Holbrook soundalike spoke the words, "The Hoffman Family of Fine Funeral Homes."

For the next five minutes, I was seduced by the lush score and happy faces depicting the joys of working and dying in the bosom of Hoffman Enterprises. The producers approached their message as if it was some kind of eternal timeshare instead of a burial service. I could see them adding a shot of Freddy, Uncle Wayne, and me welcoming our grieving clients as they entered our sanctuary from life's storm. Uncle Wayne would give everyone a copy of GRIT Magazine.

The slick presentation was a long way from our advertising efforts—hand fans distributed to the mountain churches with "When It's Time To Come Home..." under a picture of Jesus retrieving the lost sheep. Maybe Hoffman could hire an animal trainer and add that to the remake.

The music and picture faded. As the lights came up, Ted Sandiford asked, "What do you think?"

"Where do you show this?" I was a guest and remembered my manners.

He laughed. "As few places as possible. It's a fifteen-thousand-dollar stroke for the stockholders. Makes them feel good about their investment. Hope it didn't scare you off."

"It's just that Gainesboro's a pretty simple community."

"I know," he said. "Hand fans. They were big in Irondale, Alabama." He used his home town as a starting point to outline the acquisition process. It was a more detailed version of our phone conversation, but with added emphasis on the business policies of Hoffman.

"We have the economy of scale in buying equipment and supplies," he explained, "and we're vertically integrated."

"Our clients are all horizontal."

"That's corporate-speak to mean our funeral homes are both profit centers and markets for our products. Hoffman owns significant shares in the companies whose products we buy. We try to pay ourselves at every level of the industry."

I broached the subject that most concerned me. "What are your staffing plans—short term and long term?"

"A fair question, particularly since you're a multigenerational business. Like I said, we'll want a contract with you. Initially I don't see any changes. Your uncle will probably retire soon anyway, and you have a part-timer."

"Freddy Mott," I said, anxious to make him more than a personnel slot. "He's been with us over ten years."

"A smart way to run," agreed Sandiford. "Pay help as needed. Any staff additions or replacements will then come from our intern pool."

"Intern pool?"

"Hoffman has relationships with mortuary science colleges across the country."

"Like summer jobs?"

"Year-round job training," he said. "They get course credit for working at one of our operations for a semester. Everybody benefits."

Especially Hoffman. Free or near free labor. But, it was real-world experience and I couldn't fault the practice.

At eleven, we were joined by an employee from a funeral home in Marietta, outside of Atlanta. She went through illustrations of how the central business office made administration so much easier. I was vulnerable to her dog-and-pony show after spending two weeks preparing year-end reports.

The Vice President of Operations treated us to lunch at a restaurant whose menu was pricier than any evening dinner in Gainesboro. He wanted to know the ratio of indigenous family funerals to those of relocated newcomers, both in terms of number and the average expense per funeral. Those were statistics I'd never dreamed of compiling.

When we returned to the conference room, I found my folders neatly stacked on the table. Beside them lay a sealed manila envelope.

"You don't need these files?" I asked Sandiford.

"We've made copies. I'm sorry. I should have cleared that with you."

"It's all right," I said. I picked up the nine-by-twelve envelope. It was about an inch thick. "What's this?"

"Some general information for you to review this weekend. The products we use, our stock-option plan, 401-k benefits, health coverage, the usual personnel packet."

"What happens next?"

"I expect I'll be in touch the first of the week." He looked at his watch. "It's nearly two. Unless you've got questions, I'm good to let you head back. Can't have you late for the visitation."

Sandiford walked me to my jeep. The vehicle was coated in muck and salt from the road.

"Guess you need four-wheel drive."

"Yes. We've got families living alongside logging roads."

"Approval should be no problem."

"Approval?"

"Normally we buy our funeral directors a Cadillac or Lincoln. We can make it a luxury SUV. Then you can have whatever you want for a personal car. Me, I'd love a convertible in the mountains."

I thought about Sandiford's hairpiece blowing off as he tooled around a hairpin curve.

As I hit the first ascent beyond Greenville, I thought about Susan and me driving through Pisgah Forest in a red Miata convertible. I reached out, patted the manila envelope beside me, and wondered what Hoffman Enterprises gave their Funeral Director of the Year.

Chapter 11

Although it was only six when I returned to Gainesboro, the short-lived December sun had long left the sky. The street lights in front of the funeral home, laced with the green and red Christmas decorations the town hung every year, cast enough light to show puddles of water dotting the sidewalk. These remnants of melted snow threatened to become hazards as the night temperature plummeted.

Icy spots would also form in patches on the backcountry roads traveled by the McBee family and friends. Uncle Wayne and I needed to use diplomacy to end the visitation early so mourners could beat the hard freeze home.

I found Mom and my uncle in what we euphemistically called the Slumber Room. Mom mixed some of our stock greenery with the few floral arrangements delivered earlier, and Wayne bent over the casket, making last-minute adjustments to Claude's final wardrobe.

"How was your trip?" asked Mom.

"Good. Hoffman is a big operation. They know how to put the business in funeral business."

"They make an offer?" asked Wayne.

"They bought me lunch. I guess that's a good sign. We're supposed to hear something the first of the week."

"Did you like them?"

"Ted Sandiford seems like a regular guy. The others are corporate types. Not enough personality to like or dislike."

"Corporate types," repeated my uncle, with the same inflection the Tucker brothers used for "No-Reb Caleb" and "Turncoat Turner." Uncle Wayne wouldn't be in the promotional video.

"What can I do to help?" I asked.

"We're in good shape," said Mom. "Did you eat? There's meatloaf I can reheat."

"I stopped at Bojangle's in Hendersonville. Wayne, if you don't need me in here, I'll spread rock salt on the walk. Don't want to be sued for any broken hips."

"Fine. First, take a look, would you?" He stepped back from the body. "Family's coming at six-thirty for their private viewing."

I studied the old gentleman resting peacefully in the silver-gray casket. He wore a brown tweed sport coat his daughter had chosen and a string-tie now only in style for bluegrass fiddle players. A green sweater vest was sandwiched between his coat and western cut, pearl-buttoned white shirt.

"They've got him bundled up," I said.

Wayne chuckled. "That was his daughter Darlene's idea. She brought it this afternoon. Said he was always cold at the nursing home."

"He looks good."

"I darkened his moustache. Took a few years off him."

A family's reaction to a loved one in a casket is impossible to predict. We liked to get a favorite recent photograph as a guide, but that wasn't always possible. Wayne was particularly sensitive to moustaches since he had once shaved the stubble of a man who had been sick for a week before he died. When the widow peered into the casket, she fainted. Wayne had inadvertently shaved off her husband's moustache, and the shock of seeing the strange face knocked the poor woman off her feet. Smelling salts for the wife and spirit gum and hair trimmings for the husband saved my uncle from disaster.

Promptly at six-thirty, a four-wheel-drive pickup and two cars pulled into our parking lot. Eight adults and a five-year-old boy piled out of the vehicles. One of the men immediately lit a cigarette and sucked on it while coming down the walk.

I met the family on the steps of the front porch to ensure no one tripped.

Darlene Anderson, Claude's married daughter, must have been around sixty. She was escorted by her younger brother, Claude Junior. The other six were an assortment of the deceased's grandchildren, and a tyke who was a great-grandson. The only one I remembered was grandson Stony McBee because Tommy Lee had warned me about him. I had to stop him at the door and coerce him into finishing his cigarette outside.

Wayne and I stood a respectful distance away while Darlene and Claude Junior led the family to the casket. Only the upper half of the split lid was raised, and the relatives huddled close together as everyone wanted to see at once.

"What's wrong with Paw-Paw's legs?" asked the child.

Wayne and I exchanged a smile. Nine times out of ten, a youngster wanted to know why the casket covered the lower half of the body. Usually, a grownup explained the family's preference not to put the entire length of the loved one on display.

"Yeah," said Stony McBee. He glared at me. "You didn't take his shoes, did you?"

His accusation stunned me. "No," I said, louder than I should have.

"Hush," said Darlene to her nephew.

"No. I wanna see." Stony grabbed the edge of the lid and tried to lift it.

"Stop it," Claude Junior told his obstinate son.

"It's locked," Stony said. "Why would they lock it? Paw-Paw ain't getting out."

Wayne stepped closer. "It's not locked, it's latched." He slid two bolts and lifted the lower half.

Claude McBee's trousers were neatly pressed and his brown shoes tied and buffed to a soft shine. Even the argyle socks were stretched tightly over the old man's thin ankles.

"Happy now?" snapped Darlene.

"You can't be too careful. Daddy, I'm going for a smoke." He turned, glowered at me, and headed for the porch.

The room was silent. Then Darlene sighed.

"I know what's wrong."

Wayne and I edged nearer. What had we forgotten?

"Daddy needs his pocket watch." She reached in her leather handbag and pulled out a gold watch and chain. With practiced skill, she looped the chain through a vest buttonhole and slid the watch into a pocket. After studying her father for a few seconds, she extracted it. She opened the case and set the hands to match the time on Claude Junior's wristwatch. She wound the stem and replaced the watch in the pocket.

No one spoke. The steady click of the second hand sounded from the casket.

"There," she said.

Over the next hour, about twenty people came to offer condolences and view the body. Preacher Calvin Stinnett met with Wayne and me to go over last-minute details for Saturday's service. I asked him if he would suggest to the family that we conclude the visitation a half-hour early given the road conditions.

After the last visitor left, Wayne invited the family to view the body one final time. Preacher Stinnett joined them and offered a prayer.

While Mom and Uncle Wayne went for the family's coats, I stood with Darlene and Claude Junior as they reviewed the Those Who Called register. I told them I would bring it and the flowers to the church the next day.

Then Darlene returned to the casket.

"It's gone," she screamed. "Somebody's done stole Daddy's watch."

Each of us ran to join her, as if her eyes weren't good enough to see it.

"You're responsible for this," Stony shouted at me.

I gently grabbed Darlene's arm to comfort her. "Quiet," I said.

Stony stepped beside us. "Don't you tell me what to do."

"We need quiet," I repeated firmly.

Darlene looked up at me, and I saw comprehension dawn in her eyes.

"Shut up, Stony," she ordered. "Everybody stand still."

The room fell silent. Then, like a distant radio station growing stronger, the tick of the watch broke through.

"I hear it," said the three-foot kid, and he leaned his ear against Stony's sport coat.

The man's face went pale as his family stared first at his ticking pocket and then at him.

"Stony!" cried Darlene in horror.

"You planted it on me, you son of a bitch."

Before I could move, Stony's fist caught me full force on the nose, sending me into a wreath of flowers to land flat on my back. Through the petals draped across my bleeding face, I saw Stony grabbed by two burly cousins. Then Darlene swung her handbag and hit her thieving nephew across the throat. He started coughing for air and struggled to break free. Someone twisted his arm behind his back so hard Stony screamed and lurched onto the casket. The full lid crashed down with a resounding boom that stopped everyone. Claude had spoken.

I saw Mom and Uncle Wayne enter the room, coats on arms and mouths agape.

Welcome to Clayton and Clayton, one of the Hoffman Family of Fine Funeral Homes.

I sat in the den recliner, my head tilted back and mouth open to breathe. Cotton swabs were jammed up my nose and an ice compress lay across my eyes. Uncle Wayne had administered first aid while Darlene Anderson hung over his shoulder, begging me not to press charges against her nephew, the one whose Adam's apple she had cored. She knew I had been with her when the watch was pilfered.

Stony had been hustled away, his arm wrenched so high behind his back he practically floated out of the room. I figured the family would exact punishment more severe than the legal system.

Uncle Wayne gave the opinion that my nose wasn't broken, but would swell to Rudolph proportions. Instead of a reindeer, I'd look like a raccoon as both eyes blackened. Mom forced me to take two Tylenol and to promise to stay over. She called Freddy Mott to assist Wayne with tomorrow's funeral. It was more a precaution against me attacking Stony if he showed up at the service. That he had sucker punched me hurt worse than anything else.

About an hour after the McBees wreaked their havoc, I felt well enough to get ready for bed. The packing in my nose had stopped the bleeding, and I carefully cleared my swollen nostrils. The first breath stung, but the nasal passages seemed in working order. A stranger stared back at me from the mirror. Too bad we were approaching Christmas and not Halloween.

Mom brought a cup of weak tea and a plate of gingersnaps to the bedroom. As she set them on the nightstand, she said, "I used to worry about you when you were a policeman."

I laughed. "Then I never so much as stubbed my toe. I'm convinced mortuary science courses need to include self-defense."

"People are just so stressed when a loved one dies."

"So stressed they rob the body?"

She shook her head. Mom always looked for the good in everyone. Stony McBee proved too much of a challenge. "Well, I'm glad you'll be staying in tomorrow."

"I can't hide from an entire family. I'm only skipping the service to avoid upsetting Darlene."

"You can sleep late, can't you? I'm going to the grocery store early and I'll take your dad. He likes to push the cart."

"I've got some paperwork from Hoffman to go over. And I need to see Susan. She's going through a tough time."

Mom sat down on the edge of the bed and looked away. "How anyone could accuse a sweet girl like her of murder is beyond me. Is there anything you can do?"

"Get to the truth. Fight those slurs in the press."

"Oh, no," Mom exclaimed, and turned to me wide-eyed. "I forgot."

"Forgot what?"

"A reporter called this afternoon. The one that wrote that article about Susan in the Vista."

"Melissa Bigham?"

"Yes. She wanted you to call her. Left me a bunch of numbers. I got so wrapped up with the McBee arrangements and then the fight."

I thought Mom was going to cry.

"It's all right. Probably just had a question."

"I didn't tell her you were in Atlanta." The tears began to trickle. "I didn't want the newspaper to think we have to sell the funeral home."

I sat on the bed beside her and put my arm around her shoulders. I could feel the tremor of silent sobs. In all the turmoil of the past few days—Dad's wandering off, Susan's troubles, and the prospect of selling a huge part of her life—Mom had never let her feelings come through. Now, looking at her balloon-nosed son in the room where he grew up must have broken the emotional dam. I wasn't sure what the true issue was behind her tears. Probably Mom wasn't sure either, but the tears were real, and we sat together and let the moment play out.

I looked at us in the mirror, a battered face and a wrinkled face. Mom's was the more shocking. I realized she had gotten old, and I had no clue how many more years I would be able to wrap my arm around her.

"We don't have to do anything you don't want to do," I told her.

"I know. You're a good son, Barry."

We sat a few more minutes, and then she stood up. "Well, let me get the numbers for you now. I might forget in the morning." She smiled. "You'll know you're in trouble when your dad has to remind me of things."

Mom brought back a sheet of paper with four numbers—cell, work, home, and pager. The note "call anytime" was written under them. It looked like Melissa had more than a simple question. I waited until I heard Mom close the door to her bedroom, and then tiptoed downstairs to the office.

Since it was after ten, I tried the home number first.

"Barry?"

Even she had my number in caller ID.

"Yes. Sorry to get back to you so late. I got tied up."

"I've got something for you that might help Susan."

I grabbed a pen and notepad. "I'm all ears."

"After my story ran yesterday, I got a call from Annette Nolan."

The name sounded familiar. "Who's she?"

"My predecessor at the paper. She worked there for years."

"Right."

"Annette retired five years ago. I interned with her the last year and then got hired when she left. Every couple months we have lunch, and I thought that's why she telephoned. I didn't return the call until today."

"She knows something about Sammy Calhoun?"

"She thinks so. He'd come to her about a story."

I felt the tingle in the back of my neck. That fit with Cassie's information. "Did she contact Ewbanks?"

"No, and she won't. She's afraid."

"Of Ewbanks?"

"She just said she couldn't trust anyone in the system. Sammy Calhoun was proof of that."

"Are you printing her story?"

"What story? She won't talk to me. Says she doesn't want to get me killed."

"How about Tommy Lee? Will she tell him?"

"She wants to talk to you."

"Me? I don't know the woman and only vaguely remember seeing her byline."

"She knows we worked together on the Willard murders," said Melissa. "She guessed you helped get the information for yesterday's story. Annette's sharp. She figures you've got a vested interest since Susan's involved."

That's the problem with a small town. Everybody knows your vested interests. "Where does she want to meet?"

"Her place. It's off the road to Chimney Rock."

"Can we go tomorrow?"

"You can. I'm shut out."

"Shut out?"

"She's scared," said Melissa. "Scared for me. And Annette Nolan doesn't frighten easily. She told me she's afraid I'll stick my nose in some hole and end up buried in one like Calhoun." Melissa laughed. "For some reason she thinks you'll keep your nose out of trouble."

I touched my nose and the pain shot up to my eyes. "Okay. Give me her number."

"Sure," she said, and the lilt in her voice told me what was coming next. "For a price."

"You'll get the story, Melissa."

"The exclusive story," she corrected. "You talk to no one until it clears my paper and the wires. Including Susan's aunt."

"I promise." What did I have to lose? When Annette Nolan saw my nose for trouble, there'd be no story.

Maybe she'd believe I was injured in a high-speed funeral procession.

Chapter 12

The night passed in fitful chunks. At one in the morning, I took two more Tylenol and got three hours' sleep out of the next five. Dawn was another hour away when I gave up and went downstairs to the office.

I reviewed the packet of material from Hoffman Enterprises. Their fringe benefits were far greater than what we could afford as an independent operation. Even Freddy would qualify for the 401-k, and I knew he had trouble squirreling away money for a rainy day. The supplies Hoffman used weren't my first choice, but I might be able to supplement their basic stock with my preferences, particularly the restorative cosmetics. I thought about applying a heavy coat to my own face.

At seven-thirty, I heard Mom and Dad stirring upstairs. I started a pot of coffee to greet them and returned to the Slumber Room to get things ready for transport to Crab Apple Valley Baptist Church.

Claude McBee had been whisked away to the cooler temperature of the back room last night. A scattering of loose petals and leaves marked the spot where I had crashed through the largest floral arrangement. I carried the remaining ones onto the back porch where it would be easier for Uncle Wayne and Freddy to load them later.

A check in the downstairs bathroom mirror showed me I did indeed look worse. My nose needed only horn-rimmed glasses to pass for the joke disguise kids bought from novelty shops. The color under my eyes had darkened from blue-green to black, and I was glad I wouldn't be giving Stony McBee the satisfaction of seeing his handiwork.

I poured myself a cup of coffee as Mom and Dad entered the kitchen. They were dressed and ready for their morning outing. A flash of alarm crossed Mom's face at the sight of my bruised features. Then she managed a smile.

"How are you feeling?"

"Like Muhammad Ali's sparring partner," I said.

"Can I bring you anything from the store?"

"Just a grocery bag to put over my head so I don't scare small children."

Dad came right up to me and stared. He reached out and gently touched my nose. "Football?"

I knew he wasn't commenting on the size. His mind had jumped back fifteen years to when I'd taken a cleated foot to the face. My unorthodox defensive move had tripped the opposing fullback short of the goal line and stopped the game while the referees removed his shoe from my helmet. At least I'd gotten a standing ovation as they carried me off the high school field.

"Yeah, Dad. Big game last night. I knocked them dead."

I helped my parents navigate the ice to their car and gave Mom a warning to watch slick spots in the Ingles supermarket parking lot. I told her I felt well enough to return to my cabin and I'd call later to let her know how I was doing.

At eight-thirty, I telephoned Annette Nolan, afraid if I waited any longer, she'd leave for a day of Saturday errands. A woman creaked a hello. She sounded as ancient as the hills.

"Miss Nolan?"

"Yes, who's this?" she demanded, her voice suddenly stronger.

"Barry Clayton. Melissa Bigham suggested I call you. I wondered if you'd have time to see me today."

"Right now."

It wasn't a question.

I crossed an ice-choked creek and wound the jeep up through a barren apple orchard. The road had been plowed, and the gravel was thick enough to provide good traction. Annette Nolan said her farmhouse was about halfway to the top of the ridge.

She had described her home as two storied and white sided, which fit most farmhouses that were better than a tarpaper shack or the abandoned homestead collapsing beside the next generation's mobile home.

The road turned onto the ridge's southern exposure where patches of rock and weeds broke through the melted snow. The apple trees stopped at the edge of a barbed wire fence encompassing several acres of sloping pasture. Beyond the enclosure stood a barn and what I gathered to be Annette Nolan's residence. It wasn't what I expected.

The paint was dingy, but the architecture appeared wondrously Victorian. A corner turret contained round windows with mullions shaped like the steering wheel of a sailing ship. One would expect to stare out those glass panes at the ocean, not the Appalachian mountains.

The road split, with a branch headed to the barn and the other looping back to form a circular driveway in front of the house. I parked beside the stone steps to the porch. Embedded in the side of the top step was a tarnished plaque reading CONNEMARA II—1955. I recognized the word Connemara as the name of the poet Carl Sandburg's home over in Flat Rock and knew this structure must hold an interesting story.

I rapped on the door and then listened for footsteps. Hearing none, I peered through the window. A log burned low in the living room fireplace. The glow flickered across an afghan-covered sofa and a couple of dilapidated easy chairs. Hundreds of books were piled along the floor and jammed into shelves that lined the walls.

I stuck my head in the door and called for Miss Nolan. Somewhere out of sight, a cat meowed. Hesitant to wander in uninvited, I left the porch and followed the cleared road around to the barn. A green Subaru Outback sat next to the windowless side of the rough plank building. The snow lay heavier in the protection of the barn's shadow, and my boots crunched through the crusty surface as I sought an entrance.

The barn's doors were wide open, but an inner gate of unfinished slats barred the way. An old man with a long gray beard studied me from the other side. He let out a sharp raspy bleat that made me jump. A billy goat.

The chilly breeze bore the pungent odor of livestock. Even my swollen nose caught a strong whiff. I heard more bleats and a chanting chorus of goats emerged from the depths to see what triggered the alarm. They crowded together, jostling their brown fur hides against each other and eyeing me suspiciously. Over their cries, I heard, "Let yourself in. They won't hurt you."

I opened the gate just enough to squeeze through. My original greeter met me and immediately pressed his knobby head into my thigh. I scratched him behind the ears. He eased the pressure, content to be rubbed in a place he couldn't reach. We walked in step in the direction of the voice, my guard nudging me forcefully each time I stopped petting him.

Inside the first stall, I saw a tethered nanny goat standing broadside. Underneath her belly, hands rhythmically squeezed the dangling teats, sending short bursts of milk into a pail. A pair of brown scuffed brogans held the shiny aluminum receptacle in place.

"Miss Nolan?" I asked, finding it hard to believe the owner of the hands and shoes could be my quarry.

The milking stopped. Around the butt end of the goat appeared a smiling face whose youthful, blue eyes seemed out of place in the wind-burned features of an old woman. A black knit stocking hat almost covered wisps of gray hair, and the upturned collar of a Navy pea coat touched the lobes of her ears.

If she startled me, I, at least, jarred her expectations. "Good gracious alive," she exclaimed. "What did the other guy look like?"

"A lot like Stony McBee. We had a little disagreement about the best place to carry a pocket watch."

"You must have argued for the owner's pocket."

A hard push knocked me sideways.

"Jasper," yelled the woman. "Git!"

The perfectly named creature snorted, and then bolted away to resume his station at the barn gate.

"Sorry. Jasper's prone to forget who runs this place. Now, I just need a few minutes more with Molly."

"That's okay, Miss Nolan. I'm in no hurry."

"The name's Annette. I haven't been a Miss since three daughters and five grandchildren ago."

She returned to her milking. I stood there, not sure whether to talk to the side of a goat or not.

"Melissa Bigham says you're okay," she said.

"She's a straight shooter."

"Surprised we haven't met, Barry. I've known your dad and mom for years."

"I've only been back since my father's illness got too bad."

The milking paused as she considered what to say. Evidently, nothing measured up.

"I seem to have a knack for attracting trouble," I said.

"That's what happens when you're the clearing house for all the bodies. My cousin runs a funeral home in Brevard."

"Bryant and Son?" I asked. "They've been in business forever."

"My uncle founded it in 1928. Same year my father started the Vista."

"You own the newspaper?"

"No. Dad sold it in 1955."

"And built Connemara the second," I said.

Annette Nolan stood up from behind the goat. Her surprise lasted only an instant. "Oh, you saw the plaque." She bent over, lifted the pail, and unhooked Molly from her tether. "After I put this in the fridge, we'll have a cup of hot tea."

As we left the barn, I asked, "What's the connection to Sandburg's Connemara?"

"My father and Sandburg were friends. When he moved to Flat Rock in the late Forties, Sandburg gave my father an interview. He was an old newspaperman himself and they hit it off. He didn't socialize much with the locals. Most people knew him as Sandburg the goatkeeper, not Sandburg the poet."

"Goatkeeper?"

"Actually it was his wife. Mrs. Sandburg developed her own breed. You just met some descendants."

"And the house?"

"My father admired Connemara. He knew the Smythe family who lived there before the Sandburgs. Our home isn't a carbon copy, to use a word lost in today's computer age, but the inside has the same feel. My father built it on land the family had owned since his grandfather ran the inn and tavern on the coach road from Shelby to Asheville. When Daddy sold the paper, he secured a lifelong position for me, built Connemara the second, and put the rest of his money in a company called International Business Machines." She winked at me.

Even I knew International Business Machines became better known as IBM, Big Blue. I suspected Annette Nolan didn't need to sell goat cheese and apples to supplement her social security check.

We entered the house through the back porch, and she pointed me to a chair at her kitchen table. The cabinets and counters were white with red enamel trim, a color scheme shared with some cars of 1955. Mismatched appliances told me replacements had been made upon the death of the old ones and not before.

Annette hung her pea coat and cap on the knob of the pantry door and revealed a pair of bib overalls and a red flannel shirt underneath. She wore her gray hair close cropped, and her short, wiry body moved around the room without signs of arthritis common to most of her generation. She set a pot of tea, two mugs, and a pitcher of goat's milk between us.

"Sugar?" she asked.

"No, thanks."

"Then try this." She pulled a mason jar from a cabinet and slid it over to me. The light golden color of its contents tipped me off.

"Sourwood honey," I said.

"Make it myself. Or rather my bees do." She shook her head. "Don't know for how much longer. Something's destroying them. Mites or pollution. There's a reason we call sex the birds and the bees. That we're killing off both of them doesn't bode well for humanity's future."

I stirred a thick teaspoon into my mug.

Without missing a beat, Annette continued, "So, somebody killed off Sammy Calhoun and bunked him with Pearly Johnson."

"Shot him right between the eyes." Annette was a woman for whom I didn't feel I needed to sugarcoat, or rather honey-coat, anything.

"Well, that makes me feel better."

She couldn't help but see the shock in my blackened eyes. "I didn't want him murdered. I'm just glad he didn't cheat me."

"Cheat you?"

She took a sip of tea. "I guess it's about time we got down to it. I suppose Melissa told you she's mad at me because I'm going to tell you things I wouldn't share with her."

"She says you shut her out, but she's negotiated for my exclusive story."

Annette chuckled. "Glad to know I trained her well. But I didn't train her to take on a killer." Her expression turned deadly serious. "This was nearly seven years ago. I was seventy-three and figuring to retire at seventy-five. Maybe just write a weekly column. My husband had died the year before and I was taking stock of life. As a reporter, I regretted that I'd never broken a major story. Those don't come along in a small town like Gainesboro."

"That's the trade-off for living in a place where you leave your doors unlocked."

"You're right, and I had almost made peace with that. Then Sammy Calhoun came to me with a proposition. He claimed to have evidence of sexual misconduct in the justice system."

"In Laurel County?"

"Why not? We have sex in Laurel County."

"But Tommy Lee is such—"

She cut me off. "A straight arrow? Calhoun didn't say it was in the Sheriff's Department. Wouldn't say much of anything other than the story was too hot and could be squelched. I was skeptical and he knew it."

"Did you turn him away?"

"Sammy was a slick operator. Somehow he read me like a book, knew I wanted the story for my own ego." She laughed. "Remember, I was young and foolish."

"A mere seventy-three."

"And there was something else. Calhoun told me he suspected some of the girls were underage, maybe acting out of fear. I thought about my own granddaughters and the idea made me furious."

As a news story, sex in the justice system would raise a public outcry, but not nearly as loud as if juveniles were involved. I understood why Annette bit on Calhoun's proposal.

"Did he have proof?" I asked.

"Claimed he was lubricating a source. Lubricating was his exact word. Said he'd have irrefutable evidence."

"How much did he want?"

"Two thousand dollars."

"That seems like a steep price for the Vista."

"Any price was too steep for the paper. That money was coming out of my own pocket, and Sammy knew it. Was counting on it. And these past seven years I thought he'd played me for a sucker."

I studied the determined face across the table. I wouldn't want Annette Nolan mad at me. Give me Stony McBee any day.

"You gave him two grand?"

"I gave him a thousand—cash. He said he'd collect the rest after the story broke, and if he didn't deliver, he'd give me back the thousand minus the cost of his equipment."

"What equipment?"

"He didn't say exactly. I assumed he would put a wire on someone or take those grainy black and white photos detectives were famous for. I took the chance."

"How much time elapsed from when you gave him the money and he disappeared?"

"Week or two at most."

"When we dug up the skeleton, we found about four hundred dollars in cash in his wallet. He must have bought something."

"I have no idea what. I gave him the money and never saw him again. Like everyone else, I figured he skipped for Texas."

"Someone went to great lengths to create that story."

She drained her mug and set it on the table with a thud. "I know. That's why I want Melissa safely on the sidelines." Her sharp eyes bore in on me. "You, on the other hand, can't seem to stay out of the line of fire."

"It's a talent I've gone to great pains to cultivate." I took another sip of tea and my mind started making connections. "You ever hear anything else about sexual misconduct, either in the juvenile or adult divisions?"

"Not a word," she said, "and I did some digging around. Talked to released inmates, women serving probation, anybody I thought could be pressured by those holding power over them, from guards to court officials. Nothing turned up."

Just like Cassie's investigation in Buncombe County. Was it an identical scam Calhoun was playing on each of them? If so, a third person took it deadly serious.

"Did Calhoun specifically tell you the scandal was in Laurel County?" I asked.

"You found Calhoun buried in Walker County," she said.

I knew her mind raced step by step with mine. What if Calhoun had been protecting his story all along? He had first gone to Cassie Miller, but she blew him off and then had a reporter snoop around. Calhoun had played it smart, letting her think the story was based in Asheville, in Buncombe County. It made sense he would do the same to Annette Nolan so she couldn't stiff him either. Not Buncombe, not Laurel, but Walker County.

Sheriff Ewbanks and his department were investigating a crime that might have been committed by one of their own, and that someone had a very good reason to pin on Susan or her father.

"You've got your work cut out for you," Annette Nolan said.

I had the eerie feeling she had read my mind.

The Cardinal Café was crowded for a Saturday afternoon. The sun and thaw had lured cabin-fevered diners out in droves. I spotted Tommy Lee's wave from the rear by the swinging kitchen door.

"You boys having the usual?" Helen asked the question as I slid into the pink booth across from the sheriff.

"Yes," we answered in unison.

She didn't bother to pull the yellow pencil from the bun in her hair and deposited two glasses of sweetened iced tea on the table.

"Nice shiners," she said to me, as if discussing the weather, and then disappeared into the kitchen. Tommy Lee's plate of tuna fish salad and my roast beef sandwich would be out in short order.

"I told you Stony had magnetic fingers," said Tommy Lee, after hearing about last night's brawl. "Didn't realize he had an iron fist."

"Lucky punch," I muttered.

"Right. So what's up?" he asked and took a swallow of tea.

I'd telephoned him en route from Annette Nolan's asking for a cheap date. Cheap was our shorthand for the Cardinal Café.

"I spent an interesting morning with Annette Nolan," I said.

He took his one eye off the glass and looked at me quizzically. "Annette. She's a sharp old bird. How's she play into this?"

"Carefully. She's scared for anyone getting involved because she thinks she knows what got Calhoun killed. I think she's on to something."

"Yeah? And?"

I gave Tommy Lee the details of our conversation and the background Cassie had shared on Calhoun.

"How much cash was in his wallet?"

"The crime lab tech said about four hundred. I didn't hear an exact count."

"Let's assume it's the money from Annette Nolan. We can also assume Calhoun didn't buy a gun since he borrowed Susan's."

"And he wasn't wearing a wire, unless they stripped him of it before burying him."

Tommy Lee made circle patterns on the Formica with the condensation from the bottom of his tea glass. "Where else would nearly six hundred dollars have gone?"

"Maybe he just spent it on his rent or groceries," I said.

"But that doesn't take us anywhere. I'd at least like a wild goose to chase."

"Lubricating his source. That was the quote Annette gave me from Calhoun."

"I wonder," said Tommy Lee, and his voice trailed off as he kept a thought to himself.

"Wonder what?"

"His source. His snitch. Is that where the money went? I wonder if there's another extra body in Eagle Creek cemetery."

"We can't go digging up every grave."

Tommy Lee shook his head. "No, and a re-dug grave would have been noticed. On the off chance, check with Reverend Pace to make sure no one else was buried in that cemetery at the same time as Pearly Johnson."

"If not, then the source might still be around. Maybe he killed or betrayed Calhoun."

"And left four hundred dollars in the wallet? Somebody selling out the story would've been greedy enough to have looked for more."

"Greedy," I repeated, pausing as the idea took form.

"What?" Tommy Lee prompted.

"It may be your wild goose," I warned. "Cassie told me Calhoun had fled New York because he tried to blackmail a mobster with information he'd uncovered for a client. What if he tried that double play again, only this time he got nailed."

"You're saying he carried Susan's gun to the meeting because he was going face-to-face, not with his snitch, but with the target of his investigation?"

"And he got popped with Susan's gun," I said. "A service revolver would have left an identifiable slug, traced back to an issued weapon. Walt got stung because he'd registered his gun."

"It's hard for me to believe this could happen in Ewbanks' department," said Tommy Lee. "But, I know you have to go where the evidence leads you."

"When did your man Bridges start with Ewbanks?"

Tommy Lee jumped in his seat. "God damn it, Barry," he whispered harshly. "Where'd his name come from?"

I'd forgotten Tommy Lee hadn't shared his own source with me. "I met him at Walt's with Ewbanks. He said some things about you being a good sheriff and I figured he was your contact. No one else would brag on you."

"Well, keep your figuring to yourself," he ordered.

"Can you answer my question? Bridges told me his wife died ten years ago and you got him hired in the Walker County department. Was that right after his wife's death?"

"Within a couple years I guess. Hated to lose him but he felt strongly about his family responsibilities. You can understand that."

Helen appeared beside us, her arms loaded with two plates and a pitcher of iced tea. "I'll let you keep your own glasses filled," she said, and set everything in the middle of the table. "Need anything else, just holler." She turned to go, and then looked back. "Oh, and I had them leave off the horseradish, Barry. Don't think your nose can take any more abuse."

Tommy Lee laughed. We sorted out the food, and I picked up my sandwich and the conversation.

"Did you get to tell Bridges that Sammy Calhoun went into that grave before he could testify against the contractors?"

"He said Ewbanks is already on it. Talked to the state boys and the lead prosecutor. They agree it's a possibility, but none of the men had a history of violence or known connections to hit men."

"Cassie said Sammy's disappearance didn't affect the verdict."

Tommy Lee nodded. "That's what makes this line of inquiry low priority. Ewbanks doesn't have the manpower to mount a broad investigation."

"Did Bridges say they know Walt Miller was Duncan Atkins' accountant?"

My question surprised him. "No, he didn't. But sharing that information might have crossed the line, if Ewbanks is quietly trying to make it into something."

"Walt Miller didn't kill Sammy Calhoun."

Tommy Lee reared back. "Hey, you don't have to convince me. But there's the problem of the damn gun. It's Walt's and it's the murder weapon."

I didn't have an answer for that fact and took a big bite of my sandwich. We ate quietly for a few minutes, and then my mind returned to the conversation with Annette Nolan.

"So, Bridges was in Ewbanks' department when Calhoun was killed, when Sammy told Annette Nolan about a scandal."

"Not in his current capacity. The only opening at the time was as a juvenile probation officer. He spent a few years there before Ewbanks moved him back into active investigative duty."

"He worked with juvenile offenders?"

"He's not a sexual predator," said Tommy Lee.

"A lot of Catholics said the same thing about their priest."

"And the vast majority were right." He picked at his tuna fish for a few seconds. "All right," he conceded. "I'll keep Bridges in the dark, but we'll need another way to find Calhoun's source."

"Any ideas?" I asked.

"Sounds like you got all the information Annette Nolan had. If some of the victims were underaged girls, we're talking juvenile detention. Those records are hard to get. We'll have to start with who was in charge at the time."

"What if Calhoun did spend that money as a bribe," I suggested. "Paying off his source. He might have gotten the hard evidence he needed and then approached the culprits without revealing his contact. The guy could still be around."

"Can you backtrack who Calhoun hung out with?"

"I can ask Cassie. And there's his landlady, she might remember somebody coming to the apartment."

"Don't be blind to another possibility."

I stared at him and read the concern in his eye.

"I can handle it," but I felt my stomach tighten at the prospect. "I'll talk to her tonight."

Chapter 13

When we left the Cardinal Café, I knew Tommy Lee wasn't happy. He suspected Ewbanks would seek out anyone who could shed light on Susan's relationship with Sammy Calhoun, and he wanted to tip off his friend Bridges to Annette Nolan's lead. Until I had the chance to follow up with Susan and Cassie, I insisted that investigative angle be withheld.

On the way to the cabin, I called Mom for an update on the McBee funeral. Wayne had returned with news all had gone smoothly, including Claude's descent into the ground. My uncle said Darlene had decided to leave the pocket watch on her father since it held too painful a memory to be a comfort. My nose felt comforted when I heard Stony had stood sullenly at the edge of the graveyard, his arm in a sling.

I reached Susan at home, where she'd just come in from her father's.

"How's he doing?"

"Not so well. He had a long talk with Cassie. She told him everything they're reporting is circumstantial and the worst is over. But it's all still hanging over him."

"How about you?"

"I'm scared for him. He doesn't need this stress. Not at his age. I tell you, being a murder suspect is not a good way to lead your life. I'm lucky I've got my job. Once I'm behind my surgical mask, this other stuff no longer matters."

"Any contact from Ewbanks."

"He dropped by my father's this afternoon. Good thing I was there so we could keep our stories together. Ewbanks was civil. Apologized again for my name getting in the press."

"Social call?"

"Hardly. He wanted to know more about the gun. Why I had it. When I last fired it. I told him Dad made me take it because my residency schedule was so crazy. I was living at home at the time and driving in and out of the hospital at all hours."

"That's true, isn't it?"

"Of course it's true." She sounded put out. "At least the crazy hours part. I never drove with the gun. Just kept it in a clothes drawer with the clip out for safety. I told Ewbanks that was why my prints would have been all over it."

"He'd have to admit it's a plausible explanation."

"And Dad backed up everything I said." She sighed. "What a nightmare. What are we going to do?"

I caught the "we" and felt encouraged to include myself. "We'll get through it, Susan. I've been doing a little investigating of my own."

"Are you calling from the emergency room?"

"Not yet." Susan knew that my efforts at amateur police work and my time spent in the hospital had a direct correlation. "I'm on the road and about to lose the cell signal. How about dinner tonight?"

"Sure. You want to come here?"

"I thought we'd go out. A real date. Sullivan's?"

"You always say that place is too dark."

I glanced at myself in the rearview mirror. "Believe me. Dark is good."

The numbers for Cassie Miller were at the cabin so I had to wait before calling her. First, I fed and watered George, then grabbed a clean legal pad. Cassie answered the first ring of her cell phone.

"What's up, Barry?"

I was ready for caller ID. "Nothing new," I said casually. "Thought I'd check in. I know you're not officially on the story so I figured you're free to talk about it."

"So you can give leads to your friend Melissa Bigham?"

I should have anticipated that Cassie would deduce where the Vista reporter got the background on Sammy Calhoun.

Cassie laughed. "It's okay. She did me a favor by showing up Cliff Barringer. Maybe I should hire her."

"As Cliff's replacement," I suggested.

"I can only dream. So, what do you want to know?"

"I figure Ewbanks won't let go of Susan until he has something more promising to track. That could be the last story Calhoun tried to pitch you." I left it there. Cassie might be excluded from covering Calhoun's murder, but I didn't trust her to sit on the news that the sex scandal had been in Walker County, not Buncombe.

"Could be," she agreed. "I've been thinking about that myself."

"Have you got any names of people Calhoun hung out with? Did he have an office? Did he always call you or come to the station?"

"He didn't have an office, but I had a couple of numbers. Not a bad idea, Barry. I'll check my phone logs."

"Your what?"

"Notes of my calls. In my business, I keep an informal record. Just a small steno pad I can even use with my cell. Jot down date, time, key tidbits. Now I do it unconsciously."

I looked at my legal pad where I had written "sex scandal," "office," and "phone log."

"Really? And you keep them?"

"Got an attic full. Amazing how often they come in handy. I should be able to find the right one pretty quickly." She paused. "I'll expect an exclusive on this."

Reporters, I thought. Must be something in their DNA. "Sorry. I've already got a date for the prom. I was hoping we were working for Susan, not NEWSCHANNEL-8."

Silence greeted my statement. Then Cassie said, "Serves the bastards right if the Vista beats them. I'll call you back."

I wore a hat with a brim pulled down over my eyes so the light from Susan's front porch lamp couldn't penetrate the shadow on my face. As she closed the door behind her, I slouched back against the wrought-iron railing that bordered her stoop.

"Oh, are we Sam Spade tonight?" she asked.

"More like Ricky the Raccoon." I doffed my hat politely, letting the light fall upon me.

"Barry!" She jumped back against the door. If it hadn't been latched, she would have tumbled over the threshold. "What happened?"

"Sorry. I should have warned you."

"You're lucky you look so bad or I'd hit you."

"Too late. Stony McBee already did." On the drive to dinner, I told her the story.

Sullivan's is Gainesboro's special event restaurant. Proms, Valentine's Day, anniversaries, marriage proposals—all celebrate with a four-star meal that impresses tourists from Manhattan to Miami. Yet Sullivan's is locally owned and priced to attract the winter people with more limited finances. I had had the foresight to make a last-minute reservation, requesting a quiet corner away from any Christmas or birthday parties.

Our table was lit by a single white candle floating in a crystal bowl. I could have had two noses and three eyes and gone unnoticed. The perfect atmosphere for a romantic interrogation. Over a glass of white wine and shrimp cocktail, I summarized my conversation with Annette Nolan.

"So, you think Sammy was pulling a fast one on Annette?" Susan asked.

"Not necessarily. He was covering his options. If the blackmail angle didn't work, he had another thousand coming for the story. If he could squeeze more, probably a good bit more, from his target, then he'd pay Annette back and say the story hadn't worked out."

"Why bother to come to Annette in the first place?"

I held up answering while the waiter cleared away our appetizers, replacing them with two Caesar salads that could have fed his Roman army.

"It gave him two things," I continued. "A real threat of exposure for his quarry and working capital for his sting. Maybe he had a copy of a receipt from Annette he could brandish as proof the paper would print the story. And the money would be needed to bribe his snitch and acquire any equipment. We know he spent six hundred dollars somewhere."

"And you're following this lead by yourself?"

"There's Tommy Lee."

"But he can't do anything officially, and you don't know who in Walker County is clean or dirty."

"That's why I've got to deliver evidence they can't ignore. Tommy Lee agrees. Otherwise Ewbanks will just keep building a circumstantial case against you until he can get a warrant and that hotshot Claiborne can use you as fodder for his law-and-order campaign for attorney general. Someone's already prompted Calhoun's landlady into remembering events in the most damning sequence. Claiborne may time a high-profile trial so a verdict isn't reached till after the election. By then, what does he care if the case wasn't strong enough."

"And I'll always be that woman charged with murder," Susan admitted. "Where are you going to start?"

"Right here. Right now." I lowered my voice to a whisper. "There're questions I have to ask." I leaned across the table, ostensibly so only Susan could hear, but really because I wanted to study her face. "Did you ever meet Calhoun at a place called The Last Resort?"

She looked away and her jaw muscles tightened. "No, but I think Sammy used to hang out there. Who told you about it?"

"Your Aunt Cassie keeps phone logs. The last month before Calhoun disappeared she returned calls that weren't to his apartment. This afternoon I telephoned the number she gave me and got The Last Resort. What's it like?"

"From the outside, it looks like a real dive of a bar." Her eyes widened. "And it's right across the line in Walker County."

"Listen, Susan, you've got to tell me everything about Sammy Calhoun so I don't go stumbling around making things look worse for you."

"I know," she conceded, and all trace of defensiveness evaporated. "Sammy came to Asheville and thought he could re-start our relationship. He kept playing up the story about accidentally shooting the girl to make me feel sorry for him. And I knew his work with Cassie gave her station a tremendous ratings boost."

"Why'd you give him the gun?"

"He told me he was working on another investigation and needed it for protection. He said even if I didn't care about him, at least think about Cassie. She was counting on the story."

"But you were still hesitant."

"Hesitant? I was angry. He had come to the hospital trying to see me. Told security he was my brother and insisted they page me for a family emergency. I had gotten the message in surgery and was so mad I told the guards to escort him off the hospital grounds. When I left O.R., I found him waiting by the parking lot gate."

The memory kindled a fire in her voice. She took a deep breath and regained control. From out of the shadows stepped our waiter with an expression of concern that rivaled the best in the funeral business. He looked at our untouched salads.

"Is something wrong?"

"No," I assured him. "We haven't seen each other in a long time and I'm asking too many questions to let her eat."

"I can request the chef delay the entrées."

Susan shook her head. "I'm about out of answers. He'll be talking to himself in another minute."

"Very good," he said, and then looked aghast that he'd somehow insulted me.

As he withdrew, Susan said, "He's kissing his tip goodbye."

"You said Sammy was at the gate. Did you talk to him?"

"I yelled at him. I was furious. He'd told hospital security he was Stevie."

For all his slick manipulations, Sammy Calhoun had pushed one button too many using the name of the dead brother she idolized. Susan was the sweetest girl I knew. She also cut people up for a living.

"What was so urgent he'd resort to a trick like that?"

"The damn gun. Had to have it before that night. Promised me he'd never ask for another thing."

"How long after that did he disappear?"

"Like I told you before, a few days later I heard he left for Texas and I never saw him again."

"Then our only link is that bar, The Last Resort. Aptly named."

"I asked Sammy why he hung out in such a dump. He laughed and said it was a gold mine and you never knew when you'd discover a nugget."

"Then that's where I'll start," I said. "We need a nugget of our own. Do you still have a picture of Sammy?" A part of me wanted to hear no.

"Maybe. A loose one in a drawer of photos I've been meaning to organize. Why?"

"It's been seven years, but I want to see if anyone there remembers him."

Susan reached around the salad and candle to clutch my hand. "Barry, if he found something in that bar, it got him killed with his own gun."

"Don't worry. I won't have a gun." I meant it as a joke, but Susan didn't laugh.

A soft cough sounded from my left. The waiter was back with our main course. "The petite sirloin for the lady, and the gentleman's wild trout almondine."

I looked at my dinner and it looked at me. The black, lifeless eyes of the fish reminded me what can happen when you're lured into biting off more than you can chew.

At eleven-fifteen, I pulled into the parking lot of what had once been a Pure service station. The pumps were gone, but the cracked cement islands still marked their spot. A windowless, plywood addition had been built out of the double garage bays and "The Last Resort" scrawled across it with all the care of New York subway graffiti. I doubted the designers spent much time debating the font style.

In Laurel County, we have a bar called Clyde's Roadside. Its cheap beer, all-encompassing menu of peanuts and beef jerky, and full-volume jukebox are the qualities that make it a watering hole for the locals. You would never confuse it with the bar at Asheville's famed Grove Park Inn unless you had come directly to Clyde's from The Last Resort.

Outside flood lamps fixed to the building's corners provided illumination. The Saturday night crowd nearly filled the plowed gravel lot with cars and pickups, but the temperature was too cold for patrons to lean on hoods or tailgates and swig beer and swap lies. All the action was inside.

I stayed in the light as I crossed to the front door. Extra slogans had been painted under the arc of The Last Resort sign. "We don't care how you did it up north!" was ever popular with this crowd. "What do you call a Yankee with a pension? A Floridian." Nice spot for Sammy Calhoun to hang out. His New York accent had to have come across like asking for grits in William Tecumseh Sherman's chow line.

I could hear the bass beat of some country song blaring through the door. I patted my shirt pocket to make sure Calhoun's picture was still there. The shot of Susan and Sammy grinning in front of the Biltmore House like they owned the mansion had pained me a little. But she said it was the only one she could find.

I opened the door slowly in case someone tumbled out. Another slogan greeted me. "Your sh*t is our bread and butter!— Po' Boy Plumbers." Catchy. I wondered if it looked as good in the Yellow Pages as on the yellow tee shirt of the long-haired local swaying in front of me.

Now that I was inside, the basic fact that I had no plan meant I had no next move other than look around. The décor on the walls consisted of vintage auto product posters mixed with license plates dating back to the Fifties. Some of the bar customers might have made them.

Most of the tables had been created from telephone line spools upended with oil cloth draped over them. A token of the season could be found in the frayed silver garlands tying the cloth around the spindle of each table.

I estimated the size of the crowd to be between forty and fifty, counting the line sitting along the bar. The structure had a certain uniqueness, charm being too complimentary a description. The bar consisted of an oak tree split lengthwise and laid in cradles. Rough bark sheathed the underside and coats of shellac built an uneven glaze on the surface. No women occupied the barstools. I noticed only a few sprinkled among the tables, arms linked with a boyfriend.

The talk was loud, spirited, and jumped from table to table so fast I knew everybody knew everybody else. This was the membership requirement for those whose only access to a country club would always be the delivery entrance.

Ages ranged from early twenties to a seventy-plus guy in a corner debating with himself. The man working behind the bar looked about fifty. He carried on three conversations simultaneously while popping bottles and pulling drafts. He scanned the room frequently, watching for warning signs of a spontaneous argument about to become a brawl. When I caught his eye, he nodded, and I took that as an invitation to introduce myself.

I maneuvered to the nearer end of the bar and yelled "Bud" at him. He pulled a mug from a hook in the ceiling, filled it with a fair ratio of beer to foam, and walked over.

"Two bucks," he said. "We don't run no credit."

"Hard to get your product back once I've used it."

"Not in a form even these pissers would drink," he said, and took a quick glance around the room. "Course, there's just the plain fun of beating it out of you."

I reached into my pocket and took my time pulling out the bills I'd folded there. My wallet was safely locked in the jeep in case I stuck my nose into trouble two nights in a row. The bartender grew annoyed until he watched me slip an extra five on the two.

"You buying two and a half beers in advance?" He knew I wanted something. Tips were few and far between in this dive.

"Two and a half questions."

"What's half a question?"

"One I get to ask but you don't have to answer."

He nodded. "Don't expect much. People come here to get lost, not found."

"I've already found this person, or what was left of him. How long have you worked here?"

Someone shouted "Mike, beer here!"

"Hold your horses," yelled the bartender, waving off the customer. He turned back to me. "That one of the questions?"

"Sure."

"Eleven years."

I slipped the photograph out of my shirt pocket and held it up to him, keeping my thumb over Susan. I didn't even want her picture in the scuzzy place. "This guy hung out here for awhile, about seven or eight years ago."

"Yeah, I remember him. So what?"

I pulled the picture back before he could study it closer. "This guy have any friends here? He was a New Yorker, and from the signs out front, I'd say he might not have been popular."

"He bought drinks for some of the regulars." Mike the bartender laughed. "This is an old gas station. Like cars, you keep people oiled and they don't squawk."

Annette Nolan's words rang in my head—"Claimed he was lubricating a source."

"And the names of the people he bought drinks for?" I asked.

Mike grinned. "That's the half question I don't have to answer."

"You're right," I said, and slid my hand out of my pocket again. I opened my fist enough for him to see the fifty. "You don't have to tell me anything. But I'd be much obliged if you would. Names and why he might be interested in them."

Mike leaned across the bar and whispered, "This is the guy they dug up at Eagle Creek, ain't it?"

"This is the guy I dug up at Eagle Creek. You have any information or should I bury President Ulysses S. Grant back in my pocket?"

As I moved my hand, he grabbed my wrist.

"I only remember one person he was tight with. Skeeter Gibson."

"He here?" I asked, keeping my voice as low as his.

"Nope. Saturday night Skeeter's at the courthouse."

"Courthouse? You mean the jail? Is he a weekend drunk?"

"Nah, he's a full-time drunk and part-time night watchman. Good thing he's Sheriff Ewbanks' cousin or he'd lost even that job years ago." He lifted the bill from my hand.

My neck tingled. Sammy Calhoun had been right. The Last Resort was a gold mine, and I'd just found my mother lode.

Chapter 14

At nine the next morning, I called Tommy Lee. As a regular churchgoer, he should have been somewhere between a shower and breakfast.

"He's not here," said his wife Patsy. "Kenny, Samantha, and I will see him at church. Can I give him a message?"

"Is he on duty?" I asked.

She laughed. "He wishes. He's singing in the choir and has a special rehearsal."

"I didn't know he was in the choir."

"Just started a couple weeks ago. He arrested Stu Callahan on a fourth DUI. Now Stu's in weekend lockup and Tommy Lee got coerced by our preacher to sing Stu's bass part. A solo. I've never seen him so scared."

Tommy Lee scared? If so, a few musical notes on a page had finally done what the Viet Cong and our resident bad guys couldn't. "Should I show up for moral support?"

"Good gracious, no," Patsy said. "That would push him over the edge. And don't you tell him I said he was scared."

"Okay, but if he's wearing angel wings and a halo, I wouldn't miss it for the world."

"I'm afraid a red choir robe is as holy looking as Tommy Lee gets," she said. "Kenny offered to make a matching eye patch. That went over real well." Patsy thought for a second. "You might just catch him on his cell phone before he gets to church. You have my permission to give him something else to worry about."

"Thanks, Patsy. Ask him to call me if I haven't reached him."

"And remind him to turn off his phone," she instructed. "With his luck, it'll ring during his solo and he'll answer it."

I dialed his number from memory. Tommy Lee spoke a gruff hello. It wasn't a joyful noise.

"Patsy said I could bother you."

"She tell you why I have to be at church an hour early?"

"Something about serving Stu Callahan's sentence."

He laughed so hard I was afraid he'd lose control of his car. "You got that right. He did the crime, I'm doing the time." Then Tommy Lee grasped at a straw. "Why are you calling? Please tell me it's an emergency only I can handle."

"Sorry, pal," I said. "Strictly information. Ever hear of a guy named Skeeter Gibson?"

"No. Can he sing bass?"

"I need to get him to sing about Sammy Calhoun. Calhoun bought him drinks at a joint called The Last Resort. He's a security guard at the Walker County Courthouse, and he's Sheriff Ewbanks' cousin."

"Never heard of him," said Tommy Lee. "Bridges might know something."

"Would you check with him today? I want to talk to this Gibson as soon as I can."

"Sure," said Tommy Lee. "Right after church."

"You mean right after your encore."

He hung up on me.

The parking lot behind the Walker County Courthouse was a black void fringed with a wall of dirty gray snow. A sign under a sodium vapor lamp at the entrance directed traffic to different ends. One way led to the courts and county administration building, a domed structure from the 1920s, the typical courthouse gracing town squares across the South. The other direction was for the law enforcement center with subcategories of municipal police, the Sheriff's Department, and the Walker County jail. I could make out several tan cruisers parked near a building complex resembling an aluminum beehive. A ring of small apertures on the third floor must have been jail cell windows.

I chose to park near the courthouse, sliding my jeep between a van equipped to transport the handicapped and a herd of meter maid scooters.

It was a few minutes after eight on Sunday night. Bridges had told Tommy Lee that Skeeter Gibson worked a three to eleven shift. The man was a joke to his job and an embarrassment to his cousin, but Ewbanks had promised his mother to watch out for her dead sister's only child. The sheriff had tried everything to give his alcoholic relative a break. Gibson had first been hired as a jailer, but too many incidents of open cells and open whiskey bottles had demoted him to guarding empty offices.

I reached under the seat for the brown bag sheathing a sealed pint of Wild Turkey. No ABC stores were open on Sunday, so I'd raided my father's liquor cabinet that hadn't been touched in five years. If Skeeter Gibson needed lubricating, I wanted a good supply of oil, and Wild Turkey was premium grade. I had no doubt Skeeter Gibson wouldn't at least offer a bit of conversation in exchange for a pull on the bottle.

The ramp to the courthouse entrance nearest my car glowed with an eerie aura breaking through from snow-covered walk lamps. The interior of the building shone faintly in the light of exit signs and widely spaced fluorescents that provided just enough illumination to navigate the halls.

I peered through the pane, hoping to rap on the glass when Skeeter made his rounds close to the door. I was prepared to wait until my thermos of coffee ran out or plunging temperatures forced me back to the jeep. Almost as an afterthought, I yanked on the brass handle of the double door. To my surprise, it clicked open. Skeeter Gibson was living down to his reputation.

The damp rubber soles of my shoes squeaked as I walked the corridor. I made no effort to quiet the sound because I didn't want to sneak up on a half-tanked man who carried a firearm. When I stepped under the dome and into the main rotunda, I decided to risk calling my quarry. Even if someone else answered, I was ready with the cover story that I'd pulled into the lot with car trouble.

"Hello," I shouted. "Anybody here?"

My voice came back from the curved canopy overhead and vanished down the hallways. No answer returned. I went to the front doors, looking for a guard station where Gibson might be sleeping. A gunmetal desk sat unoccupied with the Sunday Asheville Citizen-Times spread open to the sports section. I noticed a wet spill on the NBA box scores. A quick sniff identified the source as cheap booze.

Maybe Skeeter was on rounds in one of the upper level wings. I could wait at the desk or I could explore.

The layout of the government complex sparked an idea that fit with Calhoun's tease to Cassie and Annette. He had said the scandal was in the criminal justice system, not simply the jail. Prisoners could be easily walked to the courthouse, a building more deserted in the evenings and yet still accessible by someone like Skeeter. He had even been a jailer at the time of Calhoun's murder. If sex for favorable treatment had occurred, the liaisons might have happened here rather than in a cell or interview room, either of which could be called into use anytime. I doubted I'd catch anyone in flagrante delicto unless Calhoun's snooping hadn't deterred the participants. Still, I decided to look around.

Three hallways intersected the rotunda. I had come in from the rear and that corridor had nothing but tax offices, the Register of Deeds, and other paperwork factories jammed with computers, cubicles, and file cabinets. I walked down the west wing, which ran along the right side of the building. The prosecutors' offices were on the front with the end suite assigned to District Attorney Darden Claiborne. I jiggled a few of the door handles, but they were all locked.

Across the hall, a bronze plaque beside double doors identified the Senator Hugh Richards courtroom. Enough tarnish had formed that I knew the tribute hadn't been made in the week since his death. Senator Richards must have had the honor bestowed several years ago. Funny how he kept crossing my life.

One of the doors was cracked open several inches. I slipped inside and found there was just enough light to see walls of fine wood paneling and a judicial bench that would have intimidated Perry Mason. This was a courtroom in the grand sense, and I walked down the aisle with reverential appreciation for its history.

The carpet muffled my footsteps. I heard only the ragged whisper of an antiquated heating system and a rhythmic buzz that grew louder as I approached the bench.

Snoring. The unmistakable sound vibrated through the back wall. I noticed a broad black seam along one of the panels and realized it had to be a door left ajar. Although my eyes had adjusted to the dim lighting, the room beyond was too dark to see anything.

I pushed the door open wider, merging its creak with the raspy snores. If the sleeper awoke, he would now see my body outlined against the courtroom, a silhouetted target. Searching for a light, I used my left hand to feel along the paneling inside the doorjamb. My fingers found a double faceplate, and I flipped up both switches simultaneously.

Overhead, fluorescent fixtures hummed as the tubes came to life, their greenish-white glow illuminating walls of law books, a mammoth desk with a scarred surface cleared of everything except a leather-bound blotter and telephone, and to my left, a long leather sofa bearing the body of a man. He lay flat on his back, black shoes propped up on the padded armrest near me and his head lolled against the far one.

His tan shirt and trousers were a spiderweb of wrinkles, and one missing button above his belt buckle revealed a dingy undershirt. The green plastic nametag, askew over his chest pocket, read GIBSON.

The narrow visor of his hat covered his eyes, and unshaven stubble covered his chin. His holstered revolver was wedged between the cushions so deep he'd have to roll over to reach it. His right arm bent back against the sofa and his left dangled to the floor. A silver flask lay a few inches from his fingertips. He was scrawny and smelly, a pathetic excuse for a law officer.

I kicked the bottom of his shoe. "Hey, buddy," I shouted, "you okay?"

He snorted and jerked his head up. His hat tumbled off and his bleary brown eyes struggled to focus.

I held out my hands to show empty palms. "It's cool, man," I said. "I'm just looking for some help."

He swung his legs around and sat up, shaking his head in a losing effort to think. He reached down and nudged the flask under the sofa, and then looked at me, squinting against the light. "You hurt?"

I realized he wasn't so intoxicated that he couldn't see Stony McBee's handiwork.

"Walked into a door."

To a drunk, the answer made perfect sense.

"What do you want?"

"Can you believe my car overheated? It's twenty degrees outside and the radiator's boiling over."

He looked to the desk. "Need the phone?"

"No. Used my cell. A friend's driving over from Gainesboro. But I can't run the heater without the engine. Glad the building was open. I was getting cold." I reached into my jacket pocket and pulled out the Wild Turkey. "Mind if I take the chill off?"

His eyes stared at the bottle as if it would disappear if he looked away. "Nah," he whispered.

I broke the seal, unscrewed the top, and tipped the bottle back. Although the motion was exaggerated, I let very little of the liquor into my mouth. After a noisy swallow, I wiped my other hand across my lips like the cowboys in the movies. "You want a nip?"

Without waiting for him to answer, I walked over and handed him the whiskey. He grabbed it with a trembling hand and took three quick swallows. I eased into a side chair in front of the bookcases. Gibson clutched the bottle as he leaned back against the sofa and closed his eyes.

I knew there was a good chance he'd drink himself back into a stupor. Interrogating an unconscious man was beyond even my police training. The dilemma was to extract information without coming on so strong I spooked him or waiting too long and watching him pass out.

"When do you get off?" I asked.

He opened his eyes and looked down to make sure he still had the bottle. "What's it to you?" he mumbled.

"I might need to be here awhile. My friend's at a party. If somebody else is coming on duty, he might not be as considerate as you are."

Gibson took another hit. "Relax. It's just me."

"Guess Sunday nights are pretty dead," I said.

He took a deep breath, but didn't answer. I was going to have to jump-start the conversation soon or listen to his snoring again.

"Course, I guess something's always going on over at the jail."

"Yeah," he muttered. "The jail."

"You work over there as well?"

He shook his head. "Use to. I like it quiet."

"Officer Gibson, right?"

He looked at me, surprised that I called his name, oblivious that I could read it on his chest. "I know you?"

"From The Last Resort," I said. "Somebody introduced us once."

He blinked a few times, and I knew he didn't have a clue as to whether I told the truth.

"Take as much of the Wild Turkey as you want," I said. "Won't find that behind Mike's bar."

He grinned and tipped the bottle toward me. "Yeah, now I remember you."

"My buddy said if I ever needed to meet a woman, Skeeter Gibson was the man to see." I winked at him. "He said you had a whole stable of fillies locked up and waiting." The cowboy lingo sounded a bit much to my ear, but the drunk grinned.

"Some of them wimmen," he slurred, "some of them wimmen let you know right quick what they'd do for a break."

"That's what I heard. Guess you have to be careful they don't try to use it against you."

"Against me?" he said, and took another heavy swallow. "Shit, I know how to cover my ass." He leaned forward and tried to focus on my face. "Give ya some advice. Always make sure somebody else has farther to fall, and they know you can take 'em with you." He knocked back the bottle again until it was two-thirds gone.

"Some big names, huh?" I asked.

He eyed me warily. I had crossed a line and sealed his lips.

"I just know you have to watch yourself around women," I said. "Even the young ones. I heard sometimes the jailbait's already in jail."

He studied the bottle, turning his talk more to it than to me. "I never cottoned with that."

"Who was involved, Skeeter? Did Sammy Calhoun know?"

He worked his mouth like he was sucking up every molecule of the whiskey before taking another shot. "Ghosts," he whispered. "All ghosts but one."

I decided to let him drift in his fog. If he started talking to the bottle, he might tell it more than he'd tell me. I stood up from the chair and looked around the room. An oil painting of a foxhunt hung over the sofa. Various plaques and framed certificates dotted the one wall not covered with bookshelves. At the far end was a door that must have been a private entrance. This was the judge's chambers, shared by whoever held court. There seemed to be no permanent occupant.

The shelves were crammed with old legal books, many of which must have been there since the courthouse was built. I ran my finger across the tops of the volumes. The dust was more in need of an archaeologist than a maid.

"No, I never cottoned to that," murmured Gibson. "Sammy knew."

I froze, hoping he would continue on his own.

Instead, he fell back against the sofa cushion, holding the bottle against his chest. I walked over and knelt in front of him. "Sammy told me," I said. "He told me you were right."

Skeeter Gibson opened his eyes, but he looked up at the ceiling. "Warned him," he whispered. A half whimper came from his throat. He raised the bottle toward some spot beyond this world. "Sammy," he said almost reverently. He looked at me and I thought he was going to cry. Then he passed out.

I stepped away. There was nothing more I'd get from him tonight. And what could I do with what he'd said? Confront him when he was sober? Bluff that he'd told me more than he had? Say I'd go to the press unless he came clean? Even in his drunken state, Skeeter Gibson had been scared of someone, someone whom Sammy Calhoun had crossed and then been murdered as a consequence.

Although Skeeter was already snoring, I left the room brightly lit so he might wake before his relief arrived. I was a few paces from the main hallway when I heard a click behind me. Turning around, I saw the lights in the judge's chamber had gone out. Maybe Skeeter had roused himself enough to turn them off.

I continued down the courtroom aisle. When I neared the door, a whine and gunshot came so close together as to be one sound. A chunk of paneling splintered less than six inches from my head.

I dropped to the floor and rolled through the doorway. A second shot shattered the milky white pane in the door to the D.A.'s office. I crawled clear of the line of fire, scrambled to my feet and ran for the safety of my jeep. As I crossed through the rotunda, I heard a third shot, muffled and echoing off the dome. No footsteps pursued me.

The cold hit me like a wall as I burst out of the courthouse. My lungs ached as I sucked in the frigid air. My first thought was to call the police from the jeep, and then I remembered the Sheriff's Department was right across the parking lot. I jogged along the sidewalk, careful to watch for icy patches.

When I burst into the office, the night duty deputy looked up from his desk of paperwork. "Help you," he asked out of reflex. Then his eyes widened at the sight of my bruised face.

"My name is Barry Clayton," I panted. "I'm a former Charlotte policeman, and I was just shot at inside the courthouse. You're going to need backup. Someone should call Sheriff Ewbanks."

He stared at me like I'd beamed down from the Starship Enterprise.

I heard the door to the outside open and turned to face Deputy Bridges.

"Clayton. I saw you run in here. What's up?"

There wasn't time to lose with a second explanation. I wheeled around and yelled at the desk deputy. "Move, man. There's a killer in the courthouse."

I ran behind Bridges and two other officers, filling them in as I could gasp out the words. Bridges made me wait outside the courtroom while he and his men approached the judge's chambers as if an armed suspect were still inside. One officer reached around and flipped on the lights while Bridges and his other partner stormed in. After a few seconds of silence, Bridges called, "Clear."

Skeeter Gibson still sat on the sofa where I had left him. The bottle of Wild Turkey had slipped from his grip, the few remaining swallows pooled in the folds of his lap. His service revolver was out of its holster and in his right hand.

His head slumped at an angle against his chest, ringed by a halo of blood and brains on the sofa and painting behind him. A bullet hole in his right temple seeped a slow, thin trickle that flowed along the bridge of his nose and fell in red droplets to mingle with the puddles of whiskey. Skeeter's final legacy—alcohol and blood and death.

Chapter 15

"So you came to talk with Skeeter Gibson and brought him a bottle of Wild Turkey?" Sheriff Horace Ewbanks asked the question without any effort to hide his incredulity.

He sat across the table from me in a small, bare interview room in the Sheriff's Department. Deputy Bridges stood behind him. The door was closed. A cassette tape recorder squeaked as it captured our voices.

"That's right," I said. "I'd heard he liked a good drink."

"From the bartender at The Last Resort?"

"His name is Mike."

Ewbanks took a drag on his cigarette. He'd lit it as he sat down, and although it was only half gone, the smoke filled the air.

The sheriff had arrived within five minutes of our discovery of Gibson's body. He'd said he'd been on his way to check the duty roster for the next day, and none of his deputies thought it odd he'd appeared so quickly on a Sunday night. Everyone thought it odd I'd come to the courthouse. From their perspective, I'd discovered Calhoun's body, I'd been unexpectedly present at the first interrogation of Susan's father, and now I'd been the last to talk to a man whose brains were splattered on county property. Horace Ewbanks had every reason to be suspicious.

"You say you found Skeeter already drunk?" he asked.

"He had a flask. It's under the sofa."

"We found it," interjected Bridges.

"But you came prepared to get him drunk," accused Ewbanks, dismissing the confirmation of my story.

"I came prepared to be sociable."

"Sociable? With Skeeter? You came prepared to ask questions."

My temper flared. "Because someone I care about seems to be the only suspect in your investigation, an investigation that's ruining an innocent woman's reputation." The words came out harsher than I'd intended.

Bridges shook his head, cuing me to back off.

Ewbanks' eyes narrowed to slits. "And what do you know about my investigation?"

"That it's none of my business," I admitted. "I wasn't asking Gibson about your investigation. His name surfaced through Sammy Calhoun."

The sheriff pulled another cigarette from his pack and lit it from the butt of the first. I coughed and took a drink from the iceless water glass I'd been given.

"We're too old to be playing games with each other," said Ewbanks. "If you think my investigation's in the crapper, then tell me what you've got. How'd you wind up at The Last Resort?"

Before I could answer, a rap sounded on the door. Bridges opened it and a man in dress slacks and button-down blue shirt came in. He looked familiar.

"For the record," said Ewbanks, "the interview with Barry Clayton has been interrupted by District Attorney Darden Claiborne."

The D.A. reddened at the admonition. I couldn't tell if he was embarrassed or angry.

"Mind if I join you?"

"Listen all you want," said the sheriff. "Go ahead, Mr. Clayton."

I nodded to Claiborne as he stood beside Bridges. The D.A. looked grim. He didn't like having both his window and security guard shot.

I took another sip of water and cleared my throat. "As you know, Walt Miller's sister Cassie is the news director at NEWS-CHANNEL-8. She had employed Sammy Calhoun as an investigator in the past, and I asked her if Calhoun had been working for her at the time of his murder."

"That's good thinking," said Claiborne. "Was he?"

"I believe Mr. Clayton was about to tell us that," snapped Ewbanks.

At this point, I decided to begin selecting what truth to tell and what to omit. "Not that she specifically recalled. But, Cassie Miller kept phone logs and she went back to the spring Calhoun disappeared. He'd called her several times, pitching a story idea. She gave me the return numbers and one of them was for the bar."

"And the bartender remembered Calhoun by name?" asked Ewbanks.

"His face. I had a photograph."

"Did you bring it to show Skeeter?"

I retrieved the picture from my jacket pocket and handed it to the sheriff. Claiborne leaned over his shoulder.

"Isn't that Dr. Miller with Calhoun?" asked the D.A.

Ewbanks ignored him. "Mind if I hold onto this awhile?"

I shrugged.

Ewbanks passed it back to Bridges. "How'd Skeeter's name come up?"

"I asked if there was anyone Calhoun hung out with. The bar's not user friendly to Yankees, and Calhoun's accent must have sounded like fingernails on a chalkboard. Mike said Calhoun frequently bought drinks for the locals and Skeeter latched onto him."

Both Bridges and Ewbanks nodded at that truth.

"What did Skeeter tell you?" asked Ewbanks.

"Not much. He drank the Wild Turkey like it was water. I asked him about Calhoun, and he clammed up. All ghosts but one, he said. Any idea what that means?"

No one answered me.

"Then he passed out," I said. "I left him on the sofa just where we found him."

"Take us through what happened then," ordered Ewbanks. "After he passed out. Don't leave out a sight, sound, or smell." He leaned over the table so far the smoke from his cigarette nearly gagged me.

I stood up for clearer air and started talking. No one interrupted until I stopped with my entrance into the Sheriff's Department.

Claiborne immediately asked, "How do we know you didn't kill Skeeter and then fire two more rounds to make it look like he shot at you?"

I stared at Ewbanks and he nodded for me to answer the question.

"Atomic absorption test," I said.

"What?" huffed Claiborne. "How'd you know about AA?"

Ewbanks chuckled. "He used to be police. He knows all about blow back too, I'll bet. Blood splatter flying back on the shooter. Gunpowder traces on his hand. Clayton knows if he fired the shots, an atomic absorption test will show residue on his hands. Same thing for Skeeter. I've already ordered a test on the body."

"I'll submit to one voluntarily."

"You'll be swabbed all right," he assured me. "Though the damn lab's not likely to get the results back till after New Year's."

"I'll put the pressure on," said Claiborne. Then he looked back at me. "But you could have washed your hands."

"I'm having all the lavatories and sink traps checked," said Ewbanks.

My opinion of the sheriff's thoroughness jumped up several notches. "How about blood tests on Gibson?" I asked.

"Ordered," he said. "I suspect they'll show Skeeter was too drunk to unholster his gun, let alone aim at anything. And why turn off the lights before shooting at you?"

That was the question I'd been asking myself. The point wasn't lost on the D.A.

"You're saying this isn't an attempted murder and suicide?" asked Claiborne.

Sheriff Horace Ewbanks got up from the table. "I'm saying until I see proof otherwise, I'm treating it as a homicide. Mr. Clayton, we'll get that AA swab now. That is if you've told me everything."

I let my gaze shift across the three men. "Gentlemen, I'm afraid everything may have died with Skeeter Gibson."

"I don't think so," said Ewbanks sharply. "Your problems in this case are very much alive."

The temperature must have dropped another ten degrees since I'd run from the courthouse to the Sheriff's Department. I zipped my jacket tight to my neck and walked alone to my jeep, glad to be shed of the questions and implied accusations, yet apprehensive that the night concealed a killer who wanted me silenced. I was halfway through the darkest area of the parking lot when I heard the sound of a car engine behind me. No headlights gave warning of its approach. I quickened my pace and glanced back over my shoulder. A black Crown Vic eased alongside and the passenger window rolled down.

"Talk a minute," said Darden Claiborne.

"I'm talked out," I said, never breaking stride. As far as I was concerned, the D.A. could have pulled the trigger of Skeeter's pistol as easily as anyone else. Either that or he was about to offer me a plea bargain.

"I think your girlfriend's being set up."

"You're the prosecutor. You do something about it."

"I will. If someone will help me." He braked to a stop, letting me walk on.

The bait was too enticing. I turned around and returned to his car.

"Get in," he said. "Let's take a little ride."

I leaned in the window where I could see Claiborne in the glow of the instrument panel. Both his hands were on the steering wheel. He smiled and gave a slight nod.

"I'm fine here."

"But I'm not. If I'm going to stick my neck out for you, I don't want to do it publicly till I've got more to go on. There are too many eyes and ears around here."

I pulled open the door and the dome light illumined the plush interior. The putty-colored leather seats and wood trim were options not found on ninety-nine percent of the police vehicles manufactured by Ford. Claiborne wouldn't be worrying about drunks puking in the backseat or junkies pissing on the floor mats.

A console housing a police radio and mobile data terminal fit flush between the bucket seats. I heard the dispatcher trying to raise a unit.

"Nice rig," I commented, and buckled up before slamming the door.

"It's the way I heard about the shooting, in case you were wondering how I showed up so fast. On my way home from church. Had to drop the family at the Krispy Kreme."

Sunday night service. Baptist, I thought. Good religion for a southern politician.

He drove the car slowly until we were a good distance from my jeep. Then he flipped on his headlights and pulled out of the parking lot.

"Why don't you want to be seen with me?" I asked. "Am I bad for your campaign?"

"Unsolved crime is bad for my campaign. But not as bad as prosecuting the wrong person."

Claiborne steered his car down a side street and through a neighborhood bedecked with colored lights on the lawns and Christmas trees in the front windows.

"I have to go where the evidence leads," he said. "Ewbanks is providing that evidence. He works his own way and doesn't want anyone interfering. I have to respect that he's an elected official just like me. He reports to the voters."

"And if he sees you talking to me, he'll think you're meddling in his affairs."

Claiborne sighed. "I wish it were that simple." He reached down and killed the radio, as if it could inadvertently broadcast his words. "I'll cut straight to the point. Ewbanks doesn't care for me. He thinks I'm a hotdog. Well, I'm a damn good D.A. and I'll make this state a great attorney general. But to win a statewide election you've got to trumpet your own horn and get a strong organization behind you. That means the party has to believe you can win. Next spring we have the primaries and I need all of western North Carolina unified if I'm going to be the candidate."

"Solving a high-profile murder case makes a great spotlight."

"Yeah, that's an upside, but if that same case uncovers a scandal in my own backyard, a scandal I should have known about, then the party will shun me like the bastard child at a family reunion."

"You think Ewbanks would hold out on you just to bring you down?"

"I think something's not quite right in the Sheriff's Department and he would put protecting his men above pursuing justice."

Claiborne's accusation merged onto the path I'd been blazing alone. The stakes in his game were high. He could lose two ways: confront Ewbanks and be wrong or ignore the possibility and look like a fool if it was true.

"I hope you can appreciate my position," he said.

We rode in silence for awhile. Claiborne let me think about what he had said. I stared out the window. We had left the neighborhoods behind and now drove down the bypass. The Wal-Mart parking lot overflowed with Christmas shoppers hemorrhaging money.

At last, I asked, "Why are you telling me this?"

"Because you connected Sammy Calhoun and Skeeter Gibson, something no one in the Sheriff's Department was either smart enough to do or willing to let come out. Right now I don't know which."

"Just because I got lucky doesn't mean there's a scandal." I still didn't trust Claiborne enough to reveal all my cards.

"That's right, and if this were the first time I'd suspected something I'd let it go."

"This isn't the first time?"

"No. About six years ago I fired an assistant D.A. for improperly handling pending cases. The guy's name was Nick Garrett. He was dismissing charges even though we had sufficient evidence to prosecute. Small things, nothing like major felonies, but still well within the guidelines for what I recommended we take to trial."

"This would have been after Sammy Calhoun died?"

"Yes, so I didn't make any connection until you mentioned Sammy Calhoun led you to Skeeter Gibson."

"Why Skeeter?"

"Because I'd seen Skeeter and Nick talking around the courthouse and jail. Skeeter dealt with the prisoners day to day. Here's the thing. All of these dismissed cases involved women. Younger women who still had their looks. Do I need to paint you a picture?"

"No."

"Well, if I made a mistake it was that I fired Garrett for mishandling cases without looking into any sexual improprieties. Then I pushed Ewbanks to get rid of Skeeter, but the best he would do was assign his cousin to courthouse guard duty."

"You think Skeeter and this Garrett were having sex with female prisoners?"

"Or letting others. Together they were in a position to do whatever they wanted. All I know is you started investigating and Skeeter got shot. If it's suicide, fine. Maybe that ends it. But if it's not, then someone else must have been involved and that someone will stop at nothing to avoid exposure."

"And you can't trust Ewbanks to thoroughly investigate."

"And I can't afford to have it blow up in my face while I'm sitting on my hands. It might not be anyone in the Sheriff's Department at all. It could be someone with enough power and money to put outside pressure on Skeeter or anyone else involved."

We headed down Main Street back to the courthouse. I sensed Claiborne was winding up for his final pitch.

"I can tell you're not going to let go of this," he said. "I think it would be good to have outside police experience working around Ewbanks' department. But I can't give you any direct help. I'll be upfront about that. But any backdoor information I come across, I'll pass along. I hope you'll do the same. I don't want to be blindsided."

"I'd say the first thing you need to do is check on the location of this Nick Garrett. Somebody killed Calhoun, and the discovery of his body has ratcheted the scandal from sex to murder. If that somebody is your former assistant D.A., then he might have come back to tie up loose ends."

"I'm afraid he has an airtight alibi. Nick Garrett died of pancreatic cancer a year ago. One thing I do know. A ghost didn't shoot Skeeter. Watch your step."

With that warning, Claiborne turned into the courthouse parking lot and killed his lights. "Sorry to be overly dramatic, but I hope you understand why I wanted this conversation to be just between us. Everything I say in the Sheriff's Department winds up coming out of Cliff Barringer's mouth. Even a hint that I suspect a scandal and Barringer would interrupt a presidential address to get it on the air."

As I got out of the car, Claiborne reached into his coat pocket and extracted a card.

"Call me, day or night." He leaned across the seat and handed it to me. "I promise it won't hurt to have a friend who's the Attorney General of North Carolina."

Then the Crown Vic and the worried candidate disappeared into the night.

Chapter 16

The drive to my cabin gave me time to think through the mess I left behind in Walker County. The conversation with Claiborne had been a surprise. I had to remember his candor had been self-serving. But was that a problem if our interests were the same?

As to the interrogation by Ewbanks, at least I'd managed to avoid revealing any particulars of my conversation with Skeeter Gibson and to conceal Calhoun's reason for buying him drinks. Mike the bartender would verify he had told me about Skeeter, but he knew nothing about why the two men hung out together.

A shot in the temple proved someone realized Skeeter was a danger. Perhaps his killer had stood outside the second door to the judge's chamber, a door Ewbanks said provided an exit to a side hall where a judge wouldn't come face to face with his docket when arriving. If so, that person had heard me question Skeeter and knew I posed a threat.

Was I being foolish not to bring Ewbanks into my confidence, or was Ewbanks involved and had pulled the trigger on his own cousin? Did Claiborne really believe there might be corruption in the Sheriff's Department, or was he just trying to cover himself in case his own department was implicated? I remembered Ewbanks had come alone to investigate Calhoun's remains. Was that to find evidence or to conceal it? And Bridges. He had appeared so quickly after the shooting. Was a senior deputy normally scheduled in Sunday nights? The more I thought about my predicament, the more I wished I were safely minding my own business: somebody else's funeral.

I was nearly home when Uncle Wayne reached me on my cell phone.

"I tried the cabin first," he said. "Hope I'm not interrupting anything."

"I was in Walker County. I'll be home in five minutes."

"Drive carefully. There's been a wreck on 176. The two older Metcalf brothers hit black ice. They were killed at the scene."

I slowed the jeep. Black ice was invisible until you were on it. "Oh, God," I said. "Should I come in tonight?"

"Bodies are at the hospital morgue. We'll work out transfer in the morning. I expect the family will be by early."

"I'll be there at eight," I promised.

The next morning would be tough. I didn't know the Metcalfs that well, but to lose two teenage sons was a life-crushing tragedy. I turned off the Christmas music on the radio.

George Eliot was eating lettuce and I was drinking a cold Bud for a nightcap when I saw Tommy Lee's patrol car pull up in my driveway. I met him at the front door.

"What the hell's going on?" he said, barging past me.

Somehow I found his rough entrance comforting. "Have a seat and you tell me. What did Bridges say was going on?"

"That you got Skeeter Gibson killed and pissed off Ewbanks. I don't know which is worse." He sat on the sofa and sank back into the cushions. He looked exhausted.

"Did he bother to mention someone tried to blow my head off?"

"In passing."

"What's Ewbanks' beef?"

"You're a loose cannon and you said his investigation sucked. And it doesn't help that you're the prime suspect for Skeeter's death."

"You don't believe that, do you?"

"It doesn't matter what I believe. Look at it from Ewbanks' point of view. You're the last person to see Skeeter alive. You came there to confront him about a murder in which your girlfriend is implicated. Bridges said Ewbanks is on a hair trigger to arrest you. One piece of hard evidence and he'll book you."

I turned away and walked to the window, raising my voice in frustration. "Is that a threat? Stay clear or we'll put you behind bars? Are you supposed to rein me in?"

"Even a loose cannon sometimes hits the mark. Bridges' words, not mine." Tommy Lee paused, letting me think about it.

"Bridges always work Sunday nights?"

"What's that supposed to mean?"

"Just that you had asked Bridges about Skeeter. He sure was Johnny-on-the-spot after Skeeter bought it."

"It's a small department. Smaller than mine and we're already running a holiday duty schedule that's shifting everyone around. Hell, I was working tonight."

I could only come back to his first question. I pivoted and stared straight in his eye. "Then what the hell's going on?"

"Ewbanks has his sights on you. You were the last one to see Skeeter Gibson alive, so he's got to take a hard look at you. Then you threw Calhoun's case in his face. Bridges admitted they hadn't connected Skeeter to Calhoun and they hadn't gone back to Cassie Miller. Score two for Buryin' Barry."

"So Bridges called with halftime stats?"

"No," said Tommy Lee. "He wants me to keep my mouth shut, not that I'd say anything. Like it or not, you're now part of the investigation and some reporter might connect us and ask my opinion."

"And you'd tell Melissa Bigham I'm an idiot."

"Nah, she'll want new information. Bridges was tipping me off that Ewbanks is going to keep things tight on Skeeter's death until he figures out what's going on. You've dumped this right in his lap. Claiborne's on his ass for an arrest, but even that media hound won't want to draw attention to an unsolved murder on his doorstep."

"Literally," I said. "The bullet hole through his window makes great news footage." I told Tommy Lee about Claiborne's secret meeting with me.

"Sounds like he's pumping you for information so that he can spin anything that might make him look stupid with the voters."

"What about Skeeter and the assistant D.A.? You ever hear about that before?"

"No, nothing involving the two of them, but I rarely deal with the Walker County prosecutors unless there's a jurisdictional issue. I do remember a shakeup a few years back and Garrett getting fired. I can ask around."

"I don't want it getting back to Claiborne," I said. "Then he'll realize I talked to you. It's enough to know it happened."

"All right," agreed Tommy Lee, "but I still think Ewbanks is right. Claiborne's a hotdog."

"Oh, yeah, even he admits it, but that doesn't mean he can't be a source of information."

"True. Well, my advice, since you didn't ask for it, is to lie low for a few days and see what bubbles up from the pot you've stirred."

"You think I'm in danger?"

"Were those shots in the courthouse meant to kill you or scare you?"

"Somebody wanted my name in the obituary column."

"Then I don't want to stand beside you in a crowd. Be my luck they'd miss you and hit me. Keep your extracurricular activities limited to fistfights at the funeral home."

His remark put my problems in perspective. "You hear about the Metcalf boys?"

"I helped pull them out of the ravine," he said somberly. "When I leave here, I'm going home and hugging my kids."

"It's been a day, hasn't it?"

"Yeah," he said, and then brightened. "After I sang, there wasn't a dry eye in the church."

"Good."
"Bad. It wasn't a sad song."

The Vista printed a short news item headlined "Shooting at
Walker County Courthouse." The bare-bones account identified
the victim as Mosely Gibson, a security guard. I wasn't mentioned by name, only that the body had been discovered by a
courthouse visitor. The article stated the Sheriff's Department
was investigating all possibilities, including that Mr. Gibson
might have taken his own life.

Mosely. He must have been tagged Mosquito as a boy, short-
ened to Skeeter.

The next morning's TV coverage of Gibson's death was limited to the anchorman reading what sounded like the newspaper
text. The newsman made an awkward toss to the weatherman,
and the next day's forecast for a wintry mix of sleet and ice over-
whelmed interest in a non-celebrity suicide. Whoever had been
leaking tidbits to NEWSCHANNEL-8's Cliff Barringer hadn't yet
divulged any information beyond what Horace Ewbanks and
Darden Claiborne authorized.

When I arrived at the funeral home, thoughts of Gibson and
my entanglement in the case took a backseat to my duties for
the Metcalf family. Uncle Wayne came at nine with news he had
already spoken with the Metcalfs' minister, Lester Pace. I took
comfort that the old circuit-riding preacher would be shepherd-
ing the family. Pace never claimed to have all the answers and
never made trite comments like God needed their children in
heaven more than they did on earth. Yet he had an authority
earned by his constant ministry to the mountain people for over
half a century. Their grief was his grief.

"Pace will be driving in with them about ten-thirty," said
Uncle Wayne. He sat with me at the kitchen table and enjoyed
the last cup of coffee from the pot.

"Both parents coming?" I asked.

"Yes. Pace is particularly concerned about Libby. She collapsed last night, and Pace would prefer she let Maynard make all the arrangements. Libby thinks otherwise and insists on being here."

I anticipated the problem. "How bad?"

Wayne understood what I meant. "Don't know. The younger boy went through the windshield. Hospital morgue attendant said lacerations were deep and ragged. Nearly took his head off."

I pushed my coffee away, the taste suddenly bitter. "And the other one?"

"Chest crushed by the steering column. They were in an old pickup. No airbags."

I stood up and walked to the sink. Through the frosty glaze on the window, I could see patches of brown grass breaking through where the sun penetrated the backyard pines. A brilliantly red cardinal scratched for grubs venturing up into the warming topsoil. The day promised a thaw, a brief reprieve before the ice storm advancing across the gulf states struck. It could bring no greater devastation to the Metcalfs.

"She'll have expectations," I said. "How can you have one casket closed and the other open?"

My uncle took a deep breath. "We don't know yet," he said. "Reconstruction might be possible. Your hands are steadier than mine."

To give a grieving mother a final memory of her child was an awesome, awful responsibility. Sometimes the kindest action meant leaving that memory embodied in a photograph rather than a stitched and painted countenance that would forever haunt her.

"Freddy should be here in a few minutes," said Wayne. "He and I'll go to the hospital. If the Metcalfs come before we return, I'll give you a nod as to what I think we can do."

I turned around from the window. "Have you mentioned it to Pace?"

"No. Maybe you can catch him alone."

"If the subject doesn't come up, I'll talk to him afterwards. He's the best one to tell them. I think it's both open or both closed."

"I agree," said Wayne. He looked up at me, his lined face troubled. "Life sure can deal some tough cards."

While Wayne and Freddy went for the bodies, I double-checked our inventory. Reconstructive cosmetic work can be tedious and delicate, and I wanted to make sure my efforts would not fall short through a lack of proper supplies. Satisfied that the anticipated materials were on hand, I took a few minutes to apply makeup to my face. My nose had lost most of the swelling, and my eyes were now the bluish-yellow tinge that can linger for days. I was putting on the finishing touches when the doorbell rang.

They were early and Mom was still upstairs with Dad. I gave a final check in the mirror. I looked like a poster for a tanning salon, but at least I wouldn't have to give the Metcalfs an explanation for my appearance.

A FedEx man stood on the front porch, trying to peer through the door's decorative windowpane. He held an express envelope in one hand and a clipboard in the other. His truck idled noisily at the curb.

"For Barry Clayton," he announced.

He thrust the clipboard into my hands and indicated where my signature should go. Although it was only ten-fifteen, the blank space was at the bottom of the page. Even little Gainesboro wasn't immune to the demands for immediate deliveries.

"Will you get home before the storm?" I asked, handing him the clipboard.

"If it holds off till eight tonight." He gave me the cardboard envelope and backed away. "Christmas," he added. "We're swamped." Then he jogged to his truck, no time for chitchat.

Ten days till Christmas and I was no more prepared than if it were the Fourth of July. Always a last-minute shopper, I'd lost the past week in the turmoil created by a photo in a skeleton's wallet. Not a single gift had been purchased. Susan deserved something special, but I was afraid the present she wanted most lay beyond my ability to give. Nothing would make her happier than to have the shadow of Sammy Calhoun lifted from her life.

The FedEx truck roared away from the curb. I looked at the return address on the envelope. Hoffman Enterprises. An offer had arrived for the business my grandfather had started over seventy years ago. Before I could pull the open tab, Lester Pace's maroon Plymouth turned into our parking lot. My future would have to wait for a few hours. Clayton and Clayton Funeral Directors had no greater mission than to serve the grieving mother and father who were calling up every ounce of energy and faith to simply walk through our door.

"Please come in," I said. There was no point in saying "Good morning" or asking "How are you?" I gestured for them to enter the parlor on the right of our foyer.

The gas logs burned low in the stone fireplace. A small Christmas tree with only white lights and brass ornaments filled the far corner of the room. Pace assisted Libby and Maynard to a sofa and then sat in the chair nearest them. I took one with my back to the fire.

Libby Metcalf perched on the edge of the cushion and clutched a holiday shopping bag from Belk's Department Store. She stared into the flames. Maynard reached out and gently clasped his wife's wrist. Both were dressed as if they were going to church.

Pace cleared his throat. "I've told the Metcalfs that you can guide them through what needs to happen."

"Yes," I said. "Have you discussed the service?"

Maynard spoke up in a voice close to breaking. "We've not had a funeral before. One that we've had to arrange. All our parents are still living."

"I understand, Mr. Metcalf. And we'll get through this together."

My assurance broke Libby's spell. She held out the bag. "I bought Mike and Ned new sweaters for Christmas." She reached in and pulled out a fold of forest green wool. "I hadn't had a chance to wrap them yet, and—" A half-swallowed sob cut the words short.

I got up and took the bag from her hands.

"We'll take care of it."

"There's underwear and pants too," said Maynard.

"Are they here?" asked Libby.

"Not yet. My uncle's gone to the hospital."

"I'll want to see them."

As I struggled for a way to sidestep her request, I heard a footstep in the foyer. Uncle Wayne joined us.

"Libby, Maynard, I'm so sorry," he said. He turned to me and gave a distinct nod.

Relief welled up from the pit of my stomach. "We were just beginning," I said. "They brought some clothes."

"The boys will look fine," he said gently.

Maynard put his arm around his wife and they wept.

An hour later, Pace and the Metcalfs left us to our work. The funeral was set for Thursday at Hickory Nut Falls Methodist Church. Pace had told me a donation fund was being established to help defray burial expenses. The Vista had been flooded with calls from generous donors wanting to make contributions. The holiday spirit carried beyond tinsel and gadget gifts.

The cosmetic reconstruction for Ned, the younger boy, was not simple, but the lacerations were deepest through the scalp and back of the neck. He must have turned in his seat as the truck skidded off the highway, and he'd been hurled backward through the windshield. The top of his head caught the inside edge of the roof. The teenager had died before he hit the ground.

Wayne and I worked through lunch, anxious to know that the Metcalfs' trust in us would prove true. It was nearly three when I washed up and came to the kitchen in search of a late lunch. Mom stood at the counter, slicing a cold ham.

"Wayne said you were finishing," she said. "I thought you'd like something quick."

"I'm famished." I realized I hadn't eaten since lunch the day before.

Mom set a sandwich layered with ham and cheese in front of me. "You had a call from Susan this morning. I told her the situation and she said not to bother you. But she sounded anxious to talk to you."

"Was she at the hospital?"

"I don't know. She said try the cell first."

"Thanks. I'll eat this in the office," I said, and picked up the plate. I hadn't talked to Susan since Saturday night's dinner and I owed her a report.

"How are things with the Metcalfs?" Susan asked the question immediately.

"Tough. Very tough."

"Such a waste of life. And so young."

"Tommy Lee thinks they might have been driving too fast for conditions, but not speeding. No drinking involved." I remembered Susan's brother Stevie and knew that would be important.

She didn't comment. To say that was good only magnified how senseless a tragedy it was. Explaining God's ways was Pace's job, and I didn't envy him.

"I'm sorry to be out of touch," I said. "Some things have happened."

"We're not talking the Metcalfs, are we?"

"No."

"Barry, who's Skeeter Gibson?"

"The guy who got killed at the Walker County Courthouse last night."

"Do you know why Sheriff Ewbanks thinks I know him?"

Her question caught me off guard. I didn't know of a connection Skeeter Gibson had to Susan, and Claiborne had been the only one to mention her name when he saw her photograph with Calhoun.

"Where are you?" I asked.

"Heading from the clinic to the hospital. I've got late rounds."

"Okay if I meet you tonight?"

"Sounds like you're bringing a story."

"I'm afraid so. And I'm right in the middle of it."

I hung up, amazed that my efforts to get Susan cleared were only making things worse. Maybe Ewbanks was just fishing for a connection between Skeeter and Susan. But he seemed like more of a hunter than a fisherman. Now I was his suspect as well. But someone didn't just want me in jail; he wanted me dead.

With that pleasant thought, I reached for the second half of my sandwich and noticed the FedEx envelope at the edge of the desk. Might as well see what lowball figure Hoffman thought they could pay to snatch up a business owned by an Alzheimer's victim and run by a reluctant undertaker. Maybe half a million.

A gold paperclip held several pages together. The cover letter was addressed to me and the opening paragraph gave the expected niceties of what a privilege it had been to meet me.

The second paragraph stopped me as cold as when I had seen Skeeter Gibson's body in the courthouse. "Hoffman Enterprises is pleased to tender an offer for the purchase of Clayton and Clayton Funeral Directors in the aggregate amount of two million dollars."

The ham sandwich tumbled to the floor.

Chapter 17

"Someone shot at you?"

I looked away. The intensity of Susan's question forced me to acknowledge how the stakes of my amateur investigation had skyrocketed. "Yes," I said, "and it couldn't have been Skeeter."

We sat beside each other on her sofa. The lights of the angel tree and glow from her fireplace belied the mood my story had created.

Susan trembled. "I nearly got you killed."

"You weren't responsible. I got into this mess all by myself. I have a knack."

"Barry, we're no longer talking about a murder seven years ago. Last night somebody put a gun to a man's head and pulled the trigger."

"I know. I'm going to take Tommy Lee's advice and lie low for awhile."

"But what if the killer comes after you?"

"That's not going to happen. I got away and then said nothing that could incriminate anyone. The murderer must ask himself if Skeeter had told me something, why would I be holding it back? Killing me now would only raise more questions."

The logic sounded good. I almost believed it myself.

Susan calmed down. "Then promise me you'll stay out of it. Let Ewbanks run his tests and follow up."

"I promise. One good thing should come out of this."

"What's that?"

"It should be clear somebody other than you killed Calhoun because you didn't kill Skeeter. And you wouldn't shoot at me. I'm your boyfriend."

"That carries a lot of weight," Susan said. "They think I've already killed one boyfriend."

Fortunately a phone call saved me from further comment.

She took it in the kitchen. I heard her say "Hi, Cassie," and then "Barry's here" with an inflection that sounded like her aunt had asked for me. As I got up from the sofa, a knock came from the front door.

I opened it, and there on the opposite side of the threshold stood Sheriff Horace Ewbanks and his faithful companion Bridges.

"Clayton, I see you more often than my wife."

I wanted to reply "And she should thank me," but I restrained myself. Instead I asked, "Why do you want to see me now?"

"I don't. We're here to speak to Dr. Miller. May we come in?"

Stepping back, I said, "She's on the phone. Have a seat."

The two men settled in chairs, leaving the sofa for me. There was no small talk. Too late I realized I should have initiated some to keep them from overhearing Susan's phone conversation.

"That's ridiculous," we heard her say. "Cliff Barringer is wrong."

Ewbanks shot a glance at Bridges.

"If he says Barry's a suspect, then your station's going to look foolish."

Ewbanks muttered under his breath and reflexively patted the cigarettes in his chest pocket. Bridges looked at me and scowled.

I yelled, "Susan, you have company. Sheriff Ewbanks and Deputy Bridges."

Her voice dropped to a whisper, and in less than a minute, she emerged from the kitchen, pale but valiantly trying to smile.

"Would you like something to drink?" she asked. "Coffee?"

"No, thanks," said Ewbanks. "We just have a few questions and we'd like to speak to you alone."

The condo wasn't large enough for Bridges to escort me to another room like he had done at Walt Miller's house. I was being told to leave.

"Barry's my guest," Susan said curtly. She came over and sat close beside me. "You can either talk to me in front of him, or make an appointment."

"Suit yourself," he replied. "We're only protecting your privacy."

"And you've done a hell of a job with that so far," she snapped. "Now Cliff Barringer is going on the air reporting Barry Clayton, boyfriend of Dr. Susan Miller, the prime suspect in Samuel Calhoun's murder, is your prime suspect for murdering Mosely Skeeter Gibson. Why don't we all just ride over to the TV station and you can interrogate us on the news set."

If Ewbanks was surprised by Susan's outburst, he didn't show it. The sheriff looked at me. "I can't control what that asshole reports or where he gets his information."

"You're saying it's true?" I asked. "You think I killed Gibson? What's the evidence? What's the motive?"

"You know I can't go into the details of an investigation," said Ewbanks.

"So, you're just going to let us be crucified by Cliff Barringer? I thought we all wanted the truth here, or does it work differently in Walker County?"

"It works the same way it does here or on the police force in Charlotte," he said. "You start telling me the truth, I tell you the truth."

"I've told you the truth. I'm the guy who reported the shots. If I killed Skeeter, why wouldn't I wipe the judge's chambers clean and leave? No one saw me."

"Someone did wipe the judge's chambers."

"What?"

"The gun had been cleaned except for a neat set of Gibson's prints. Too neat. There should have been smudges all over it. And the inside and outside knobs of the hall door had no prints or smudges either. You can bet the cleaning crew didn't single out that one door for their attention."

"That's the point," I protested. "Whoever killed him came in and out of that door."

"That would explain it," agreed Ewbanks, "except you were once a cop and would know how to set the scene to look like someone had used the door."

"That's absurd. Why bother?"

"To substantiate your story."

"It substantiates my story because my story is true." His catch-twenty-two logic infuriated me.

"I can't dismiss that possibility," he argued. "You're a smart guy, Clayton. We found traces of blood in one of the lavatory sinks. I suspect we'll get a match to Skeeter. Whoever shot him cleaned up. I expect your AA test will come back negative and prove nothing one way or the other."

"And why would I kill Skeeter Gibson, a man I didn't know till Mike the bartender gave me his name?"

"That's why I'm here to talk to Dr. Miller," said Ewbanks. "I spoke to Mike this morning. He remembered Calhoun from the photo just like you said. He also remembered the woman with him."

"Susan's never been in that bar," I said.

I looked to her for support. She stared at the floor.

"Susan," I said. "Tell them."

She turned to me and said through clenched teeth, "I'm sorry, Barry."

Ewbanks and Bridges didn't need a polygraph test to validate that I was astonished. "But you told me—" I let the words hang, unable to complete the sentence.

"I was embarrassed and scared," she said. "I didn't think anyone would remember one more woman yelling at a man in that bar."

"You're not their typical patron," said Ewbanks. "At least not the type who threatens to kill someone."

Suddenly, no one in the room could be trusted. Not Ewbanks, not Bridges, and not Susan. She had first lied to me about her relationship with Calhoun and now about a confrontation with him. There was no wiggle room for any misunderstanding. I had asked point-blank if she'd been in The Last Resort and she had said no.

The anger surged up and I lost it. "Great. Just great." I got to my feet. "You want to talk to her alone," I told Ewbanks. "Fine. Have at it. I'm out of here."

I slammed her door so hard it sounded like a pistol shot. Halfway to the jeep, I realized I'd left my jacket and the cold, damp air of the coming storm bit to my skin. But there was no way I was going back in that condo. Ever.

By the time I pulled into the cabin's driveway, my thoughts had focused on one course of action, and I had two million reasons for taking it.

Susan was on my answering machine. I stopped the tape as soon as I heard her voice. I locked up the cabin and nestled into bed under a heavy down comforter, licking my wounds. Pellets of ice began blowing against the window with the rhythm of a snare drum, a steady roll portending dramatic events unknown but unavoidable.

From the depths of sleep, I heard the phone ringing on the night stand. I grabbed the silhouette of the receiver etched by the glow of the clock radio. Five minutes after two.

"Hello," I mumbled, hoping for a wrong number.

"Barry, it's Tommy Lee. There's been a death."

I shouted the first name that came to mind. "Susan? Something's happened to Susan?" I was wide awake and panicking. Had my temper tantrum pushed her over the edge?

"No. Nothing like that. Do you know a Gentle Deal?"

"Gentle Deal?" The words meant nothing.

"She's in her early twenties. Looks like a drug overdose. But underneath her phone is this morning's newspaper article about Skeeter Gibson, and someone's written Sammy Calhoun in the margin. I thought you'd be interested."

Gen-tle…Gen-tle…The wiper blades beat the rhythm of the two syllables as they cleared the sleet from my windshield. I had never heard the word as a proper name before. Tommy Lee had said very little other than in addition to Sammy Calhoun's name, a phone number had been jotted down. It belonged to Reverend Lester Pace.

I insisted on going to the scene and Tommy Lee didn't discourage me. In fact, he wanted me up there as soon as possible. He gave directions to a gravel lane off Red Fox Road which was less than three miles from my cabin. He offered to send Deputy Hutchins to lead me from that point. As I turned off the blacktop, Hutchins activated the flasher bar atop his patrol car, and I followed the strobing blue beacon into the mountain cove.

The storm wasn't so severe that I couldn't make out my surroundings. After a quarter mile, we pulled into a small clearing on the left side of the road. A stone chimney rose as a solitary sentinel guarding the approach and marking the spot where a cabin once stood. Behind it, a single house trailer perched on a cinder block foundation. All its lights blazed, spilling out a yellow glow through thin sheer curtains and illuminating four other vehicles parked in an erratic semicircle around the center door.

One was an ambulance with two Emergency Medical Technicians sitting in it, drinking coffee from a thermos. Evidently, there was no need for their skills, and the EMTs waited patiently to carry their lifeless cargo to the morgue. Tommy Lee's patrol car was beside the ambulance. It was flanked by a mid-Eighties Camaro with a splotched paint job and a PIZZA HUT delivery logo mounted on the roof. Closest to the door was a Ford 150 pickup truck with the mandatory gun rack in the cab's rear window.

Reece Hutchins and I parked our cars in the crowded yard and trudged through the layer of coarse sleet granules now coating the ground. I was surprised to hear the sheriff's engine idling, and I looked back through his windshield to see the dark shape of someone in the backseat.

"Don't know what he thinks you'll find," muttered Hutchins as I walked by him.

Tommy Lee opened the metal door of the trailer and pointed to a white plastic garbage sack he had flattened on the threshold. "Step on this," he ordered. "Then put these over your shoes." He held out a pair of small bags with drawstrings like those worn by an operating room team. "I don't want to contaminate the scene. The crime lab and coroner are en route."

The narrow confines of the door allowed only one of us to prep at a time. Hutchins waited outside while I donned the shoe coverings. While tying the string around my ankle, I managed a quick glance at the interior of the trailer. The kitchen and living room were separated by a counter which came two-thirds across the width. The low ceiling and tight quarters had the feel of a boat except this one wasn't shipshape. Plates and glasses were wedged in the small sink; a pot and pan were on the stovetop; clothes and magazines lay scattered around the floor and on sparse furnishings. I took all this in with a sweeping glance that ended on a girl slumped in a beanbag chair.

"Oh, God," I mumbled. My fingers froze, suddenly incapable of tying a simple knot.

"Come on, Barry," urged Tommy Lee. "The ice is blowing in."

Quickly, I looped the strings of the shoe bags around my ankles and tucked them in my socks. I stepped closer to the corpse, my eyes drawn to the bloodless cheeks and bluish lips. She looked young and innocent, a little girl's face on a woman's body. Her head lay back against the white vinyl cover of the amorphous chair, and her long, sandy-brown hair flowed across her shoulder and down her bare left arm. The long sleeve of the loose-fitting flannel shirt was rolled up above her elbow, and a black rubber tourniquet dangled at the edge of the fabric, pinched in place by the weight of her arm. A plastic syringe had rolled against her left thigh as if it had been dropped. Her right hand was in her lap, palm down on the fly of her jeans, the sweep hand of her oversized wristwatch ticking off meaningless seconds.

A footlocker served as a makeshift coffee table. Its brass-plated clasps and lock created the only facade of style in the room's simple décor. A candle had been stuck to the locker's black, scuffed surface by its own wax drippings. Beside it was a smoke-smudged spoon, a half-empty folder of matches from *Pizza Hut*, and a small clear plastic bag with a white residue inside. I guessed I was looking at an addict's works, the paraphernalia for cooking and shooting the poison. Heroin, most likely. Poor Gentle had mainlined herself out of existence.

"Who found her?" I asked.

"The kid out in my patrol car. A Wade Ryan. He and Gentle worked the late shift at the Pizza Hut in Gainesboro. She was a waitress and he did deliveries. I think he's a wanna-be boyfriend. He's only eighteen, a high school senior who works after school. He was worried when Gentle didn't show up for work or answer the phone. He got the manager to give him her home address and he dropped by when he got off. He peered in the window and saw the body. Shook him up pretty bad. I don't consider him a suspect."

"Suspect?" I asked. "So, this isn't an overdose?"

"Oh, it's an overdose all right. I just don't believe she took the injection willingly."

"Did she write Calhoun's name?"

Tommy Lee handed me the news item on Gibson torn from the *Vista*. I saw "Sammy Calhoun" written above the headline and a seven-digit phone number I recognized as Pace's.

"You call him?" I asked.

"No. Figure it can wait till morning. Handwriting matches other notes she's got posted on the refrigerator. She had to know something. No link between Calhoun and Gibson has been made public."

"This was under the phone?"

"It makes sense. That's where she'd keep it to call Pace. I found an Ingles receipt in her trash for a newspaper and some groceries.

Time is stamped at two-ten this afternoon. She probably called Pace when she got home."

"I doubt if she reached him," I said. "He was with the Metcalfs all day."

"I'll know tomorrow," said Tommy Lee.

"Wouldn't be the first time an addict calls a preacher."

"But it's her first time for shooting up. There're no other needle marks on her arm. Also, the trailer is too neat for a druggie."

"Too neat?" I looked at the mess around me.

"Yes. Someone tried to create the impression that Gentle was a stoned slob, but I've noticed very little dust in this place." He bent down and sniffed the small, marred table which held the phone. "Lemon Pledge. The bedroom has bureau drawers left out and the closet in disarray, but that could be because someone was searching for something. We also found a sandwich bag of grass in the bedroom, but no ashtrays, no roach clips, and no rolling papers. I asked Ryan, the delivery boy, if she ever tried to sell or buy drugs. He said she didn't even drink. And then there's the guitar in the bedroom."

"Guitar?"

"Yeah, the advantage of my son playing in a bluegrass band. I ran my hand across the strings to hear if something was stashed inside the soundboard. The strings are tuned backwards."

I looked at the tourniquet on the girl's left arm and understood.

"She's left handed."

"Yeah. Calluses are on her right-hand fingers from fretting the strings, and her writing has a backwards slant." He took a deep breath and shook his head. "Even if this is a first-time fix, odds are she would have used her left arm to inject her right. This girl was set up, Barry. Set up by someone who thought her death would be dismissed as the unfortunate end of just another junkie. Write her off as trailer trash." Tommy Lee was so angry his jaw trembled. "But the son of a bitch who killed this girl made the mistake of doing it in my county. Sheriff Horace Ewbanks just got himself an unwanted partner."

"We have to link her to Sammy Calhoun," I said. "How are we going to do that?"

"Through an anonymous source close to the investigation."

"Who?"

"You."

"Me? Why?"

"Because you have means, motive, and opportunity," he said, as if that made it crystal-clear.

I just stared at him.

"Look. I want this handled by my department. Any connections between Gentle Deal and Sammy Calhoun are to come to me where they can't be buried or ignored by Ewbanks." Tommy Lee stepped around the footlocker and walked between Hutchins and me. "At this point, I don't think Ewbanks has any information to give us." He turned his back on his deputy and mouthed the word "Bridges."

I realized the well-placed informant was a secret not shared by Hutchins. Through Bridges, Tommy Lee could learn everything he needed from the Walker County department while keeping Ewbanks out of the Gentle Deal case. That was assuming Bridges himself wasn't involved, an assumption I wasn't willing to bet my life on.

"I don't need to trade Ewbanks anything," said Tommy Lee. "Let him figure it out."

"And somehow I'm going to help you do what Ewbanks can't?"

"Right. Means—NEWSCHANNEL-8, motive—clear Susan and save your own ass from whoever's trying to kill you, opportunity —as soon as you can get in touch with Cliff Barringer."

"Barringer? The creep's a hatchet man. Look at the job he did on Susan and her father."

"The creep's heading the coverage of Sammy Calhoun's murder investigation. If he thinks he's getting an exclusive, he'll work with us."

I still didn't understand where Tommy Lee's grand scheme was leading, and from the look on Hutchins' face, I knew the deputy was just as confused.

"First, make sure Susan has an alibi for the time of Gentle's death," said Tommy Lee. "We'll have a better idea after the coroner's report." As if summoned by the words, the sound of arriving vehicles rose above the staccato beat of the sleet against the trailer. "Reece, go tell the crime lab what we've got. I'll be out in a minute."

His deputy nodded and dutifully tended to business.

"Okay," Tommy Lee told me. "I'll make this quick. We know Gentle was supposed to be at the Pizza Hut at five and she bought groceries at two-ten. Assuming she would have left for her shift twenty to thirty minutes ahead of time, the killer probably crossed her path here between two-thirty and four-thirty. We'll check the other residents along this road to see if they remember another vehicle during that time, but that's a long shot. Tell Barringer a source close to the investigation reports a suspected link between Gentle Deal and Sammy Calhoun. He'll soon learn we're friends and figure it's from me. He can broadcast that NEWSCHANNEL-8 has learned the Laurel County Sheriff's Department is questioning anyone who might have known the two victims. Tell him your name is to be kept out of it. I'll give my no comment statement when the press comes asking. Then he should encourage any viewers harboring such knowledge to step forward and call the Laurel County Sheriff's Department, like it was the station's idea to see justice done."

"You think that will work?" I asked.

"Barringer's a snake, but he won't turn down an exclusive, and right now, until I learn more about Gentle Deal, it's all we've got. We need to move fast because the killer beat us here." He stared at the dead girl. "And we all know who else he's trying to eliminate."

I shivered. "You keep trying to scare me."

"Do I now? Then why don't you listen for once. I'm getting tired of sounding like a broken record. Maybe I should try singing a warning. That should frighten you."

The storm ended as I returned to the cabin. It was nearly five-thirty, and the pale silver of the moon set the world alive with the glow of a million iridescent icy pearls. The temperature hovered just below freezing, cold enough to create a crystal wonderland, warm enough to keep the roads passable.

I decided to get on Cliff Barringer's voicemail at the station, requesting a callback after ten. Four hours of sleep would at least make my brain functional again. Instead of a menu of automated phone options, a real person answered the newsroom number. I realized NEWSCHANNEL-8 was preparing for their six a.m. broadcast.

"I'm calling for Cliff Barringer."

The young woman laughed. "You won't find him here. Not at this time of the morning. Can I help you?"

"Thanks but I need to talk to him. Does he have voicemail?"

"He does, and sometimes he even checks it. If it's urgent, I can call his pager and he'll phone in."

Power in a newsroom is the control of information. I understood the young reporter was curious as to why I'd be calling so early in the morning. "Tell him Barry Clayton has information regarding the Sammy Calhoun murder. He should call me after ten." I gave her the number, and she repeated it for accuracy.

"I'll see that the message is passed along. He can probably call before ten."

I could hear the excitement in her voice.

"Ten will be fine. Thank you."

I hung up while she was still saying the company slogan, "Thank you for making NEWSCHANNEL-8 your choice for news."

I tumbled into bed, my mind so numb that even the murder in the trailer and the questions it raised couldn't keep me from sleep.

Chapter 18

"This is Nelson Darius calling for Barry Clayton."

"Nelson Darius?" I answered. I knew who he was. I couldn't believe he was asking for me. I checked the bedside clock. It was only nine.

"I'm the president of NEWSCHANNEL-8. Is this Mr. Clayton?"

"Yes."

"Our early morning producer notified me that you telephoned for Cliff Barringer. As you may know, I'm personally supervising and coordinating our coverage of the Sammy Calhoun murder investigation. I wondered if you wouldn't mind meeting with me rather than Cliff. I'm trying to approach this story in a fair and balanced manner. I know your name is associated with certain aspects of the case and I'd like the opportunity to talk directly."

Tommy Lee hadn't mentioned Darius as our contact person, but Barringer was only a means to an end. Enlisting the cooperation of the station owner seemed a much more productive idea.

"Have you discussed this with Barringer?"

"No. And for right now, I'd like to keep this between you and me. I'm home this morning and can meet anywhere at your convenience."

"Your house is fine," I said, preferring to stay away from the prying eyes at his station. Darius must have felt the same way.

"Very good," he said, and then his presidential authority resurfaced. "I'll expect you at eleven."

Nelson Darius lived in one of those houses most people in the mountains never see. Plain stone columns marked the driveway entrance, and a mile of winding road climbed under bordering pines whose ice-coated boughs sparkled in the morning sunlight. The fairytale approach ended at a white mansion. The size was appropriate for a multimillionaire. The only surprise was that Nelson Darius lived in Walker County.

My jeep emerged from the tree-lined lane and approached the stately historic residence. It must have been erected by some long-dead plantation owner who shipped his family to the mountains each summer to escape the lowland heat of South Carolina. Instead of a horse and carriage, the circular loop in front of the house was blocked by a black Lexus with the trunk open in a half salute. I parked behind it close enough to read the Ingles Supermarket logo printed on four brown bags which had toppled over on the trunk's plush gray carpet. Darius may have been a multimillionaire, but he or his wife did their own shopping and chose paper over plastic.

I looked up on the wide, wrap-around porch and saw that the front door stood open. Someone must have had an armful of groceries and couldn't close it. I grabbed a couple of bags and had started up the two steps when Darius came through the door.

"Mr. Clayton?"

"Barry," I corrected.

"Good. I was afraid you'd beat me here. My wife is in Florida for the week. After we talked, I realized I didn't have any decent food to offer you, so I ran down to Ingles."

"That wasn't necessary," I said as I reached the door. The aroma of fresh muffins rose from the bag in my left hand, and I was hungry enough to eat them through the paper.

"Just set those inside the foyer. I'll fetch the rest."

I placed the groceries at the base of a walnut grandfather clock and walked back out on the porch. Darius hoisted the remaining two sacks in one arm and lowered the trunk lid to a point where a motor hummed and closed it automatically. I stood aside and then followed him into the house.

"Give me a minute to put these away," he said. "Just make yourself at home in the living room." He nodded to an open double doorway on the left.

The room must have been at least twenty feet by thirty. I have an untrained eye, but the eighteenth-century furnishings didn't appear to be reproductions. The room's dark hardwood floor matched the crown moldings, and the chalk-white walls were liberally hung with period portraits and landscapes. One wall was dominated by a finely carved gilt mirror. It was nearly six feet tall and four feet wide and crested with an ornate pagoda top. Nelson Darius seemed too down to earth to be caught preening in front of the slightly milky glass.

I was walking the perimeter, admiring the artwork, when the brightness of the gold chandelier in the center of the ceiling suddenly increased.

"There," said Darius, twisting a dimmer. "I hope that will make it seem less like a museum. I realize everyone doesn't find my wife's Chippendale taste as livable as she does."

I made the obligatory complimentary comments to the contrary, which Darius graciously accepted without indicating he knew I was full of it. My honest reaction was that velvet ropes, stanchions, and a tour guide could easily be a part of the room's décor. Resisting the urge to dust off my butt, I sat on a green velvet upholstered chair whose mahogany legs ended in elaborately carved claw-and-ball feet.

"Where'd your wife go in Florida?"

"Disney World," he said, and smiled as he saw my surprise. "She's with a group taking some underprivileged kids down there during the Christmas holidays. I don't know who was more excited, the children or the chaperones. We've both worked with troubled kids for years, but I decided to stay home when the mess broke about Cassie's niece and Calhoun. I put my wife on a charter bus yesterday afternoon and they rode all night. Got out ahead of the storm, thank God." He glanced at his slim gold wristwatch. "Right now, she's probably in line for the Tower of Terror."

I took another look at the elegant room in which I was sitting and tried to imagine its designer plummeting thirteen stories, surrounded by screaming juveniles.

Nelson Darius chuckled, and the distinguished, tanned, silver-haired seventy-year-old looked more like somebody's fishing buddy than a CEO. "Neither Hazel nor I should be considered stuffy," he said. He sized me up as I sat self-consciously on the velvet chair. "What say we move to the kitchen? We'll both be more comfortable and closer to the coffee."

To the degree that the living room was formal, the kitchen was just the opposite. The historical purity in the front of the house had been abandoned for ease of modern living. A wall of thermal-pane windows faced the morning sun, letting an eclectic collection of indoor plants and herbs thrive in the light. The stucco walls of the kitchen were trimmed in gray barn wood, the floor covered in adobe brick, and the exposed ceiling beams decorated with vintage kitchen utensils. If not for the spectacular view of the mountain lake and sharp granite bluff behind the house, I would have thought we were in the Southwest.

Darius pulled two mugs from hooks in a rafter and grabbed the coffee pot from the white-tiled counter.

"How do you like it?" he asked.

"Black, unless it would dissolve a spoon."

"It's stiff, but I haven't lost a guest yet." He poured me a full cup, and then started putting the muffins on a plate. "I'll pop these in the microwave. We can sit at the table or stand and eat if that's okay with you."

"I'm happy here," I said and sipped the gourmet coffee.

"Me too. You know, most of the big decisions of my life have been made in the kitchen."

"Well, I don't know how big a decision I'm bringing you, but it's sure important to me."

"You or Susan Miller?"

"Both of us."

The timer went off on the microwave, and he set the plate of warm muffins between us. I broke one in half and watched the steam rise off the exposed surfaces of corn meal and minute pieces of apple.

"Tell me about it," he said.

"I got some information this morning from a source close to a murder investigation."

"Sammy Calhoun's?"

"No. A young woman overdosed in a trailer in Laurel County yesterday afternoon. The circumstances are very suspicious. The authorities think someone made it look like a heroin self-injection. But a newspaper account of Skeeter Gibson's death was found with Sammy Calhoun's name written on it."

"Whose handwriting?"

"The victim's."

Nelson Darius studied me carefully. "Why would she make that connection?"

"Exactly the question I'm asking."

"I held back a story last night linking you to Gibson's death. Barringer's getting his own inside information, but Cassie speaks too highly of you for me to air uncorroborated speculation."

"Thank you," I said. "I think there's a good chance your station is being manipulated."

"And that's not what you're doing?"

I smiled. "At least I'm being upfront about it. Sheriff Tommy Lee Wadkins is looking for a concrete tie-in between Sammy Calhoun and the woman, not just the newspaper article."

"Of course," said Darius, his blue eyes flashing with a comprehension that anticipated my request. "Let's say, for argument's sake, she did know something about Calhoun and Gibson. Now she's dead. If Claiborne and Ewbanks are building a strong circumstantial case against Susan Miller, they'll dismiss this piece of evidence as simply a note jotted because both men were murder victims recently in the news. The woman followed crime stories. A name is no real proof of anything."

"That's why we need more."

He nodded. "So, my role is to broadcast the possible link as a NEWSCHANNEL-8 exclusive."

"You've got it."

He smiled. "Tempting, but what confirmation do I have? Will the sheriff comment that such a piece of evidence exists, or that the apparent suicide is murder? Our news department could look foolish if we make some unsubstantiated claim that turns out to be false. I know your vested interest is in protecting your girlfriend."

Great, I thought. Just my luck. A journalist with ethics. "That's true. And I'm also under suspicion for Skeeter Gibson's death. I want that cleared up as well. I'm doing what I can while Sheriff Wadkins is proceeding along more traditional investigative lines."

"And if we find other people who knew of a relationship between Calhoun and this woman?"

"Then the game changes," I interrupted. "You've broken the story and Sheriff Wadkins will have a trail to follow which the D.A. and Sheriff Ewbanks can't ignore. I think that's worth the risk of your news department looking foolish."

"Well put," he agreed. "I didn't get where I am by not taking risks. Okay, your name stays out of it and we go with our source close to the investigation line. We'll ask people to volunteer any information that could help the authorities establish the link. Who's the victim?"

"I can't tell you until I know her next of kin have been notified."

"All right." He thought for a second. "If she knew Calhoun, how old would she have been when he was killed?"

"I'd say sixteen or seventeen."

He took a sip of coffee. "Interesting. You know Calhoun had approached Cassie with a story about allegations of sexual misconduct with minors in the justice system."

"Cassie thought he meant Asheville."

"Calhoun was cagey, wasn't he? We're the dominant station in Walker County. We would have gone for it in a heartbeat."

"The story's still out there," I said. "Bigger than ever."

"I think I'll keep Cliff Barringer out of the loop," he said. "I'm going into the station this afternoon. E-mail me the girl's name and photo by five-thirty, and we've got a deal. Your story will lead the six o'clock broadcast."

"Thank you."

"I'm going to call Cassie right now and have her reserve at least ninety seconds. She says that's an eternity in news time." He excused himself and went to a back office.

I took my coffee and walked around the spacious kitchen. A wall of photographs caught my eye. Nelson Darius was in many of them, and I quickly determined an older woman with him must be his wife, Hazel. Some of the pictures were with kids on camping trips and other outdoor activities. Not their own children because the groups were large and racially diverse. Probably YMCA or church field trips. I saw a younger Cliff Barringer standing with Darius and some kids by a waterfall. Good public relations for the then NEWSCHANNEL-8 anchorman. Barringer was flashing a canned smile. My gaze froze on the photo beside his. Darius' wife was in a whitewater raft with five teenagers. Even in the safety helmet, the face of Gentle Deal was clearly recognizable.

I telephoned Tommy Lee from the jeep and we agreed to meet at the Cardinal Café for a late lunch. When I arrived, he had my roast beef sandwich and iced tea waiting for me.

"So, what's the word?" he asked.

"Nelson Darius is breaking the story at six tonight."

"Well, that's some good news," he said. "You didn't have any trouble convincing him?"

"He was cautious, but he couldn't resist. He wants the information to continue to go to him rather than Barringer."

"That's great. Sounds like he doesn't trust his own reporter."

"I told Darius we were waiting to notify next of kin."

"Not much to notify. The trailer and the pickup had been her father's. He died a couple months ago, and Gentle moved in. A neighbor said she'd been living with her grandmother in Tennessee. We're working through the Pizza Hut personnel records for an address and phone number. I should have something within the hour."

Helen came up to our booth. She replenished our iced tea without asking. No matter that it was winter. If the sun ever burned out, southerners would still drink iced tea until the air froze around them.

"Those eyes are coming along nicely," she said. "How can I get some of that makeup?"

"Easy, Helen. All you have to do is die."

"Thanks, Barry. I'll pass on it for as long as I can." She moved her snappy banter on to the next table.

I waited until she was out of earshot. "I found something else. Darius has a photo of Gentle Deal on his wall."

"What? Are you sure?"

"She's in a raft with some other kids, but, yeah, it's her. That girl's face is etched in my brain. She looked about sixteen."

"Did you ask him about it?"

"No. I didn't want him to know her name or that I recognized her. What's his story?"

"He's a homegrown multimillionaire. Made his money in timber and real estate and then bought the station. Has the Midas touch all right."

"No scandals?"

"Not that I've ever heard. He and his wife are on half the charity boards in western North Carolina."

"Can you check on him?"

"I'll ask around. Anything special about the photo?"

"No. It was one of many. Looks like he and his wife do volunteer work with kids."

"Maybe Gentle Deal happened to be one of them."

"Yeah," I said. "The one we found dead. Have you talked to Pace yet?"

"Yes. He said Gentle never reached him or left a message."

"How did he know her?"

"She'd started coming to church. They had a conversation about forgiveness last week. Pace said she carried a burden, but she hadn't confided in him."

"Too much to expect he'd break the case for us."

"We're on to something, Barry. Too many dead bodies prove it."

"What should I do now?"

"Lie low and get on with your life."

"Get on with my life? With a killer after me?"

"Get on with your life with Susan."

His statement surprised me. I knew he saw the color rise in my face.

"Did she say something to you?"

"No. Bridges told me about the incident in her condo last night. How you were blindsided that she and Calhoun had a confrontation at The Last Resort."

"She lied to me, Tommy Lee. I asked her if she'd been in the bar and she said no."

"And after you stormed out, she told Bridges and Ewbanks she blew up at Calhoun. He had pretended to be her dead brother to pull her out of the operating room. She was furious."

"I know about that."

"So her only lie was about threatening Calhoun in a cheap joint she'd never been in before or since. She knocked over a whole table of drinks she was so mad. I'd say she was embarrassed to admit it. She didn't want to appear foolish in the eyes of someone she respects. Maybe even loves."

I didn't say anything.

"Look," he continued, "you don't take my advice about things to keep you alive, and I've got no reason to believe you'll listen to advice about things that make it worth being alive. But I'll just say the best thing to happen to me was Patsy and I almost blew that."

"She lied to you?" I asked.

"I lied to myself. I thought no one could love a guy with one eye and half a face. I didn't want to be pitied. I pushed her away."

"What changed?"

"She told me I was right. She did pity me. Pitied me that I was hell bent on shutting out anyone that might keep me from pitying myself. 'Go ahead and wallow in self-pity,' she said. 'I love you too much to watch it.' She nailed me, Barry. That was exactly what I was doing."

"The truth," I said. "Not a lie."

Tommy Lee pushed his half-eaten tuna salad sandwich aside and leaned over the table. "The truth came out at two o'clock this morning. I told you there was a death, and you cried Susan. That came straight from the heart, pal. And you're a damn fool if you don't see it."

I left the Cardinal Café and got on with my life. Things were quiet at the funeral home. Arrangements had been completed for the Metcalfs' service on Thursday, and I spent the afternoon in the office, reviewing the paperwork from Hoffman Enterprises.

Two million dollars sounded straightforward enough. The sum was nearly twice what I'd valued the business. The more I studied the documents the more I realized the words "aggregate amount" required interpretation. I called my attorney, Carl Romeo, and my accountant, Josh Birnam, and asked them to analyze the proposal. Scanning and e-mail provided the fastest means of getting the information to them. We set up a meeting for the next afternoon in Carl's law office.

While I was attaching the file in preparation to send it, an e-mail message arrived from Tommy Lee. He had attached a photo of Gentle Deal from the Department of Motor Vehicles along with the contact instructions that Nelson Darius could give his viewers. I forwarded both immediately.

It was three-thirty, well ahead of his deadline, but cutting it close for mine.

I parked at the far end of the lot, tucked behind a GMC Suburban. Through its windows, I had a clear view of Susan's front door. The reserved space beside her walk was empty.

Thirty minutes later, it was still empty. I was tempted to start the jeep and blow some heat. My jacket hung in her condo, and I hadn't brought another. I was afraid the sound of the engine and the vapor from the exhaust would draw attention to me. She should have been home around five given her early surgeries. Maybe there'd been complications; maybe an emergency.

At five-thirty, I started the engine and was speed dialing her cell, when her Subaru zipped into her spot. She emerged with a small bag of groceries, and, without so much as a glance in my direction, hurried inside. I waited a minute to make sure she wasn't returning for something else. Then I walked to her condo while dialing her home phone.

"Barry?"

Count on caller ID to eliminate phone surprises.

"I have something I want to say," I began seriously. I pressed her doorbell.

"Wait," she interrupted. "Somebody's at the door. Hold on, I'll get rid of them."

I stepped to the side where I wasn't visible through her window. She opened the door, still holding the cordless phone to her ear. I was gratified to see her amazement.

"I left my jacket," I said into the phone. "I can't stand having a cold shoulder."

Chapter 19

I not only got my jacket, but also an invitation to stay for dinner. I had planned to calmly and maturely explore why Susan had been less than candid with me about Calhoun and the bar. We couldn't let that fester between us. But it was nearly time for the newscast and I was anxious to see how NEWSCHANNEL-8 handled the Gentle Deal story.

I told Susan about the murdered girl and my visit with Nelson Darius. She was distraught that a young woman might have become another victim of Sammy Calhoun's blackmail scheme.

True to Nelson Darius' word, Gentle Deal was the lead story. Her blurry driver's license photo appeared over Matt Markle's shoulder. The anchorman detailed her suspected murder in a few short sentences which could have been lifted from the crime scene report. Then Matt uttered the words "a NEWSCHANNEL-8 exclusive" and the camera zoomed back to include Charlene Kensington seated beside him.

Charlene moistened her lips as her colleague introduced her. The script in her hand shook slightly, and I realized this woman who deftly hosted "Pastors Face Your Questions" was nervous. Perhaps she had never faced so large an audience; perhaps she had never been on the air live with the owner of the station standing only a few feet out of camera frame; perhaps she realized Cliff Barringer had to be fuming that she was reporting his story.

"NEWSCHANNEL-8 has learned that yesterday's death of Gentle Deal may be tied to the murder of Sammy Calhoun nearly seven years ago." Charlene's confidence returned as she raced through the first sentence without stumbling. She even managed to keep her eyes from wavering back and forth across the TelePrompTer. "A source close to the investigation has told NEWSCHANNEL-8 the Laurel County Sheriff's Department is questioning anyone who may have known both the victims. Gentle Deal would have been sixteen at the time and a resident of Walker County."

"Walker County," I said to Susan. "I didn't know the girl had lived in Walker County."

Charlene continued, "Sheriff Tommy Lee Wadkins would neither confirm nor deny that his department was pursuing such a connection, but he did say his inquiry into the girl's death was independent of Sheriff Horace Ewbanks' investigation. At this time, the Walker County Sheriff's Department has made no arrests in the Calhoun case."

"Interesting that neither of our names is mentioned," said Susan.

"I think Darius wants to avoid having a suspect also declared a source."

Charlene took a breath and managed a smile before continuing. "Meanwhile, in the interest of justice and cooperation with law enforcement officials, NEWSCHANNEL-8 is making every effort to assist the investigation. Anyone who may have information regarding Gentle Deal and Sammy Calhoun should telephone the Laurel County Sheriff's Department." A phone number appeared on the bottom of the screen. "The NEWS-CHANNEL-8 team will continue to cover this major story as it unfolds. This is Charlene Kensington on special assignment."

I clicked off the set. "Well, I guess we'll know soon enough."

Soon enough came twenty minutes later as Susan and I sat down to tortellini, French bread, and a garden salad. My forkful of pasta was in midair when the call came.

She rose from the table. "If it's for you, I assume you'll want to talk."

"Unless it's Tommy Lee interrupting our dinner for the hell of it."

It was Tommy Lee, and he had news.

"I tried your cell first. Glad I found you where I found you," he said.

"Just getting on with my life. Did you get a call?"

"Calls," he corrected. "Three of them. The first one within five minutes of the newscast."

"It connected Gentle and Calhoun?"

"Darden Claiborne wanted to know what was going on."

"What did you tell him?"

Tommy Lee laughed. "I asked him if he believed everything he saw on TV. I said I had no idea where they got such a cock and bull story, but as a concerned officer of the court, he must appreciate I was doing everything I could to bring this poor girl's murderer to justice. He told me to watch my step and not compromise his case."

"What case? He means he doesn't want his innuendos to unravel. Who was the second call? Sheriff Ewbanks telling you to stay out of his county?"

"Close. Bridges."

"You got a warning from Bridges?"

Susan gave up any pretense of eating her dinner and joined me in the kitchen.

"Calm down," said Tommy Lee. "I made good progress this afternoon. Gentle Deal's autopsy report leaves no doubt she was murdered. Traces of chloroform were found on her lips, trachea, and lungs."

"Will that hit the papers?"

"Not if I can help it. I certainly won't be sharing it with Walker County. It does show the murderer had sophistication and that the killing was premeditated."

"Gentle had to have been targeted before she saw the article on Gibson's death. To arrange her murder in that brief time would have taxed even the CIA."

"And the CIA wouldn't have stolen drugs from the evidence room of the Walker County Sheriff's Department. That's why Bridges called."

"What?"

"Four days ago, some heroin and marijuana came up missing from their evidence room. It's being handled as an internal investigation."

"Four days ago and Bridges is just now telling you?"

"He's not running to me at every creak in the floorboard. He didn't have any reason to think there was a connection until he heard how Gentle died."

"Jesus, that means—"

"That means," he interrupted, "we either have a coincidence, or someone is very dirty in the Walker County Sheriff's Department. You know how I feel about coincidences."

I did know. He hated them. In any of his investigations, circumstances were labeled coincidence only after every other possibility had been eliminated.

"If they find who stole the drugs, we've found who killed Gentle Deal," I said. "But how do we prove it?"

"They won't learn a damn thing, Barry. The murderer is either too good at covering his tracks, or too high up the food chain. All we know is what we suspected. Sammy Calhoun was onto someone in the Walker County justice system. It got him killed, it got Skeeter Gibson killed, and it got Gentle Deal killed."

I thought about the cold reality of how what he was saying would play in a courtroom without direct evidence. "But, Tommy Lee, we can't even prove it's Walker County. All I have is drunk Skeeter Gibson toasting the heavens and saying Sammy Calhoun's name."

"Yes, we do know for sure," he said confidently. "The third call came from a man named Amos Slatterly. He used to be the manager of Hinkle's Department Store in Tyler City, the Walker County seat."

"I know. I've seen their courthouse and jail."

"Slatterly's retired now, but seven years ago, he hired Sammy Calhoun to watch for shoplifters. One of the shoplifters Calhoun apprehended was a sixteen-year-old girl named Gentle Deal."

"Calhoun arrested Gentle?" I asked.

"He had her arrested, or rather the store did. Slatterly mentioned Calhoun didn't want to involve the Tyler City police. He preferred the Sheriff's Department, and he took the girl straight to Sheriff Horace Ewbanks."

A tingle ran from the base of my spine to the top of my head. Ewbanks. The man who headed the Sheriff's Department for over thirty years and could have removed those confiscated narcotics as easily as getting candy from a vending machine. Hard-ass Hor-ass. The top of the food chain for sure.

"For God's sake, tell him to come over," said Susan. "I've got an extra bottle of wine, and it's killing me to hear only half the conversation."

We sat around the fire. Tommy Lee took the glass from Susan, and then swept it in an arc from her to me. "Here's to the two of you. May you both stay out of jail."

"Amen," I said. "I'll just be happy to stay alive."

"We're working on it," said Tommy Lee. "Now here's what I learned. Amos Slatterly told me that he hired Sammy Calhoun in early 1997 because a rash of shoplifting plagued Hinkle's. Posted signs threatening prosecution had done nothing to halt the increase."

"Calhoun worked undercover?" I asked.

"Yes. Slatterly was getting pressure from upper management to do something. To take aggressive action. Gentle Deal had been the first catch made by Calhoun. She tried to take a large leather handbag out of the store. Slatterly said she had no identification and wouldn't give her name. She was afraid to have her parents notified."

"Was she an abused child?" Susan asked.

"Slatterly didn't think about it then. He was glad they'd finally caught someone, and he wasn't looking for reasons to let her off the hook."

"So Calhoun took her to Ewbanks."

"To the jail," said Tommy Lee. "He pressed charges on behalf of the store and waited while the girl was booked. But they wouldn't release her until they had family information, and she wouldn't talk. She stayed in juvenile detention three days."

"Three days!" exclaimed Susan.

"That's what Slatterly said. He asked Calhoun whatever happened to the girl and he said her father had finally sobered up enough to realize she was missing. When he came to the police, that's when they got her name."

"Was she convicted?" I asked.

"No," said Tommy Lee. "Slatterly said the charges were dismissed by the court."

"This Slatterly's got a good memory," said Susan.

"Struck me as being a little too good," agreed Tommy Lee. "I was afraid maybe his stepping forward was a setup somehow, arranged by someone to throw me off the track. I'm getting paranoid in my old age."

"That's why you're around to reach old age."

"But then Slatterly made an unprompted remark that the reason he remembered the girl is because of what happened several weeks later. Even though Calhoun was no longer working security, he came back to see Slatterly."

"What for?" asked Susan.

"To buy the purse that Gentle tried to steal."

Susan held up her hands. "Well, he didn't give it to me."

"No," said Tommy Lee. "Calhoun made a point of telling Slatterly it was for the girl. He said after what she'd been through she deserved it. And she deserved it filled with money. Slatterly thought Calhoun meant she should sue the store and he told his former detective they wouldn't pay a nickel. Calhoun said all Slatterly had to do was promise to testify Gentle Deal had been caught shoplifting and taken to the Walker County jail for prosecution."

"Did he?" I asked.

"Calhoun never came back. Shortly after that, Gentle went to Tennessee."

"I wonder how that photograph wound up on the wall of Nelson Darius?"

"Bridges said Darius and his wife have worked with troubled kids for years. They founded an outdoor adventure program that was in place when he worked juvenile. It's not unusual she would have participated."

"Did Bridges know Gentle?"

"He doesn't remember her."

"But her name's unusual."

"Barry, he says he doesn't remember her."

"So, what about next of kin?"

"This afternoon I spoke with her grandmother, Mrs. Bethel Deal, in Knoxville. She bounced back and forth between grief and anger, but she understood I was trying to find out who murdered her granddaughter. The woman confirmed Gentle moved in with her during the summer of 1997. Her son was at a loss as how to handle his teenage daughter. He might have been abusive. His wife had left him and Gentle a few years before. Gentle never gave the grandmother any trouble."

"I'll bet she was scared," I said.

"Yeah, that's what I thought. I asked Bethel Deal if Gentle ever mentioned a man named Sammy Calhoun or Sheriff Ewbanks. She said her granddaughter had had no contact with anyone here after she left North Carolina. Her father would drive over every few months and visit. Then his liver gave out on him."

"Alcoholic?"

"Sounds like it. Mrs. Deal said he was bad to drink. He died last summer. He'd moved to Laurel County and Gentle came back to watch over his land and trailer until it sold. Nobody knows where or even if the mother is living."

"Who knew Gentle moved to the trailer?" Susan asked.

"If you ever get tired of chopping up people, you'd make a good detective," said Tommy Lee. "I posed that same question. At first, Bethel Deal couldn't think of anybody. I asked if Gentle had filled out any official change of address notices. The word official jarred her memory. Last week, someone called from the juvenile records division of Walker County, or so they said. Since Gentle was no longer a minor, they wanted to update the files before reclassifying her status."

"Last week?" I said. "Amazing timing, isn't it."

"Sure is," said Tommy Lee. "Obviously, that was a ploy as there's no such procedure. Mrs. Deal asked me if she'd done all right in giving Gentle's address. I told her yes. How could I tell her she got her granddaughter killed?"

"Did she remember which day?"

"She's pretty sure it was Wednesday. She was getting ready for Wednesday night prayer meeting."

"Wednesday's right after Sammy Calhoun's body was publicly identified," I said.

"Yes," said Tommy Lee. "The person who killed him must have known he had to locate Gentle immediately. If she'd stayed in Tennessee, she might not have been a threat. But back in North Carolina, she was a time bomb. As soon as Calhoun's name hit the news, the girl would know what happened."

"Somebody had access to court records, and drugs, and the report of the body in the graveyard. Remember, Sheriff Ewbanks came up personally to investigate."

"Not unusual," said Tommy Lee, "but in light of everything else, it could be important. Right after I spoke with Amos Slatterly, I called Mrs. Deal again. I asked her if Gentle brought a leather purse to Tennessee. The old woman wanted to know how I knew about it. Gentle never took it anywhere, but kept it packed away. Mrs. Deal got the purse out of her locker once, but Gentle wouldn't carry it. She said a friend gave it to her, and she wanted to keep it new. The grandmother thought it had a lot of sentimental value."

"It did," I said. "The gift from the man who befriended her, and then disappeared."

"I asked if she left the purse behind. Mrs. Deal started crying because she had just gone through Gentle's room, looking for something to take to the funeral home for when the body arrived. The purse wasn't there."

I thought about the trailer last Friday night, the drawers scattered around in her bedroom, the closets disheveled. "Do you think that's what the killer was looking for? Did he find the purse in Gentle's trailer?"

"Maybe, but why would the murderer care about it? It's just a purse. Nothing incriminating about that. I think he was looking for something else and he didn't find it. The whole place was ransacked. Odds are he would have discovered it before tearing through everything."

The scene came back to me. The sleet blowing behind me as I stood in the doorway, looking at the body of the girl. The tourniquet, the needle, the bag and candle on the table. No, it wasn't a table. It was a footlocker used as a table. "The grandmother said she got the purse from her locker," I said.

"Right," agreed Tommy Lee.

"There was a locker in her living room," I said. "It wasn't opened."

Tommy Lee's eye sparkled with firelight. "Damn, I missed it."

"So did the killer."

"Yes, because it was used as a table, it appeared to be a table." He sprang to his feet. "We need to go back to that trailer."

I left my jeep at Susan's and rode with Tommy Lee in his patrol car. Gentle Deal's trailer was less than twenty minutes away, and we spent the first ten minutes of the trip in silence, lost in our own thoughts.

Suddenly, Tommy Lee floored the accelerator and raced down a quarter-mile straightaway. He took the next curve with tires squealing and again let the engine's full power sling the car out of the turn. We rocketed another hundred yards or so before he slammed on the brakes and skidded into a dirt side road tucked behind a cluster of full white pines. He killed the lights.

"What the hell are you doing?" I shouted.

"Losing our tail. Didn't you notice the headlights come on after I pulled out of Susan's complex?"

I had been thinking about Gentle Deal and how Calhoun had probably used her to prove his story.

Within ten seconds, a truck shot by us at what had to be seventy-five miles an hour. We lunged forward in pursuit, the blue lights reflecting off our hood as Tommy Lee lit up the patrol car like a Christmas tree. I glanced over at the speedometer, and my heart rose in my throat. The needle kissed ninety.

"Did you clock him?" I asked.

"Nah, we're not going to arrest him. We're going to play with him."

At first, I thought playing with him meant rear-ending the back of his pickup because Tommy Lee came within a yard of the tailgate in a maneuver more suited to a NASCAR track than a mountain road. Then he gave several blasts of the siren which must have rattled the driver's teeth. The pickup slowed, and Tommy Lee hit the brakes to increase the distance between us. He radioed in the tag number and kept the siren on a steady wail until the other driver found a spot along the road wide enough to pull over. Tommy Lee turned off the siren, but left the swirling lights cutting the darkness with their cold blue brilliance.

"What do you do now?" I asked.

"For the next few minutes, I do nothing. Let him stew."

I stared at the green truck with flashing bands of blue reflecting off the cab's rear window.

The voice of the dispatcher crackled on the speaker. "Tag is for a 1997 Dodge Ram pickup. Owner of record is Cliff Barringer, 465 Compton Lane, Asheville. Vehicle is negative stolen."

"Barringer," I said. "NEWSCHANNEL-8. After tonight's report, he's following either you or me."

"And I'll bet he's working for whoever's been giving him inside information," said Tommy Lee. "The pipeline flows both ways. Let's see what I can do to keep him curious. You stay here."

Tommy Lee got out of the car and stood by the open door. He unsnapped the holster strap covering his pistol. "Barringer!" he bellowed. "Out of the truck with your hands over your head." He whispered to me, "I love my job."

The cab door opened, and a pair of brown, laced hiking boots hung in the air. After a few seconds, a weasel-thin man in blue jeans and a leather bomber jacket dropped to the ground. Gloved hands stuck up above his blue knit cap, and he squinted against the high beams and flashers of the patrol car. White puffs of breath rapidly poured from his mouth, betraying either fear or excitement.

"Identify yourself, please," the man said in his best TV voice.

"You don't know?" Tommy Lee asked sarcastically. "Aren't you the hot-shit reporter?"

"Now wait a minute," Barringer protested. He lowered his hands and started walking forward. "I don't have to take this police harass—"

The boom of the pistol throttled the word in the man's throat, and I jumped with such force my head hit the roof. Barringer's arms shot up so high I thought they might leave their sockets. His face went white and his knees buckled.

"A warning shot," Tommy Lee said over the fading echo. "I told you to keep your hands in the air. I don't know if you're drunk, drugged, or armed and dangerous. I do know you were doing over eighty in my county. Identify myself? All right, I'm Sheriff Tommy Lee Wadkins, the man you were tailing, and nothing would give me greater pleasure than to run you in."

"You're crazy." A definite tremble appeared in his voice. "Okay, I was speeding. I'm late for my deadline."

"Really, what exciting things are going on in Laurel County that I don't know about?"

Cliff Barringer said nothing.

"I didn't think there was anything. That's why you're hanging on to my friend Mr. Clayton like a blood-sucking tick on a clever hound dog. I'm warning you for your own good, Barringer. The pieces are falling together, and when the picture's completed, I think it will show you've been collaborating with a murderer."

The reporter's eyes widened. "You ain't got nothing," he said, but all the bravado was gone.

"Maybe not, but you know the people up here. They don't take kindly to sex offenders who molest young girls, and they don't take kindly to creeps like you who protect them."

The white beam of the headlights magnified the surprise on Barringer's face. "What are you talking about?"

"Hey, like you said. I ain't got nothing. Now get the hell out of this county before I change my mind."

The yellow crime scene tape made the rusted trailer look like a discarded Christmas package, too pitiful to even be opened. Tommy Lee unsnapped the padlock one of his deputies had bolted to the front door and we entered.

Not much had changed since the wee hours of the morning. Of course, the drug paraphernalia had been removed, but no one had straightened up the interior. I wondered how an elderly grandmother in Tennessee would deal with such final affairs.

A couple of celebrity magazines lay on the footlocker. Tommy Lee set them on the kitchen counter next to the telephone. "If I ever get too cocky, remind me of this trunk," he said. "I should have thought to check inside it."

Tommy Lee sat down on the floor beside the trunk and unbuckled the two clasps on either side of the center spring lock. "See if you can find a pointed knife or ice pick in the kitchen," he told me. "Otherwise, I'll have to break it open."

A set of carving knives hung in a wall-mounted plastic case, but the blades seemed too broad. I rummaged through a drawer of candles, pot holders, and measuring spoons. At the back, I found a box of plastic toothpicks and tossed them over the counter. "Here, try these. I'll keep looking for something better."

"This will do," said Tommy Lee, and he knelt down to get his eye close to the small keyhole. After a few minutes, he grunted and raised the lid until the flimsy metal hinges locked in place. "Now let's see what we've got."

The trunk was filled with seasonal clothes. Tommy Lee lifted out shorts, cotton dresses, and two bathing suits, a one-piece and a bikini. "There it is," he exclaimed.

A large black leather handbag lay on top of a sleeveless blouse. He brought it into the kitchen where the light was brighter. Tucked inside was a small video camera. Tommy Lee flipped open the cassette sleeve. It was empty.

"I'm not surprised," said Tommy Lee. "Whatever was on the tape was too hot to give to the girl."

"What's this?" I asked.

"I'd say it's what Calhoun spent some of Annette Nolan's money on. An 8 millimeter video camera with extended play that could record up to six hours. It still has mounting brackets on it. Calhoun must have given it to the girl when he'd finished with it."

"Calhoun caught somebody on videotape?"

"Yes. Somewhere there's a tape that Sammy Calhoun tried to use as blackmail."

"Could it be in Tennessee?" I asked.

"No. I don't think the girl ever had it. And I'm beginning to think Calhoun might not have been the total scumbag we've imagined. I mean, except for you, Susan can't possibly be a total misjudge of character."

A few hours ago, I would have taken offense at the comparison to Sammy Calhoun, but Tommy Lee made a good point. "You don't think Calhoun set Gentle up to be sexually abused?"

"No. It happened too fast. I think he and Skeeter had been drinking buddies for awhile and Calhoun was already onto the story. Hinkle's Department Store insisted on prosecuting Gentle and she remained in custody. Calhoun probably had the camera in place and could activate it with a remote. Some of those things can go through walls like a garage door opener. Then the girl was subjected to something. Maybe she was willing, but Calhoun had gotten her into the situation and I think he was going for a payoff for both of them. We know the charges were dropped."

"Maybe that was in exchange for sex," I said, "not blackmail. You think the killer ever found the tape?"

"No. But he knows the tape exists because Calhoun told him, or perhaps even sent him a copy. So he kills Calhoun, figuring to find the tape on his own. He pays an additional month on Calhoun's rent, and then he has Calhoun's furniture moved, supposedly to Texas. Instead, he probably goes through every item, but the tape never turns up. Gentle Deal is sent to her grandmother's soon after Calhoun disappears, and the killer figures the heat is off. Nearly seven years later, you dig up the body. Susan and her father become convenient suspects, but Gentle is also back where she'll hear about it. He can't take any chance that she'll come forward. He's still looking for the video when he ransacks this trailer."

The theory made sense. Unfortunately, it also led to one unpleasant conclusion. "Tommy Lee, if we don't find the tape, then I'll say I found it and try my own hand at blackmail. We've got to get whoever's behind all this out in the open."

"Yes," he reluctantly agreed. "We'll keep this discovery quiet. You may have to claim you came back here alone and found the camera and a tape. I hope it doesn't come to that. Tomorrow, I'll notify all the banks that we're looking for a safe-deposit box for Sammy Calhoun. That's one avenue we haven't tried. Maybe we'll get lucky."

I didn't want luck. The only luck I'd seen lately had been bad. Bad for Sammy Calhoun, bad for Skeeter Gibson, and bad for Gentle Deal.

It was nearly eleven o'clock when I climbed in the jeep and headed for home. Alone in the blackness, conscious of only headlights on faded yellow lines, my mind began to free-fall. An image formed in the dark at the edge of the farthest reach of my high beams. I saw Sammy Calhoun's skull floating on the night horizon like a macabre moon beckoning me onward. Just over a week ago, we had exhumed his remains from Pearly Johnson's grave; tonight, we had exhumed the partial remains of what might have sent him there.

Buried in Gentle's trunk, a body of evidence bore witness to the testimony of the department store manager. Sammy Calhoun had captured proof of a damning crime on a video camera. But the evidence was incomplete without those images of seven years ago, images which would speak in a way the tongueless skull never could.

Out there in the night was someone whose image on that tape would betray him as surely as if Sammy's skull had spoken his name from the grave. Was Cliff Barringer talking to that person now, telling him Tommy Lee and I were closing in on Gentle Deal's killer?

I envisioned Barringer peering at me through the patrol car window. His beady eyes and hooked nose had made him look like some great bird squinting against a spotlight. A buzzard living off the death of others.

Buzzards. Ewbanks had used the word to describe the media circling around the open grave. His distaste for them had seemed so genuine that I had trouble picturing him cooperating with someone like Barringer. It seemed out of character. But then Tommy Lee and I had planned on using him ourselves. If we didn't find the video cassette in some previously unknown safe-deposit box, how could I make the killer believe I found it in the trailer? I'd have to talk directly to him as blackmailer to victim. Who would I approach? What if he called my bluff?

Finding the tape would eliminate the need for the whole charade. What would Sammy Calhoun have done with it? Mailed it to himself at some post office box? The package would have been cleared out years ago. Left it in a locker at the airport or bus station? Those too would have been checked. All of those hiding places—safe-deposit, post office, and locker—required a key. Seven years ago, the killer had searched Calhoun's body and his apartment. If he hadn't found a key then, it was probably because no such key existed.

Who knew how Sammy Calhoun thought? Susan? Susan's father? Cassie? Suddenly, Cassie Miller's words echoed in my head. "He was always talking about how people overlook the obvious. Said that's what made him a good investigator." What were we overlooking? Was the videotape in an obvious place like Poe's purloined letter? Sammy Calhoun had been hidden in a graveyard and discovered. But I felt sure he had been clever enough to keep his damning evidence from his killer. Sammy Calhoun had known exactly what he was doing—right up to the point he was murdered.

Chapter 20

I had just walked into the funeral home the next morning when Tommy Lee telephoned.

"Bridges told me the lab work on you and Skeeter would be back today or tomorrow."

"That fast?"

"He said Claiborne twisted every arm and used his political clout to get the report expedited. It doesn't look good for a candidate for attorney general to have a murder committed on his own doorstep."

"We know what the reports will state. Skeeter was drunk as a skunk, and neither he nor I had any trace of gunpowder or blow back."

"Probably. But at least Claiborne can claim he pulled out all the stops."

"Are you going to pull out all the stops searching for the video?"

"Yeah. I've got contacts in banking security to trace a safe-deposit box, and the SBI can coordinate with U.S. Postal authorities as well as the private mailbox franchises. What's your schedule?"

I looked at my desk calendar. After the Metcalf funeral, it was wide open. "There're some things to tie up for the Metcalfs this morning, and then I've got an afternoon meeting. The visitation for the boys is tonight and their service is tomorrow. Why? What can I do?"

"Disappear. If nobody sees you, then nobody shoots you. It's as simple as that. And I figure you're due for a couple of days without the stress of the case. Can you leave town for the weekend?"

"Maybe. I'd hoped to do my Christmas shopping."

"Christmas isn't till next Thursday. That's why we have Christmas Eve. It was made for men shoppers. I thought you'd like a break."

"You mean hide out somewhere?"

"I was thinking of a romantic retreat for you and Susan."

"Keep talking."

"There's a hunt club cabin near Etowah. I'm not a member, but a friend gave me a key. One of my many perks. No one will be up there this time of year. Plenty of firewood, a pond stocked with rainbow trout, propane for cooking and heat. Just you, Susan, and nature."

I got the picture, and I liked it. I wasn't so sure how Susan would like it.

"Is this your version of a safe house?"

"I don't know how safe it will be for Susan, but nobody else will be within miles. The cabin's near the top of the ridge. Best cell phone reception in the area in case anyone needs to reach you."

"I'll check Susan's schedule. I don't think she's on call."

"Good. I'll get the key and directions to you tonight. I'm coming to the Metcalfs' visitation."

"Let me know what Bridges says about those tests," I said.

"I will. But I'm betting on a clean report too. I've also found some interesting information on Gentle Deal."

"What?"

"There's no record of her in the Walker County juvenile records. I requested information from the timeframe when Slatterly said she'd been brought in by Calhoun. Now that she's a murder victim there's no reason for confidentiality."

"Did you go through Bridges?"

"No. This was an official request from an investigating officer. Me."

"Maybe her file was pulled when charges were dropped. She was a minor and the judge had the records expunged."

"But the judge didn't issue any such order. And there's the booking log," said Tommy Lee. "An entire week is missing. I find it hard to believe arrest records would be accidentally lost that happen to contain her name."

I couldn't argue with him. Missing drugs and missing documents were too much of a coincidence.

I reached Susan at her clinic. She had early rounds Friday, but nothing that afternoon or Saturday and Sunday. I was a little surprised when she said the prospect of a weekend away was just what the doctor would like to order. With the immediate future under control, I picked up the packet from Hoffman Enterprises and began contemplating the rest of my life.

Carl Romeo led Josh Birnam and me into his small conference room. The lawyer had a few books on shelves as the obligatory display of his legal resources, but most of the wall space was filled with plaques and photographs commemorating civic and community events. Carl knew marketing was part of any business, and his name and face were attached to numerous worthy causes. He also believed fervently in those causes and was a worker, not just a name on a committee.

Josh Birnam had been our accountant for ten years, inheriting our business from his father-in-law. Josh had introduced me to the sport of archery and we had spent many an afternoon searching for lost arrows together.

Normally, a meeting involving the three of us would be informal and sprinkled with verbal jabs. But today both Carl and Josh behaved as if we were about to read the family will. Carl sat at the head of the table and Josh took the seat across from me.

"What's the matter, guys?" I asked. "Am I being screwed by their proposal and I haven't even signed it yet?"

My two friends looked at each other. Carl spoke first.

"The offer seems in order," he said stiffly, "but there are a lot of implications to consider."

"Oh, come on, Carl," said Josh. "Let's just get it out on the table. Barry, what's going on?"

"My dad's not doing well. I'm trying to plan ahead."

"No, I understand that," he said. "What's going on with this murder business? You dig up a body. Susan's dad's on the news, and then Susan. Rumor has it you were in a gunfight or watched a man commit suicide. The version varies by the hour. I'm wondering whether I need to find you bail money and Carl's going through his Rolodex of defense attorneys."

"It's just a series of misunderstandings," I said. "You know how the media has to make everything a scoop. Susan and Walt both knew Sammy Calhoun. He borrowed a gun from them and somebody used it on him. That's all there is to it."

"There's the guard in Walker County," said Carl.

"I went to see him because I heard he was a friend of Calhoun's. We don't know what happened and I've been told by the D.A. and sheriff not to discuss it. As an officer of the court, you can appreciate that."

"Okay," said Josh. "We're worried about you. And now your father's problems and the offer for the business are dumped on top of everything else, and it's got to be a ton of stress. Carl and I are here for you."

I was touched by their concern. "Thanks," I said. "You'll be a big help just navigating me through this Hoffman deal."

But Carl's mind was elsewhere. "So, you can't talk about the guard's death. He knew this Calhoun. You were investigating and the guard kills himself. Sounds like they're wrapping up the case with the suicide."

"What do you mean?" I asked.

"The guard killed Calhoun. You found Calhoun's body and the trail led straight back to him. He took the quick way out."

Carl's rapid-fire verdict left me speechless. Of course, it was wrong, but without the element of a sex scandal, the motive could have been an argument in The Last Resort that turned deadly.

For that matter, why wasn't Gibson the murderer? Because I knew he hadn't killed himself. Because Gentle Deal died after he did, and because an empty video camera told me explosive evidence was still out there somewhere.

I just nodded. "That's true, Carl. A suicide ties everything up nice and neat. You're a regular Perry Mason."

"Yeah, but can he make sense out of this contract?" asked Josh.

The question brought us to the business at hand.

"You're the numbers guy, Josh," said Carl. He leaned back in his chair and stroked his salt and pepper moustache. "You tell us when two million dollars isn't two million dollars."

"You're not as dumb as you look," replied Josh.

"He couldn't be," I said. We were back to our normal give-and-take. "I'm neither a lawyer nor an accountant, but I thought the sale price came from a lot of assumptions."

"True," agreed Josh. "The formula is basically a cash down payment, a cash installment plan, and a stock distribution running in concert with the cash payments."

"So, what do you think?" I asked. "The down payment is only three hundred thousand of the two million."

"That's fifteen percent," said Josh. "Not that uncommon. Like a down payment on a home."

"A funeral home," chimed in Carl.

"Are you charging Barry by the stupid utterance?" asked Josh.

"My humor's free."

"And worth every penny," said Josh. "Look, Barry, it all comes down to predicting the future. You get three hundred thousand in cash, plus three hundred thousand worth of shares in common Hoffman Enterprises stock at the current market price. That leaves one point four million. Over the next four years, you get one hundred thousand per year in cash and one hundred fifty in stock. At the end of the four years, you'll have gotten four hundred thousand in cash and six hundred thousand in stock for a total of one point six million counting the initial payments."

"Forget the stock for a moment," I said. "The cash will total seven hundred thousand."

"Yes," said Josh. "The remaining balance of the purchase price will then be paid in stock over four more years at one hundred thousand per year. The timeline from start to finish is eight years. During this time, you are prohibited from selling your shares on the open market. Furthermore, they have predetermined share prices of future distributions. If the stock overperforms, you get the bonus. If it underperforms, tough. You're still credited at receiving the stock at the projected value."

"Their appreciation rate is fifteen percent a year. Is that realistic?"

Josh shrugged. "It's consistent with the last five years, but as any good broker will tell you, past performance is a guarantee of only one thing—past performance. Hoffman Enterprises is a maturing corporation. Acquisitions will only take their share price so high."

"What should I count on?" I asked.

"To be safe, I'd say half. I don't think you're looking at a dot-com bust. People are still dying, and I haven't read about online funerals yet. But mortality statistics are very stable. To boost profits, they've got two options—cut costs and raise prices."

I thought about the bulk ordering of supplies for the entire chain and the use of cheaper brands. "So, I'm getting seven hundred thousand in cash and maybe seven hundred thousand in actual stock value."

"Something like that."

"Well," I said, "One point four million's not too bad."

"No," agreed Josh, "but you've got the time value of money. This is all in current dollars, and you lose the investment opportunity by having the cash payout over four years, plus you can't sell the stock for eight. Just things to consider."

I turned to Carl. "What about the proposal as a contract?"

"No surprises. You've got advantages in no longer having to administer your payables and receivables. You won't be chasing down people for money. Your employment contract has a three-year no-compete clause should you leave and decide to open another funeral home. Those are simply nuisance paragraphs. Half the time they're unenforceable if you left for just cause and are being prohibited from earning a livelihood in the field you were trained. You're planning to move your mother and father, aren't you?"

"Yes."

"Good. Hoffman Enterprises forbids use of their property as residential. That's behind this phrase—premises are for commercial practices only."

"I didn't catch that," I said. "Would they have to move immediately?"

"Negotiable, I'm sure. Might not be an issue if you're anxious to get them settled in a retirement facility."

Getting settled by choice and getting settled by eviction were two different propositions. I didn't know how Mom would take to having her holidays burdened by an imminent deportation.

Carl drummed his fingers on the edge of the table. "What's your inclination, Barry? They've asked for a fast response. Monday the twenty-second. If you've got concerns or points for modification, we'd better notify them."

"I'm not nuts about the stock arrangement, and I want to make sure we've got some transition time for my parents."

Josh flipped through his legal pad. "I took the liberty of calling an accountant friend in Raleigh. He has several funeral homes as clients, and I ran the broad parameters of the deal by him without any particular figures attached. He dealt with a Hoffman buyout last year. Basically, the same setup in terms of the ratio of cash to stock. He told me there were no negotiations. They have a business model and they stick to it like a fisherman sticks to a favorite lure. I do suspect we can get some leeway on the move."

"I haven't had a chance to go over this with Mom and Uncle Wayne. If I don't respond by Monday, what do you think will happen?"

"They have the right to rescind the offer," said Carl. "But if they're interested on Monday, they'll be interested on Tuesday."

"There was some consideration of year-end taxation and asset acquisition," I said.

"Probably for their quarterly report to the stockholders," said Josh. "Do you need more information or just thinking time?"

"I need the right time to talk to my family. We've got the Metcalfs' visitation tonight and their service tomorrow. I'm going out of town Friday and don't want to get into a discussion of this magnitude and then leave."

"Let me call Hoffman," suggested Carl. "Lawyers are always bogging things down. Maybe I can delay them a week. That still leaves three business days in the year. I'm sure they've got a legal staff ready to railroad this through."

"Going out of town with anyone we know?" asked Josh, and he winked at Carl.

"Just stick to your numbers. I'll worry about how many people are in my jeep."

They laughed. Meeting adjourned.

Libby Metcalf sat between the two caskets. Maynard and their twelve-year-old daughter, Alice, stood beside her. A line formed in front of them and stretched out our front door to the parking lot where arriving visitors waited in the frigid December air for the chance to express their sympathies.

The ordeal was grueling for everyone. Time would tell whether the parade of mourners would serve to further the family's healing. Tonight, the extended hands of condolence lifted the burden more from the givers than the receivers.

I stood just inside the front door, ushering people along as space allowed. Coats stayed on because our furnace couldn't keep up with the loss of heat. I knew many of the people had only a casual acquaintance with the Metcalfs, but the magnitude of their loss, the decimation of a family during the season when the sense of family was strongest, had touched the heart of our community.

I had worried about Libby's first sight of her sons' bodies. Wayne and I had labored over the boys, addressing not only their physical appearance, but also the lighting in the room. Libby had approached the caskets cautiously, supported by her husband and daughter. She had gone first to the older boy, Michael, and reached out a hand to touch his cold cheek. Then she let her fingers feel the nap of the new sweater. "He looks good," she had whispered, and then cried and smiled at the same time.

She had then turned to Ned and said nothing. I had placed the top of the turtleneck high under his chin to cover the marks of his lacerations. For a moment, I was afraid she would adjust it lower. She had fumbled with her small purse and pulled out a comb. With a steady hand, she guided a few errant strands of her son's brown hair off his forehead. Then she licked her fingers and patted the locks down in the same way she must have done countless times before his death.

My breath had caught painfully in my chest as I knew this final act symbolized the past, present, and future of a mother's love for her child, locked in place with the gentle press of her hand. She had looked up at me but said nothing.

I had left them to Wayne's care and busied myself where my own tears wouldn't be noticed. Dealing with death doesn't callous one to the loss of life. Libby Metcalf's grief was neither maudlin nor exaggerated, but the sheer force of its honesty engulfed me. I could do wonders in mending the physical ravages an accident made upon the body, but I could do absolutely nothing to mend the gaping hole in a mother's heart.

"This is really tough," said Tommy Lee. He stepped across the threshold as one more visitor in what seemed an endless procession.

"You're telling me. I'm by the door because I can't handle it as well as my uncle. He's with the family."

"Patsy wanted to come, but I knew we'd be standing outside for awhile. She's getting one of those colds that come from being in crowded shopping malls."

"Everything will be a blur for the Metcalfs. You're good to be here."

He cleared his throat and whispered, "I picked up some information late this afternoon."

"And?"

"Ewbanks and Claiborne have been contacted by Duncan Atkins' attorney."

"The contractor serving time?"

"He's sniffing out a deal."

"For Atkins?"

"Along the lines that for a reduced sentence Atkins will testify that Walt Miller talked about shooting Sammy."

"That's ridiculous. Why'd anyone believe Atkins now?"

"He'll claim he didn't realize Walt had actually done it until the body was discovered."

"You get this from Bridges?"

"Yeah. Claiborne talked to Ewbanks but he doesn't want to move on Walt till he sees Atkins' signed statement. The attorney wants his client sprung for time served, which Claiborne doesn't have authority to guarantee."

"But that doesn't explain Skeeter and Gentle," I argued.

"Skeeter's a suicide and Gentle's not a problem. She's my case."

"When's this going to break?"

"I don't know. Right now it's just a line of inquiry. Claiborne can't broker a deal without help at the state level."

"This will crush Susan."

We reached the open archway to the viewing room. Tommy Lee pulled an envelope from his pocket.

"Here are directions to the hunt club and keys to the gate and cabin. Forget about all this for a few days. If something happens, I'll call you. If you get a sudden insight, you call me."

"Thanks, Tommy Lee."

He gripped my shoulder. "And don't let someone who matters get away from you." He looked back at the line still coming through the door. "You of all people know how short life can be."

I couldn't imagine a sadder Thursday. We gathered under a pale blue sky as Reverend Lester Pace read the words of interment over the twin caskets. The cemetery at Hickory Nut Falls Methodist Church had never held so many for a burial. Pace lifted his head and voice to reach those standing behind gravestones at the far edges. After the Lord's Prayer, Libby Metcalf rose from her chair and spread her arms to touch both caskets.

Somewhere near Knoxville, Tennessee, a third casket was being lowered into the ground. How many mourners were standing beside Gentle Deal's grandmother as she watched her loved one laid to rest?

And how many more senseless deaths would I have to witness? At least the deal with Hoffman Enterprises meant after three years I would be free. As I stared at the mother weeping between twin caskets, I made my decision that I wanted out of this madness.

Chapter 21

Susan was late. I sat in my jeep in her parking lot, half listening to Christmas music and checking my watch with every change of song. We were supposed to leave at one. Tommy Lee had warned me that the road to the hunt club was little more than an abandoned logging trail. He'd advised me to travel it by daylight or risk winding up in a ravine. At one-twenty-five, I called her on her cell phone.

"I'm sorry," said Susan. "There were complications in surgery. Where are you?"

"Where do you think?" I snapped. "Sitting outside your condo. Are you ready?"

"My overnight case is packed. I was going to stop and pick up a few things."

"Just get here. We can do that on our way."

"I said I was sorry, Barry. Back off."

I mumbled an apology and hung up. The waiting had aggravated more than my irritation at Susan's delay. Carl and Josh had been right and I'd refused to face it. The stress on me was coming from all directions, and now I was so enmeshed that I couldn't separate Dad's condition from the personal threat of the murderer or from Susan's lies or from the horror of burying two boys for whom life was just beginning. Intellectually, I knew what was happening to me; emotionally, I was so vulnerable that even the prospect of a weekend away left me feeling miserable. The problems and a killer would all be waiting for me Monday morning.

If I ever extricated myself from the Calhoun mess, I saw the funeral home solution clearly. I'd convince Mom and Uncle Wayne to take the Hoffman deal, I'd work out my contractual obligation, and then turn a new page. Whether Susan was part of that story, or its setting was even in these hills, remained to be seen. I just wanted a fresh start.

At twenty to two, Susan's Subaru sped into her parking space. She jumped from the vehicle and hurried inside without giving me as much as a glance. Two minutes later, she came out, carrying a large brown backpack. I pulled the remote release on the rear hatch and she tossed in her weekend belongings.

She climbed in the passenger's seat and slammed the door. "Let's go," she said, snapping the seatbelt buckle for emphasis.

"You can change clothes if you want."

"I grabbed an extra pair of jeans and a sweatshirt, and then dumped everything out of my valise into that camping gear. I'll change when we get there."

"What do you want from the store?"

"Almonds, and maybe fresh lemons if they're available. You said there was a stocked pond, and trout almondine came to mind."

"I've already brought groceries and a cooler with steaks and frozen vegetables. The pond's probably iced over anyway."

"Yeah," she said. "Everything seems to be iced over."

The sharp edge in her voice was a cue for me to give an apology for my curt behavior, but I said nothing. We rode in silence out of town.

When we were still a few miles from the turnoff, I pulled into a convenience store for gas. While I charged my fill-up at the pump, Susan went inside for spare flashlight batteries and coffee. When she came back, she handed me a Snickers.

"Maybe this will sweeten you up."

"Thanks," I said. "Something needs to."

"I'm willing to listen."

"And I'm willing to talk. But let's get up to the cabin. There's nothing like a mountaintop to help you look down on your problems."

The road snaked back and forth with switchbacks more like U-turns. There were no guardrails, no caution signs, and no room to pull over should we have met another vehicle. The bare hardwoods revealed the increasing elevation, and I forced the jeep tighter against the mountainside with each breathtaking, hairpin turn.

The cabin sat in the saddle of a ridge. The structure was utilitarian, not picturesque. Instead of logs, the siding was weather-worn plywood painted battleship gray. A tin roof had become a mottled pattern of black tree sap and brown rust. The open foundation consisted of stones mixed with cinderblocks. Remodeling would require a stick of dynamite.

But the cabin wasn't meant to be a showplace. Any architectural creation would have been wasted against nature's spectacular panorama. The ridge top afforded twin vistas to the east and west, sunrise and sunset occurring behind the ripple of the Blue Ridge mountain range that stretched like waves to each horizon.

"I like it," said Susan.

"It's primitive."

We got out of the jeep and carried our first load inside. The layout resembled a bunkhouse. A small kitchen was at one end of the rectangular room. A stained sink had a hand pump for a faucet, and a two-burner propane stove served as the source for cooking and hot water.

A stone fireplace stretched eight feet along one wall and its rough-hewn mantel held an assortment of kerosene lamps and lanterns.

"No electricity," observed Susan. "Guess you don't run lines up here for one cabin."

"No." I turned around and looked at the mishmash of furniture. A sofa faced the fireplace. Given its condition, it should have been burning in the fireplace. A few folding chairs were set up, and others leaned against a card table in the corner. Poker was clearly the indoor activity of choice. A few chips were scattered on the floor.

Two doors broke the wall opposite the fireplace. One led into separate sleeping quarters where three sets of bunk beds and an army cot tossed Tommy Lee's description of "romantic retreat" out the cobweb-laced window.

The second door hid the bathroom. The word was a euphemism for a modified commode and steel washbasin. The top of the toilet's tank had been removed so that a hand pump could replenish the water before each flush. Cautiously, I lifted the seat lid. The porcelain bowl had been scrubbed sometime during World War II.

"I guess the Jacuzzi won't be installed till spring," I said.

"Where's your pioneer spirit?" chided Susan.

"You're asking a guy who owns a vehicle with heated seats?"

We brought in the cooler and set it in front of the stove.

"There's no refrigerator," I said.

"Yes, there is. It's this attractive side porch with the chicken wire to keep the animals from getting the food. The freezer's the part closest to the outside, the fridge is closest to the warmth of the kitchen."

While Susan took charge of organizing our provisions, I busied myself building a fire. As the flames began to pop sparks against the fireplace screen, I felt maybe there was something to this pioneer spirit.

"The real fire is in the sky," said Susan. "Come watch." She held out a glass of red wine, as if her smile wasn't enticing enough.

A bare patch of rock jutted from the edge of the ridge. Someone had hauled up an old park bench and anchored it to the mossy surface. We sat close together, bundled in our jackets. The swollen sun fell rapidly, slipping beneath the wisps of clouds that created the perfect canvas for yellow, pink, and magenta streaks to play across the western sky. I lifted my glass and twirled it, watching the rays refract through the liquid prism, scattering light in a wide arc.

"I'm sorry," I whispered. "I've let myself turn into a whiner."

"Better a whiner than a wino," she teased, trying to defuse the tension. "You've had a lot on your shoulders."

"But that's no excuse to make life difficult for others. Especially you."

She put her arm around my shoulders. "I dumped some of the burden on you. You had every right to be angry."

She nestled her soft hair against my neck. The curve of her ear lay cold against my skin.

"No more lies," I said.

"No more lies. Let's ship them all out to that sun and let it carry them away. Tomorrow's a new day."

Only the top half of the sinking orb could now be seen. The rim of the mountain range blazed in the final seconds of dying light. I raised my glass to eye level.

"To a new day," I said. The wine glowed blood-red for an instant, and then dulled as the ridges swallowed the last sliver of fire.

"If there are no more lies, then all we're left with is the truth," she said. "May as well start now."

"What do you mean?"

"Down at the gas station, I said I'd be willing to listen, but I need you to listen to me first."

"You don't have to tell me anything," I said. "It's none of my business."

She jerked her head up. "Don't say that, Barry!"

The anger in her voice startled me.

"Don't let me keep something bottled inside that needs to come out. I can't have it festering between us."

I stared at the horizon. The sky deepened into gold and purple. A lone hawk spiraled against the backlit clouds, searching the ground for his evening meal.

"All right," I said. "Then why did you lie to me?" I could feel the pent-up hurt rising in my throat. "Why did you continue to lie even after I asked point-blank for the truth?"

"I couldn't help it. I hated myself for those words, but continuing to lie kept me safe in my cocoon, protected in my image of little Miss Perfect."

"I don't expect you to be perfect."

"But I do," she said bitterly. "I always have. Since Stevie died."

Her last sentence opened the window into the soul of a girl watching the perfect brother die in a ditch along a mountain road.

"I wanted him to be so proud. To look down and say that's my—" a sob strangled her words— "that's my little sister."

"Susan, he is proud of you, you know he is."

"I didn't want there to be any doubt. I was a straight A student, the class president, and summa cum laude graduate from college. I couldn't accept anything less, and somewhere along the way, I believed others couldn't accept anything less of me. Then I met Sammy."

"He certainly wasn't perfect."

"No, but I'd never met anyone like him. He forced me out of that goody-two-shoes straitjacket. Took me into the backstreet bars of New York and into the lives of people I'd never met before. I mean I wasn't suddenly into drugs and orgies, but I realized I could experience life without having to master every aspect of it."

"Sounds like he was good for you."

"That's what I told myself. It provided the rationale for my new outlook on the world. Then, I realized Sammy was manipulating me, using our relationship to get more work from Cassie. And I discovered he used his undercover roles for personal advantage, playing his employer and target against one another. Revealing and concealing information depending upon the highest bidder. When I finished med school, I left Sammy and that other Susan behind and retreated into the illusion of being perfect again."

I shifted on the bench. The clouds had gone gray in the gathering dusk. The hawk had glided to more favorable hunting grounds. The cold seeped through my clothes, but I wasn't about to shut down the most important conversation Susan and I had ever had.

"Then Sammy showed up in Asheville."

"Yes. Cassie had taken the producer's job at the station. Sammy came here looking for a meal ticket when his game was up in New York. I don't know why my aunt hired him. She said he promised to stay away from me, and then he broke the big story about the bid-rigging, and everybody came up a winner. That's when he had the audacity to re-enter my life, and I guess I had a hunger for a taste of those New York days. We were on again and off again, just like I told you. It came to a head when he showed up at the hospital impersonating Stevie. Perfect Susan couldn't tolerate that, and I had a meltdown culminating in a shouting, threatening confrontation at The Last Resort, witnessed by the entire bar."

"You could have told me that," I said. "I would have understood."

"But you don't understand, even now. You were the reason I had to stay perfect. After Sammy disappeared, I immersed myself in that persona deeper than ever. And then this guy shows up. A former policeman who took the oath to serve and protect. And he sacrificed his career for his ailing father and to keep a business going that comforts people when they're most vulnerable. And for some reason, he likes me."

Her tears flowed freely. I reached down and grabbed her hand with a gentle squeeze.

"And then this wonderful man digs up the imperfections of my past. Literally. I was terrified I would lose you. You were Stevie," she said. "The kind of person my brother would have become. And last year, you laid your life on the line to bring a killer to justice. How could I admit to being less than perfect when I had found the perfect companion?"

"Oh, Susan," I whispered. "You're so wrong. I have such feet of clay that if it rained now, I'd sink to my knees. Don't do this to me. If I were perfect, I would have understood. Can't you see that?"

She took a deep breath, wiped her eyes and nodded. Before she could answer, I sealed her lips with mine.

If Susan had cooked on my scout camping trips, I'm sure I would have risen beyond the rank of Tenderfoot. The steaks were grilled to perfection, and she had managed to discover enough ingredients in the convenience store to create a fantastic sauce and intriguing salad.

Over dinner, I set aside any discussion of the murders and I tried to forget that Tommy Lee sent me to the cabin for safety. So I told Susan about the funeral home offer and how I had to make a decision that meant a life change for Mom and Dad and a new employer for me. Just talking it through lifted my spirits, as her confession on the mountain ledge had lifted the shadow of Sammy Calhoun from both of us.

"It comes down to a choice of what's best for your mother and father compared to what's best for the community you serve. You have to give the edge to your family," she said. "That's why you came back. You can't worry about what other people think." She laughed. "Aren't I the one to be telling you that?"

"You are," I said, "because no one understands better. And I have to let Mom guide me rather than persuade her to do what I think is best for me. That kind of decision will only haunt me later."

We cleaned the dishes together, which meant Susan scrubbed the cast-iron pots, and I buried the food remains and tossed the paper plates in the fireplace.

Then I sat overstuffed on the understuffed sofa with Susan snuggled against me, her shoeless feet tucked into the lumpy cushions. We watched the fire as if it were a television program.

"So," she said, "I guess there's only one more problem we two perfect people share."

"What's that?"

"We're both murder suspects. Not the kind of thing to make you Hoffman Enterprises' funeral director of the year."

"Or the person you'd want wearing a mask and wielding a knife above your body," I said.

"No, I guess not. Has Tommy Lee got any leads?"

I decided not to mention the development of Duncan Atkins' testimony against her father. It might go nowhere and it would certainly upset her. "Someone's dirty in the Walker County Sheriff's Department. Drugs like those we found in Gentle Deal's trailer are missing from the evidence room."

"Couldn't that be a coincidence?"

"It could, but you add it to Skeeter's death and Gentle's arrest and it's just one more coincidence demanding an explanation. Another funny thing's surfaced. We have only the former manager of Hinkle's Department Store saying the girl was ever in the Walker County jail. All records of her have been expunged."

"Isn't that typical when a juvenile's been cleared of charges?"

"Only if the judge orders it. And the jail's log sheet of her booking is missing. Hers wasn't the only name on that list."

"How does Tommy Lee investigate another sheriff?" she asked.

"Very carefully." I kept Bridges out of the conversation because of my promise to Tommy Lee, and because I also considered him as much of a suspect as anyone.

"Does the killer have to be someone in the Sheriff's Department?"

"What do you mean?"

"Skeeter Gibson worked there. He would have access to everything, wouldn't he?"

"But he's dead," I reminded her.

"Yes, but the disappearance of the records and the drugs happened before he died. Skeeter could have been working for someone outside the department."

I hadn't given serious thought that Skeeter might still have been in the pay of whoever killed Sammy. Susan was absolutely right. Skeeter could have been the inside man. Claiborne's words from the night in his car came back to me. "It might not be anyone in the Sheriff's Department at all. It could be someone with enough power and money to put outside pressure on Skeeter or anyone else involved." At the time, his statement had seemed like mere speculation.

"That opens up more possibilities," I said. "I'm trying to narrow the field of suspects."

"How much wider is it?" asked Susan. "The killer still had to know Gentle Deal."

A wall of photographs appeared in my mind. "Nelson Darius knew her from his charity work."

"He certainly has the money to buy a hundred Skeeters."

My skin crawled at the thought. "What a twist that would be. Cassie comes to Darius with the story idea, and he knows the trail will loop back to him."

"Why wouldn't he have squelched the story then?"

"Because it was too good. Cassie would have wondered why. But he could have encouraged her to assign their reporter, limit the scope to the wrong county, and then he could have kept an eye on Sammy."

Susan shook her head. "I just find it hard to believe Darius would be that sleazy. Sex with prisoners and a minor."

"I agree. But anything's possible. The more despicable the act, the more extreme the actions to keep it hidden."

"Did Cassie say who they assigned to the story?"

"No. Maybe their court reporter. Jesus."

"What?" she asked.

"That would have been Cliff Barringer. And he might have known Gentle." I remembered the picture of the former anchorman standing beside his boss amid the underprivileged children. "As a court reporter, he'd know all about booking records and how to track down Gentle Deal."

"Maybe that's why Darius is keeping information from him," suggested Susan. "Or maybe Darius is afraid Barringer will stumble across something that incriminates him."

"Suspects inside an institution investigating the crime. Just like the Walker County Sheriff's Department. I'm afraid our best hope is for Tommy Lee to find that videotape."

"But the killer couldn't find it, and he had free access to all Sammy's things when he gutted the apartment."

"Sammy Calhoun was too smart to hide it on his own property. We're hoping maybe there's a safe-deposit box somewhere, but after seven years...." I shrugged. "You knew him better than any of us. Any ideas?"

"No. Just what he always said. People overlook the obvious."

"I doubt we'll find it on a shelf in Blockbuster."

She laughed. "Would you like the last of the wine?"

"What are you trying to do, get me drunk?"

"I'm trying to have my way with you." She nibbled my earlobe and chills shot down my spine.

"The sleeping arrangements are challenging."

"Who said anything about sleeping?" She slipped her hands under my sweater and pressed her warm palms against my chest. "Not yet, anyway."

I lay back against the sofa arm and pulled her to me. A spring groaned in protest, but I wasn't about to give up the best love nest the cabin offered.

Then a scene burst into my mind like a flood of cold water.

"What's wrong?" asked Susan, as she felt the tension knot every muscle in my body.

"The sofa. Skeeter Gibson sacked out on a sofa in the judge's office because it was probably the most comfortable private place in the courthouse."

"That would make sense," agreed Susan. "He had the run of the building."

"And if someone wanted a sexual liaison with a female prisoner close to the jail, he'd also want the most comfortable setting."

"Skeeter brought the girls to the judge's chamber? Then where did Sammy put the camera?"

I didn't answer. I saw Skeeter sitting on the sofa, lifting the bottle of Wild Turkey and toasting Sammy. He wasn't raising it to heaven, he was raising it to where the blackmail scheme had netted its evidence.

"You said there were mounting brackets on the camera in Gentle Deal's trunk," said Susan. "Would Sammy have fastened it to the ceiling?"

"I think that's exactly what he did, but managed to hide it somehow. Maybe in a heating duct or on top of a bookcase."

"So, Skeeter must have let him in to plant the recording equipment," Susan said. "You don't think he knew where Sammy hid the tape, do you?"

"No. I'm afraid Sammy took that to his grave."

"You mean Pearly Johnson's grave. How ironic."

Yes, how ironic, I thought. A body hidden in a graveyard, and a videotape—"Jesus, that's it," I shouted. I eased Susan to the side and jumped to my feet. "We've been focusing on where the tape could have been hidden. We should have been focusing on where it could have been found."

"What's the difference?" Susan stood up and watched me pace back and forth in front of the fire.

"The difference is in the purpose. Sammy had the tape, but he didn't take it to the rendezvous. He knew once he got his money, he'd have to deliver the goods. Better to let his blackmail victim recover it after he was safely away. That meant the tape would need to be found in a place easily accessible."

"Where?"

"The last spot you would look. The scene of the crime."

"In the courthouse?"

"Why not? You tell me. Wouldn't Sammy like to put it right under their noses?"

"Yes," said Susan, and the excitement grew in her voice. "That'd be just like him."

"Maybe he set it where the camera had been, after he knew the site had been checked. He gets money for himself and Gentle Deal, and has the pleasure of telling someone to find the evidence in their own pocket."

I picked up my jacket from the floor.

"Where are you going?"

"To the courthouse. Alone. I can't take a chance someone else isn't scrambling to put these same pieces together. What if they solve the puzzle first?"

"You're crazy to go down that mountainside in the dark. Call Tommy Lee. Have him search for it."

"Tommy Lee would have to get a warrant. What if someone in the Walker County Sheriff's Department got wind of it? They might get the tape first."

"Can't he break in?"

"Then any evidence he found would be inadmissible. He's a sworn officer of the law and can't go around it. But I'm a private citizen. If I break in, I'm not bound by those same restraints. Even if I'm charged with a crime, anything I find can be used by the prosecution. You see, there's no other way. We don't know who to trust in Walker County."

Susan went to the door and held up my car keys. "I thought we were sharing our burdens. I'm in this as much as you are. If I don't go, these get tossed." She smiled. "You see, there's no other way."

Chapter 22

The drive up the mountain that afternoon had taken ten minutes. Coming down at night, we inched along at a speed that was little faster than a brisk walk. My headlights often swept a void where the road turned so sharply it simply disappeared. Fear of taking an unintended shortcut stretched our travel time to over half an hour. With simultaneous sighs of relief, we finally reached the highway for Walker County. I figured that whatever lay ahead couldn't possibly be as nerve-wracking as our white-knuckled descent.

It was about eighty-thirty when we arrived at the complex. Cars rimmed the parking lot in front of the county jail, but the courthouse side was deserted. I killed my headlights and parked in a spot outside the glow of the street lamps. A new guard would be on duty, replacing Skeeter Gibson with what had to be greater effectiveness. I hoped that meant he would be stationed at the front desk when not making his prescribed rounds. If I could get into the judge's chambers, I would be home free. No one wanted to hang out in a room where less than a week ago, a man's brains had splattered the walls.

"Now what?" asked Susan.

"I'm glad you're here," I said. "I might be charged with just entering instead of breaking and entering."

"I'm the one breaking in?" She asked the question with more excitement than alarm.

"No. You had car trouble. The jeep just died on you, and you coasted into this spot. You'll ask the guard to come look. How could he possibly resist aiding such a lovely damsel in distress?"

"What if he's a she?"

"Call her a sister and give her the secret handshake."

"Right. We are women, hear us roar. What am I doing out at eleven-thirty? Bar-hopping?"

"Don't lie about your identity. You're a doctor. You've been called over to consult on a case at Walker General Hospital. You got lost, and then had the misfortune of having your engine stop. I'm going to pull the wire on the distributor."

"And you'll walk in the front door while we're working out here?"

"Exactly."

"What if he locks the door behind him like a good security guard should?"

I was glad no light could show the blank look on my face.

"Let's add one thing," said Susan. "The car broke down, I ask for help, but I also have a stomach virus and have to get to the bathroom immediately. No one will risk witnessing an attack of diarrhea no matter how lovely the damsel."

I leaned over and kissed her. "The green apple quick-step. Excellent. I remember the bathrooms are around the corner from the courtroom. I'll slip in as soon as you're out of sight."

"How will you leave?"

"The back hall off the judge's chambers. A door has to open from the inside or they're violating fire codes. I'll call you on your cell phone when I'm back in the parking lot. I'll keep mine off until then." I grabbed my phone from its dashboard charger and pressed the power button.

In less than thirty seconds, I had disconnected the main wire to the distributor. Susan cranked the ignition until I was confident the jeep wouldn't miraculously start.

"Let me go first," I said. "See that boxwood to the right of the door? I can stay clear of the lights and crouch behind it. When I'm in position, work your magic."

"Right, but remember Houdini was good at breaking out of things, not into them."

Keeping well within the shadows, I crept along a hedge that bordered the curb. When I reached the end, I looked back at Susan. She sat in the driver's seat and appeared to be using her cell phone. Smart girl. If someone saw her, they would assume she had parked to make a call.

Between me and the boxwood lay twenty yards of open ground. Although no lamps directly illuminated the area, enough ambient light flooded it to make me visible. I needed Harry Potter more than Harry Houdini to get across that space.

With a final glance at the jail to make sure I was unobserved, I jogged through the dead flowerbed and wedged myself behind the shrub. My pulse pounded in my ears, and breath came in short jabs. Calm down, I thought. So far all I'd done wrong was trample dead pansies.

For a moment, I was afraid the courthouse glass doors would be too well sealed for me to hear Susan's conversation. How would I know when she and the guard were clear? Then I heard the squeak of a chair as someone shifted in it.

A few minutes later, Susan came down the sidewalk, clutching her hospital ID badge in her hand. I knew she'd hold it up for the guard to see, a gesture that would give her official credibility. She rapped on the glass. The chair squeaked again. I heard a voice muffled by the door.

"Sorry, we're closed," said a man.

"I'm a doctor and this is an emergency. Please let me in."

The bolt in the lock turned.

"I'm on my way to Walker General and had car trouble."

"Someone can help you over in the Sheriff's Department," the guard said through the open door.

"I've also been hit with an intestinal virus. You're taking me to the ladies' room right now or we're both going to be very embarrassed."

"But—" His protest was cut short as Susan dragged him back inside.

"Hurry," she pleaded. "I'm not kidding and I won't be the one cleaning it up."

Their footsteps echoed on the marble floor. When I knew they were safely out of sight, I left the shelter of the boxwood and walked into the courthouse. The guard's keys still dangled in the door. Susan had been magnificent.

The lights were off in the courtroom. I walked along the aisle, touching the backs of the pews for reference. I knew the door to the judge's chamber was on the right behind the bench, but I wished I'd had the sense to bring a flashlight from the jeep. Now I'd have to risk turning on a light. Susan could keep the guard occupied for only so long, and his comment about sending her to the Sheriff's Department was exactly what I didn't want to happen.

My eyes adjusted enough to see the knob in the paneled door. It was unlocked. I suspected the sitting judge had requested other quarters after last Sunday's tragedy. With the door securely closed and locked behind me, I turned on the light.

The sofa and the foxhunt oil painting were gone. The wall had been scrubbed so hard that the washed area stuck out like a huge blemish. I glanced up in the direction Skeeter had lifted the whiskey bottle. A heating vent with a grate cover was in the corner of the ceiling over the desk. The perfect position for a bird's-eye view of the room.

I stripped off my jacket and wedged it under the bottom of the door to the courtroom, hoping to block any light leakage. Then I locked the hall door and used my flannel shirt to jam its threshold. I noticed there was a second light switch mounted on the wall close to the knob. The fluorescents could be turned off or on at either door. On the night Skeeter had died, his murderer must have reached around from the hall and switched off the lights without having to expose himself.

There was no checkpoint in this office for the guard to record his rounds. Without seeing a suspicious sign, Susan's drafted Good Samaritan would have no reason to enter. I could spend the whole night undisturbed.

But I took no comfort in the security of the locked room. I wanted to get my search over and leave the building as quickly as possible. In my mind, the room reeked of death and the evil behind it could still be stalking the halls of justice. I climbed up on the desk and examined the vent. Two small screws fastened it to the ceiling. I opened the blade of my penknife halfway and used the back edge as a makeshift screwdriver. When the first screw was loose enough, I extracted it with my fingers. The second one proved more difficult. The threads had crossed the inset sleeve and jammed it in place. I could see the groove in the screw head had been damaged by someone trying to either undo or tighten it. Perhaps Sammy Calhoun had been in a hurry seven years ago, and no one had touched it since.

The desk groaned under my feet as I shifted for a better angle. For several minutes, I attempted to loosen the screw by pressing the blade deeper into the groove. I only succeeded in cutting my thumb and dripping warm blood onto the desk. More than fingerprints would need to be cleaned up.

I opened the blade all the way and wedged the sharp edge between the screw and the vent. I tried to pry the screw free, figuring my knife was stronger than its metal threads. The gap widened about a quarter of an inch. I forced the blade in farther and twisted it as hard as I could.

The screw shot free before I could catch it. The vent cover fell after it. I grabbed at the grate but batted it into the wall. The clang resounded like a gunshot and repeated even louder against the hardwood floor. I might as well have shouted "Hey! I'm in here!"

I froze on the desk, listening for any indication that the guard was on his way. If I was lucky, he was still waiting outside the ladies' room or was fiddling with the jeep's distributor wire. I heard nothing. Then a nearly imperceptible creak came from outside the hall door. I held my breath and stared at the door-knob until my eyes burned. It never moved, and the courthouse remained as quiet as a tomb.

I peered into the open vent above me. A block of wood had been inserted along one edge. Two holes were visible in its side.

Here was how Sammy Calhoun had mounted his camera. I reached in, feeling above and behind for a tape. My fingers collected only dust. The vent was empty.

I had been so sure I had cracked Sammy Calhoun's secret. The mounting bracket on the camera and the holes in the wood looked like a perfect match. Skeeter's toast to the vent had verified his complicity in the scheme, and Susan's insight that Sammy thought people overlooked the obvious had raised my hopes that the proof lay in this room. I could taste bitter disappointment and felt foolish standing on a desk with nothing in my hands but a penknife and my blood clotted with dust from seven years ago. Ashes to ashes and dust to dust. The voiceless skull of Sammy Calhoun would always taunt me, withholding the words that could have convicted his killer.

I turned to climb down and retrieve the grate. I would try and reattach it to the vent and then wipe the room clean. I took a final look from the viewpoint of Sammy's camera. Then I saw it. Atop a bookcase, out of sight from the floor, lay a leather-bound volume. A dingy piece of tape held its covers together. Dust obscured the title and signified the book had been untouched for years.

I stretched out and steadied myself by grabbing the nearest corner of the case, curious as to what would have been stored in such an unreachable spot. The bookshelf wobbled under my weight, and for a second, I thought I'd topple the whole thing over with a noise so loud the dispatcher in the Sheriff's Department would hear it. Something caught, and I realized brackets held the shelving to the wall. Their screws must have loosened slightly over the years.

I pinched the edge of the book's top cover between the tips of my fingers and slid it to where I could grab it. Then I stood up and brushed the dust from its surface. The faded gilt title on the spine sent a tingle up my own. *The Collected Works of Edgar Allan Poe.* "The Purloined Letter" was literally at the scene of the crime. With trembling fingers, I removed the gummy tape and opened Poe to the place marked by an old-fashioned ribbon attached to the binding.

A section of pages had been razor cut to form a pocket hidden within the volume. Its dimensions perfectly encased an 8mm videotape. Sammy Calhoun had provided the solution to his murder. Now I had to get it safely into hands I could trust. I would call Tommy Lee and let him take charge.

Suddenly, a creak came from the other side of the door to the courtroom. The knob jiggled as someone tried to open it. I hopped down from the desk and grabbed my shirt from under the other door. The guard would have a key and possibly enter with his gun drawn. I wrapped my shirt around the book, unlocked the knob and started to slip out into the hall.

"Barry, it's me," called Susan.

The unexpected sound of her voice stopped my flight. Why was she here? Had the guard figured out he was being duped? Was he out at the jeep and had told her to stay in the warmth of the courthouse?

"Barry?" she called again, this time louder.

Whatever had happened, I couldn't ignore her. "Just a minute," I said. "I'm coming." I removed the cassette from the book and stuck it in my back pocket. I tossed Poe up on the top shelf, turned out the light and opened the door.

The courtroom was silent and dark. Susan must have retreated somewhere into its midst.

I went halfway down the aisle and stopped. "Susan?" I called softly. There was no answer. Had she already left?

Overhead, the lights blazed to life, blinding me for an instant. Then I saw Susan at the back of the room. Her face was bloodless and winced with pain. Shielded by her body, a man stood grinning at me. I had seen him on television. We had met in person, and I had no reason to believe he hadn't been pursuing justice. That was his job. He was District Attorney Darden Claiborne.

But the smile on his face was as cold as the blue steel revolver pressed against Susan's temple.

Chapter 23

I raised my hands. "She has nothing to do with this. Call the guard and he can escort me to the Sheriff's Department."

The gun didn't waver from Susan's head.

"I'm unarmed. I was just looking for something." I started walking toward them.

"Stop!" shouted Claiborne.

"He knocked out the guard," said Susan.

Claiborne wrenched her arm higher behind her back and she cried out in pain. I dropped my hands and the D.A. swung the pistol toward me.

"Back in the judge's chamber," he said. "You can show me what you've found."

I walked slowly, but my mind raced. The pieces of the puzzle fell into place. Darden Claiborne linked them together. Like random dots that suddenly coalesce into a recognizable pattern, and then you can never see them as individual dots again. In the time it took me to return to the judge's chamber, I understood the clues that had been right in front of me.

Claiborne had given the cozy interview to Cliff Barringer that first night after the skeleton was discovered. I should have seen their relationship from the start. Claiborne had access to all the damning information leaked to the former court reporter that put Walt and then Susan under suspicion. During my ride in his car, Claiborne had convinced me he was as angry about

Barringer's revelations as Ewbanks was. Now I saw how he had zealously pursued and publicly fingered anyone who could be remotely charged for a crime he committed. He even held out the carrot of a reduced sentence to a convicted felon if he would accuse Susan's father of murder.

After Skeeter Gibson's death, Claiborne had appeared so quickly at my interrogation, not because he heard it on the police radio, but because he had pulled the trigger. He was the one who had washed up in the courthouse lavatory and then tried to project that action on me. He had also been careful to ensure no one saw our clandestine conversation in his car. He wasn't worried that Ewbanks might think he was meddling; he didn't want any visible connection to me in case I had to be eliminated. That thought sent a chill down my spine.

"Come on, move it, Clayton. I don't have all night."

"Got a date with a prisoner?" I said. "A junior high girl?"

"Shut up," he said.

The big shot with the big gun. Skeeter had told me he had covered his ass with someone who had farther to fall. That was not the sheriff but the D.A. who would have also overseen juvenile prosecutions. Who better to exploit teenage girls looking for an easy way out? Who better to expunge the records of Gentle Deal's arrest and his involvement with her case?

And now the politically ambitious district attorney had farther to fall than ever. The discovery of Calhoun's body must have been a shock to the arrogant bastard. He had thought he had gotten away with murder. I knew he would not hesitate to kill again. All I had to bargain with was the videotape in my hip pocket. Claiborne would shoot us as soon as he had it. He'd concoct some story to explain everything. If the guard hadn't seen him, I'd be the one blamed for the attack.

As soon as I entered the judge's chamber, he shoved Susan toward me and turned on the lights. Then he switched off the ones in the courtroom and closed the door.

I pulled Susan behind my back.

"He found me in the jeep," she said. "The guard had fixed the loose wire and gone inside."

Claiborne looked at the open ceiling vent. "What did you find?"

"The place where Sammy Calhoun mounted the camera," I said. "But you already knew that, didn't you?"

"You've stuck your nose in once too often, Clayton. You and that one-eyed excuse for a sheriff." He chuckled to himself. "I was damn lucky to be working late that night you came looking for Skeeter. Heard you call and then jiggle the doorknobs. But I couldn't count on luck twice, so I told the new guard to call me direct if anybody he didn't know came in after hours. Nice of you to flash your ID, Dr. Miller. Got me over here real quick."

"Why'd you have to kill Skeeter?" I asked. "He didn't tell me anything."

"I should have done it seven years ago. Never trust a drunk. Eventually he'd have sold me out for another bottle of Wild Turkey."

"You didn't kill him because he's Sheriff Ewbanks' cousin."

"I don't give a damn about Horace Ewbanks. He'll go along with what I say. I've got the killers right here in this room, returning to the scene of the crime, trying to break into my office to see what kind of case I'm putting together. You had means, motive, and opportunity. I'll make sure it's an open and shut case, and you won't be in any condition to mount a defense."

The smirk on his face told me he was enjoying describing his plan. Otherwise, he'd have already shot me. He walked over and sat on the edge of the desk. He held the pistol level with my stomach. I pivoted to keep between him and Susan.

"And that story you told me about Nick Garrett. Was he in it with you?"

"I canned Nick Garrett because he was stupid enough to say he planned to challenge me for district attorney. I threw him to you because I knew you couldn't interview him. Skeeter either. What's the old expression? Dead men tell no tales?"

Claiborne's skill at mixing truth and lies during our car ride had been masterful. Now I had to beat him at his own game.

"All right," I said. "I lied to you. I do have proof and killing us will only ensure you get the death penalty. We found the camera."

The smirk wavered. "It wasn't up there," he said. "I looked seven years ago."

"No, it was in Gentle Deal's trailer. The table was a footlocker. You should have looked inside it. Eight millimeter extended play with a fisheye lens. You couldn't find it when you cleaned out Calhoun's apartment because he'd given it to the girl."

For the first time, I saw a hint of fear in Claiborne's eyes.

"Where is it?"

"With that one-eyed excuse for a sheriff. I'm just too curious. Susan and I dropped by to see where it had been mounted. The angle on the video matches the vent's location. Tommy Lee's holding back. It's a little tricky arresting a hotshot D.A. and he's making sure everything's buttoned down. You can appreciate that."

"You're bluffing."

"How'd I know about the camera? Why am I here? You had Skeeter Gibson bring an underaged girl to this room, but Sammy Calhoun got you on tape. The quality of the picture is quite good."

"Me and who else?" asked Claiborne.

His question threw me. Someone else was on the tape with him and Gentle. Sheriff Ewbanks? Bridges? I could take a guess, but if I was wrong, my bluff was over. He read the uncertainty on my face.

"You know who," I said.

Claiborne stood up and smiled. "I'm not buying it. I know what's on the tape. Calhoun showed us a copy when he made his demand. The prick thought he could blackmail me."

I didn't say anything.

"There's no tape with just me on it," he said, "because Skeeter didn't bring that piece of white trash here for me."

"But Calhoun came to you, didn't he?"

"Yes. He thought he'd struck it rich. Gave me this bullshit about wanting money for the girl. Showed us a copy and promised to tell where the master was after we gave him fifty thousand dollars, but I knew he'd be a leech on me the rest of my life." He looked at Susan. "We met right here in this room. Your boyfriend didn't like it when I said we'd take our chances without him. He reached for that little popgun of yours, but he was too slow. I knocked it out of his hand and shot him with his own gun. He should have read my campaign literature. Four years in special forces. Amazing how that military training stays with you."

"Are you going to say Susan dug up Pearly's grave and buried Calhoun?" I asked.

"I don't have to say anything. Explaining how is Ewbanks' problem. Besides, Cliff Barringer will report whatever I tell him as long as it's an exclusive." He laughed and waved the gun. "Let's stroll over to my office."

"I can take you to the tape," I said, desperate to get us out of the courthouse. "I just haven't had the equipment to look at it."

"If you have it, I'll find it on my own. Time for talk is over."

"Time for talk is over all right," said Susan. "You've said enough." She stepped from behind me and held up her cell phone. "You should have patted me down. All I had to do was punch redial. I phoned Sheriff Wadkins from the parking lot. Woman's intuition. He's heard everything you've said, Claiborne."

Claiborne's face turned livid. "Give me that," he ordered.

Toss it and run, I wanted to say, but I knew the odds of beating a bullet out the door were slim to none.

Susan threw the phone toward the ceiling over Claiborne's head, but his eyes never left us. His expression hardened and I expected him to pull the trigger.

"Claiborne!" The voice of Sheriff Horace Ewbanks echoed from the rotunda.

Claiborne glanced back at the closed door to the courtroom. I grabbed Susan by the arm and dove for the light switch. The room went pitch black. Claiborne didn't fire. I pulled open the hall door and we stumbled through it. Behind us, a pistol roared and the plaster wall exploded over our heads.

An exit light shone at the far end of the corridor, but if we ran that direction, we would be silhouetted against its blood-red glow. That way also led to Sheriff Ewbanks, a man who likely was also on the videotape in my pocket. We had no choice but to run for the safety of the shadows at the opposite end.

"Stay low," I whispered, and pushed Susan ahead of me.

Again, I heard Ewbanks shout Claiborne's name. When they found each other, they'd make a systematic search of the courthouse. I could only hope we would find an outside exit before then.

The hall made a sharp left, taking us out of Claiborne's line of fire. A set of double glass doors promised a retreat from the shooting gallery of the narrow corridor. REGISTER OF DEEDS appeared in black lettering on the frosted pane. We found ourselves in a maze of cubicles and filing cabinets.

"We should split up," said Susan. "That doubles our chances."

As much as I hated to leave her, I knew she was right.

"Okay. Head for the back corner. Maybe there's an exit. If you can't find one, hide in a closet." I pulled my cell phone from my pocket. "Call Tommy Lee again and tell him where you are. I'll try to keep them after me." I handed her the videocassette. "I found the tape. If something happens to me, get it to Tommy Lee."

She gave me a quick kiss and scooted behind a row of file cabinets. I heard footsteps running down the hall and took off in the opposite direction, banging a few drawers along the way.

My sense of direction told me to keep moving to my right, hugging the wall that enclosed the department. I could hear Claiborne's footsteps on the terrazzo floor behind me, but my speed was limited by the unknown location of Ewbanks. I didn't want to be driven into the muzzle of his gun.

The seam of a door appeared at the end of a row of cubicles. I could only guess where it emerged in the layout of the courthouse. Instead of bolting through and into the unknown, I pushed it open, and then retreated along another line of file cabinets. If Claiborne had seen the door move, he should go through it, leaving me in the office alone. I crawled along the floor, circling like a fox behind the hounds. My safest exit lay in the route he had already searched.

I heard the door slam. Claiborne had taken the bait and headed down a wing away from me. There was only a moment or two at best to double back and run through the courtroom, cross the rotunda, and flee through the front doors. Maybe Susan had made it to the jeep and we could escape together.

I stopped at the door to the Register of Deeds before darting into the hall. The way seemed clear. Then just as I started forward, a wheeze came from the shadows. Too many years of cigarettes had marked Ewbanks. Like two wolves hunting, he followed Claiborne's trail, waiting for their quarry to double back.

I knelt behind the filing cabinets. The cold hard floor bit into my knees. At last I heard Ewbanks' labored breathing pass me as he moved on.

Cautiously, I retraced the path to the judge's chamber. The room was still dark. I knew it well enough to cross and enter the courtroom. The double doors at the other end were open wide and the light from the rotunda reflected on the polished surface of the hall floor. I was halfway there when the voice of Sheriff Ewbanks whispered from behind me.

"Clayton, stop."

Before I could run, Darden Claiborne stepped into the doorway, blocking my path. No matter where I turned, I faced a bullet.

"It's over," he said, and raised his pistol.

Suddenly a shot fired from behind him and he pitched forward into the courtroom. Lights came up, illuminating the shock and disbelief on Claiborne's face. He staggered against the back of a pew and lifted his gun again. A second gunshot exploded, this time from the judge's chamber. The impact knocked Claiborne to the floor. I turned to see Ewbanks at the door, pistol in one hand, the light switch under the other.

"The filthy son of a bitch," he said. "You okay?"

I was too stunned to answer. I looked back at Claiborne and saw Susan standing over him, a gun gripped tightly in both hands, her face etched with conflicting emotions of shock and relief. I ran to her and took the gun.

"Susan?" I whispered.

"I couldn't let him hurt you. I had to shoot." She kept her eyes glued on Claiborne. Blood gurgled from his mouth and chest.

"It's all right," I said, holding her tightly to my body. "It's all over now."

But my words were wrong. It wasn't over. I released her, ran past Ewbanks to the judge's chamber and grabbed the volume of Poe from the shelf.

"It's here," I said, hurrying back into the courtroom. "It's been here all along. Sammy Calhoun put the videotape right under your nose."

I took the cassette from Susan, placed it in the book and held it in front of Claiborne. Yes, it was cruel, but I did it for Gentle, and for Skeeter, and for Sammy Calhoun. Claiborne's mouth opened and his eyes fixed on the black cassette. Then his focus wavered and his chin sank on his chest. If there was a Hell, I knew Darden Claiborne entered it with that final vision burned into his soul for all eternity.

Ewbanks took the book from my hands and then stooped down to check Claiborne's carotid artery for a pulse. He shook his head and stood up.

He turned to Susan. "There's nothing you can do for him, doctor. Pretty fair shooting. Where'd you get the gun?"

"It's the guard's," she replied in a shaky voice. "He's injured in a hallway near the restrooms."

The sheriff grabbed the walkie-talkie from his duty belt. "Get an ambulance and some patrol units over to the courthouse as soon as possible," he ordered. "Take me to him," he told Susan. "We'll care for him and then go to my office and sort this all out."

He looked down at Claiborne's body. "Kinda fitting he died in here. And people say the court system doesn't work."

When we reached the security guard, he was regaining consciousness, dazed and unsure about what had happened. Susan examined the gash on the back of his head.

"A few stitches," she said, "and probably a mild concussion. He's earned some leave."

"That was quick thinking redialing Tommy Lee," I told her. "I hope he heard it all."

She smiled. "He didn't hear a word. The battery was dead."

"That was a bluff?" I said, staring at her as if she were a stranger.

"I did reach Tommy Lee from the jeep before it died. Someone needed to know where we were. For seven years we thought Sammy Calhoun had gone to Texas. If things went wrong, I didn't want to just disappear without a trace."

I turned to Ewbanks. "And Tommy Lee called you?"

"No, I didn't," said a familiar voice. Tommy Lee came up along with several Walker County deputies. "When Susan's phone died, I hightailed it over here. Looks like I missed all the fun." He spoke to me, but kept his one eye on Ewbanks.

I showed him the book and cassette. "We found the tape. Claiborne admitted he killed Calhoun because he tried to blackmail them."

"Them?" asked Tommy Lee. He again looked at Ewbanks warily.

Ewbanks stared back, a wry grin on his face. "Don't worry, Sheriff. I ain't the other man on the tape if that's what you're thinking, but I can tell you who it is."

"You've already seen it?" I asked.

Ewbanks pulled a cigarette from his pocket and popped a match head with his thumbnail. He took a deep drag as if savoring our confusion.

"Nah, I ain't seen it, but I got a brain. Only one man it can be. Hugh Richards."

"State Senator Richards?" asked Tommy Lee, as amazed as the rest of us.

"Bridges tells me you don't believe in coincidences, Sheriff," said Ewbanks. "Didn't it strike you as odd that Senator Richards would go to such lengths to be buried beside Turncoat Turner? Keeping his arrangement with Pearly's family a secret until he was dead? That first day up at the graveyard I knew something wasn't right. I knew Richards and I knew his family. His momma was a yellow dog Democrat."

"A what?" asked Susan.

"Somebody who'd rather vote for a yellow dog than a Republican," I replied.

"Right," Ewbanks said. "I don't care how old the man was or how long his momma's been dead, he wasn't going to plant his bones beside a carpetbagger-loving Republican without having a damn good reason."

"That will be easy enough to prove when we see the tape," said Tommy Lee.

I could tell he still wasn't sure about Ewbanks.

"But why did you suspect Claiborne?" Tommy Lee asked.

"I know my men," Ewbanks answered between puffs. "They only leak what I want them to leak. But Claiborne was suddenly spewing like a busted radiator to that reporter Cliff Barringer. And then he started crawling up my back to get warrants on Clayton and Dr. Miller when there wasn't enough evidence. That's why I fed information to Bridges to pass on to you. I wanted someone who wasn't under Claiborne's nose to know what was going on. I knew you were a good police, Wadkins, for a pup."

Tommy Lee Wadkins, twenty-year veteran sheriff of Laurel County, stood dumbfounded. He didn't know whether to be pleased or pissed.

"Oh, don't feel too bad, Sheriff," Ewbanks said. "I didn't have it all figured out myself. I was suspicious of Claiborne, but I wasn't sure until Gentle Deal was killed with the same type of drugs that were missing from my evidence room. He'd been in there just a few days before with some excuse about needing to check on some evidence for an upcoming case."

He took another long drag on his cigarette as if contemplating how much to tell us about his thought process. "But knowing and proving are two different things. So all I could do was keep a close eye on him. Tonight I was coming in to check tomorrow's schedule like I always do about this time when I saw Claiborne's Crown Vic parked out back like he was trying to hide it. Then I saw Clayton's jeep out front and knew something was bad wrong. Thanks to Clayton and Dr. Miller, evidence ain't a problem now."

I was still confused. "But if Senator Richards is on that tape, why did he want us to find Calhoun's body?"

Ewbanks' voice dropped and the sadness came through each word. "People are hard to figure out sometimes. Like I said, I knew Richards. In a lot of ways, he was a good man. But he was just as human and just as weak as the rest of us. When a man gets toward the end of his journey, I guess he looks back and the weak moments stand out as much or more than the strong. I feel sure he regretted to his dying day what he did and that includes getting mixed up with the likes of Claiborne."

"I'd have thought he'd been smarter than that," said Tommy Lee.

"Sex can be a powerful magnet," Ewbanks replied. "Friend or no friend, he was a grown man and has to be held accountable for his actions. My guess is he was with Claiborne when Calhoun was killed. Probably helped bury the body. Turns my stomach to think about it. Hugh Richards did a lot of good for people around here."

"Why didn't he just confess?" I asked.

"Same reasons. He was human and didn't want to lose his position. He surefire didn't want to go to jail. Richards was one of the most powerful politicians in Raleigh. That's why Claiborne wanted to get something over him in the first place. I suspect the real reason Claiborne used those women was to entrap men he wanted to control. I'll bet he held what Richards did over his head for the rest of his career. But Richards found a way to even the score."

"So after he died he made sure Calhoun's body would be found," I said. "Claiborne would know Richards was coming after him from beyond the grave."

"That's the way I read it," said Ewbanks. "Any hint before then as to what he had in mind would have sent Claiborne up to Eagle Creek cemetery to get those bones out of there. Claiborne had no clue what Richards was planning until you unearthed that skeleton." Ewbanks shook his head. "I'm afraid Richards didn't foresee his scheme would cost the lives of Gentle Deal and Skeeter Gibson. I can't believe he would've wanted it to go down that way."

"So now the whole story comes out," Susan said.

"Maybe." With that cryptic comment, Hard-ass Hor-ass led us to his office.

As we walked across the parking lot to the jail, I pulled Susan close to me. "You were amazing. Coming up with that cell phone ruse on the spur of the moment."

"Spur of the moment? I first thought about it as Claiborne pulled me at gunpoint out of the jeep, but the phone had already died. I did press the redial button after he knocked out the guard, hoping the battery had regained enough energy to at least make a brief connection."

"I feel like an idiot for suspecting Ewbanks."

"We knew Ewbanks was a fox," said Susan. "But fortunately he turned out to be one of the good guys."

The old fox ordered up some coffee and sent for an 8mm video player.

When it had been powered up, he stubbed out his cigarette and cleared his throat. "This could be pretty graphic," he said. He looked at Susan and actually blushed.

She remained calm. "Do you think Barry should leave?"

I was so happy to see Susan trying to shake off the trauma of the shooting I let her jab at me go unanswered.

The tape played like a cheap porno flick. Calhoun must have activated the camera over several of the escapades, maybe with a motion detector. First we saw Richards with a woman, and then Claiborne with another. There was nothing erotic about it. The senator seemed to be a pathetic old man, barely able to perform. Claiborne had to have the women tell him how good he was.

The scene with Gentle Deal was the most disturbing. Richards had her strip nude. She was crying. "You won't tell my daddy, will you?" was all the girl could say. The senator started fondling her, and then stopped. It was as if her tears had shed her years, and he suddenly saw her for the child she was. As he was telling her to dress, the tape ended.

"That's that," said Ewbanks.

Tommy Lee, Susan, and I sat silently. Ewbanks ejected the cassette.

"Proof enough, don't you agree, Sheriff?" he asked, looking at Tommy Lee.

"Yeah," said Tommy Lee. "It's clear Claiborne killed Calhoun, Gibson, and Gentle Deal. The tape shows why. Each had to be silenced as they became a threat."

"And now Claiborne's gone to face the ultimate judge and so has Richards." Ewbanks held up the tape. "So I don't see where this has any purpose now."

He set the videotape on the floor in front of his desk. He looked at each of us. No one said a word. Then he stomped the heel of his boot down, smashing the black cassette into a mangled pile of splintered plastic and twisted tape. There would be no graphic revelation of what happened in that room seven years ago, no tantalizing excerpts to boost news ratings, no bootlegged pornography showing up on the Internet.

As I watched Ewbanks destroy the tape, I wondered about his motives. I felt sure they were in part to save the good name of an old friend. An old friend who had disappointed him, but in a way tried to redeem himself. Ewbanks must have thought he'd paid enough for his sins.

As for me, I didn't give a damn about the good name of Senator Hugh Richards or how much he had to pay. Destroying the tape was fine with me. Gentle Deal had a grandmother in Tennessee.

Chapter 24

We spent the next half hour deciding how to release the story. At least Saturday would catch the local news media understaffed and without the resources to do much more than digest and regurgitate the information given them.

I insisted on honoring my pledge to Melissa Bigham for an exclusive. Since we were past her deadline, Ewbanks had no problem stonewalling as much information as he could. Sunday morning The Gainesboro Vista would break the major details without knowing that a videotape had ever been found.

Ewbanks had only one request. He didn't want Cliff Barringer given any information. He planned to tie the reporter up as much as possible with questions about his meetings with Claiborne. It's one thing to protect a news source, but it's another to have been the patsy for a murderer. Claiborne had brought Barringer's name into play, and Ewbanks encouraged me to let Melissa Bigham know the obnoxious leech had been duped.

Once Melissa's story broke, Susan would call Cassie and give her an exclusive TV interview.

"Tell her you want strong backlight," I said. "Shows off your hair."

Even Ewbanks laughed. The strain of the ordeal needed relief. All of us knew how close Claiborne had come to getting away with murder.

I took Susan back to my cabin. We'd retrieve our things from the hunt club over the weekend. Lying in bed, we quickly found ourselves picking up where we'd left off on that lumpy sofa. Because we'd been a split second from death, life felt all the more precious. The beat of her heart became a marvelous sound that converged and merged with mine, and the tender warmth of flesh against flesh buried the ache that had been unearthed in that mountain church cemetery. Afterward, we slept clinging to each other, afraid to let go, afraid for what might have happened.

The next morning I met Melissa at the paper. I was pleased to discover she'd invited Annette Nolan. The old woman had left her goats on the mountainside long enough to participate in the culmination of the story she'd given Sammy Calhoun a thousand dollars to investigate. Annette and Melissa would share the byline. The younger reporter was giving her mentor the national exposure that would complete her career.

At four in the afternoon, Cassie Miller called me from NEWS-CHANNEL-8 to say Cliff Barringer had been fired by Nelson Darius. She was so happy she forgot to cuss.

With the close of the Calhoun investigation, I focused my energy on coming to grips with Hoffman Enterprises. Sunday, I reviewed the figures and the notes I'd taken during my meeting with Carl and Josh. Under closer scrutiny, the numbers swung wildly depending upon the value of the stock and the expense of getting Mom a place to live and Dad into an assisted living community.

I spent the next two days making drop-in visits at several facilities in the Asheville area that were recommended for Alzheimer's patients. The complexes sported names like Dogwood Estates, Rhododendron Ridge Manor, and Tranquility Forest. Too bad The Last Resort had already been taken. Each was decked out in holiday décor. Christmas music played in activity rooms and on elevators, cafeterias served special menus, and church youth groups offered a perpetual parade of choirs and gift bearers to ensure the forgetting weren't forgotten. Beneath the veneer of happy times lay the inescapable core of vacant eyes and bewildered faces. Dad might be headed to that final state of mind, but what would the move do to my mother? Would Dad's professional care be liberating or usurp her role as wife and loving companion?

I asked Mom if we could invite Uncle Wayne to lunch on Christmas Eve and approach the future as a family. She fixed Cornish hens, and my father was delighted to have "a tiny chicken" on his plate. After the meal, Mom left Uncle Wayne and me with a fresh pot of coffee and took Dad upstairs where he could watch TV in the den.

"Now whatever's good for your mother and you is good with me," said Wayne.

"I want your opinion too," I insisted. "It's not just about the financial side. I want everyone comfortable with our decision."

"You're the one with your career ahead of you. Certain decisions shouldn't be made by a committee, even if it's all family."

"Hoffman's giving me a three-year contract and the authority to hire one full-time and one part-time employee with benefits. That protects you and Freddy."

"What if one of us doesn't want to stay three years?"

"No one has to, but I'd sure like things to stay the same for awhile. People in this town look to you now that Dad can't be the public face. When Mom and Dad leave the funeral home, your presence will be a comfort."

Wayne's coffee cup clattered against the saucer. "Leave the funeral home? I thought you were using the sale money to get your Mom some help?"

"Hoffman doesn't allow on-site residents. We'll need to get Dad into a care facility and find a place for Mom nearby."

"Nearby to what?" asked my mother. She came in the kitchen carrying a manila file folder.

I slid back in my chair as she sat down. The conversation wasn't proceeding like I had planned it. We were jumping straight to the most difficult part.

"Nearby to Dad. I've been looking at possible options for him, and I know you'll want to be as close as possible."

"Then you think we should sell?" she said.

"It looks like it can give you the financial security you need."

She looked at her brother, and then let her gaze wander over the kitchen she had ruled her entire married life. "Financial security isn't worth the cost of breaking up a family. If you think selling is the best thing, then your father and I will find a place we can live together. Tranquility Forest has some small cottages where couples can live." She opened the folder and pulled out a brochure identical to the one I'd collected on my visit. "It's," she searched for the word, "nice."

"Bunch of old people," said Wayne.

"I'm an old person," said Mom.

Old but full of life, I thought. She could still be a bundle of energy. The folder showed me she had been actively investigating housing possibilities and had been able to find only one. What effect would living in the midst of caregivers and disintegrating personalities have on her? How would her vital spirit survive?

"I don't know, Mom. That's a pretty drastic change for you."

"As drastic as giving up my husband?" The tears brimmed, but she willed them not to fall. "I'll be fine with him. It's what works for you and this community that's important."

The community we served. That had always been Mom and Dad's priority. How would the community adjust to a funeral home that became a funeral corporation?

"Uncle Wayne will provide the continuity," I said. "I can be the person responsible for any changes Hoffman requires. The people here don't look at me the same way."

"What put that idea in your head?" asked Wayne.

"Watching you all my life. I'll never have the trust you and Dad have earned."

"That's foolish talk," he protested.

There was no sense arguing with him. We agreed that after Christmas, Mom and I would look for more housing possibilities. Maybe we could find an option with a better mix of independent living and professional care.

For a few minutes, the three of us sat quietly, each lost in private thoughts.

The doorbell rang.

"I'll see who it is," I said.

Libby Metcalf stood on the front porch. Her blue cloth coat was pulled tightly around her waist, and the afternoon chill had turned her cheeks and ears into red ornaments. She clutched a small green package in her bare hands.

"I hope I'm not bothering you," she said. Her smile wavered as she glanced past me into the empty foyer.

"Not at all. Come in."

"I'll just be a moment."

I led her into the parlor. The gas logs burned brightly in the fireplace and the Christmas tree's white lights sparkled off the brass ornaments.

"Your decorations are so beautiful," she said. "I thought maybe—" she stopped as the words caught in her throat.

Mom and Uncle Wayne entered.

"Can I take your coat, Libby?" I asked.

"Would you like some hot coffee?" added Mom.

"No, really, I've got to get back home, but I just wanted to say thank you." She handed me the package.

"For me?" I asked, feeling stupid saying it because the small gift tag read "For Barry Clayton."

"Yes." She looked at the tree. "I thought maybe there would be room."

The green foil paper was well taped, as was the box it concealed. Inside, I found a brass oval Christmas ornament framed by angel wings. It held the picture of two boys, arms around each other's shoulders with bright smiles for the camera. They stood in front of a Christmas tree.

I couldn't get any words past the lump in my throat. I sat on the sofa and she joined me.

"You were so kind," Libby said. She took the ornament from my hands and let her fingers caress the protective glass. "They warned me at the hospital that I shouldn't try to see them again. That the damage had been too great. You proved them wrong."

I looked up at Uncle Wayne. Even after forty-five years in the funeral business, I could see this mother's words touched his heart.

"I had help," I said. "We wanted you to be comforted."

She gave me back her treasure. "I know. And I thought maybe no one ever tells you how much that means. Everything is so overwhelming when what you love most is stripped from you. But you really cared. I could tell that. You made the difference for me. I just wanted to say that in person. Now I can remember them with a peace that you made possible. I thought maybe you would hang this each year and remember them as well?"

She looked at me, hope suspended on her tear-streaked face. I saw in her features all the Appalachian women who pioneered these mountains, raised their children, and bore the hardships that nature relentlessly thrust upon them. Theirs was a heritage that would not show up on a Hoffman Enterprises balance sheet. Who would a grieving mother be looking at three years from now?

"Always," I said. "Always."

Christmas broke clear and cold. I had spent the night at the funeral home and awoke with joy to being in the place I had spent so many Christmas mornings.

I helped Mom get Dad downstairs. We had our coffee and sweet rolls in front of the tree. The fire burned, and carols played softly on the stereo.

Dad kept looking at the lights and decorations. Then he'd turn and smile at me. I tried to see the room through his eyes and thought how he as a boy had grown up in this very scene. Surely, any vestige of those memories must be bursting forth to fill his shattered mind with a sense of peace and comfort. After all, that is Christmas.

Dad stood up and walked to the tree. He picked up a bright red package with a white bow. It contained a new bathrobe I'd bought for Mom. He came over and held it out to me.

"Merry Christmas, son."

There are moments in our lives that we hope we'll never forget. I prayed that should I ever have to follow my father down the dark murky tunnel of his illness that this would be one of those moments spared from the ravages of the disease. And the moment also clarified that I wasn't ready to take these memories from my father. Would his heartfelt wish have happened if we were seated in some assisted living cottage? Would Hoffman Enterprises be cutting me off from my own past and closing one more door to my father's mind?

If I had any lingering doubts about not selling out this home and that past, they were eradicated by Dad's words and the picture of Libby Metcalf's boys hanging beneath the star. I didn't need Hoffman Enterprises. I was already funeral director of the year.

A few minutes later, Susan and Tommy Lee came through the front door. He held a large square box with the lid slightly ajar. They wore conspiratorial smiles, and I knew something was up.

The present wasn't wrapped, but a red bow had been taped to the top.

"Patsy run you out of the house?"

"Nah, we went to midnight candlelight service. Samantha and Kenny are still sleeping. Patsy will keep them from ripping through their gifts till I get back. I've had this on my hands long enough." He handed the box to Susan.

"It's from your mom and me," she said.

I turned to Mother, and she pulled a sheet of legal paper from her pocket. "You thought we wouldn't know," she said. "I found your wish list stuck in the magazine."

She read aloud, "Christmas. Bird dog. Want more than anything." She winked at me. "And that last part's even underlined."

I didn't know what she was talking about, and then it hit me. She had the list of notes I'd jotted down during my first conversation with Ted Sandiford of Hoffman Enterprises. The self-described bird dog who needed to close a deal by Christmas and who told me he'd wanted to run his family's funeral home more than anything.

I started laughing and couldn't stop. Everyone joined in, thinking I was surprised and delighted that my wish had been discovered. Susan handed me the carton. A wet black nose nudged the lid aside. Puppy breath rose into my face.

Scrambling for traction on the smooth cardboard, a yellow lab no more than eight weeks old looked up and yipped at his new master. It was love at first sight.

"Thank you," I said, and leaned over the box to give Susan a kiss.

"I had to get the puppy out of the house early," said Tommy Lee. "Samantha's fallen in love with it. She doesn't know I've gone back and got this little guy's sister from the litter for her. I'm guaranteed to be a hero for at least a few hours today."

I set the box on the floor and the puppy immediately tipped it over and escaped. He waddled with hind legs outracing his front ones until he ran into my father's shoe. Dad reached down and stroked his head. Then he looked up with the grin of, well, a kid on Christmas morning.

"You have to name him," said Mom.

"Oh, he already has a name," I said.

I whistled.

Democrat ran to me.

To receive a free catalog of Poisoned Pen Press titles, please contact us in one of the following ways:

Phone: 1-800-421-3976
Facsimile: 1-480-949-1707
Email: info@poisonedpenpress.com
Website: www.poisonedpenpress.com

Poisoned Pen Press
6962 E. First Ave. Ste. 103
Scottsdale, AZ 85251